OUR STAR-CROSSED KISS

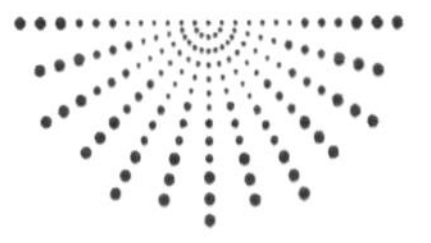

PIPER RAYNE

Cover Photo: Wander Aguiar Photography

Cover Design: By Hang Le

1st Line Editor: Joy Editing

2nd Line Editor: My Brother's Editor

Proofreader: Shawna Gavas, Behind The Writer

Our Star-Crossed Kiss

She's got two strikes against her.
Her name is Erickson and her parents own The Bagel Place.

It wasn't always that way. When we were nine, we were best friends. But then a feud between our dads ripped their successful business apart—and my best friend was ripped away too.

Our paths were bound to cross again. Now, both our families are vying for the same spot on a Food Channel's reality show. Soon, the hatred between us becomes indifference and then our friendship grows like our time apart was only hours instead of years.

So when Evan asks me to pretend to be her boyfriend, I naively assume it's to repair the rift between our families. But I wasn't only wrong, I was dead wrong. That glimpse of a future I saw with her is ripped away again just like when we were young.

The difference is, now I'm all grown up, and I fight for what I want.

OUR STAR-CROSSED KISS

CHAPTER ONE

Seth

"My fiancé would die if he knew I was here with you."

I wish I could say I'm surprised to hear my client say this, but every bridal session I shoot, the woman says that sentence almost verbatim.

"Well he's going to know once you show him these pictures, but I think he'll be too distracted to care when he's looking at them." I chuckle and snap a picture of her spread eagle, dressed in white lace and satin lingerie.

She giggles and I snap the shutter five times in a row to catch her head tipped back, smile wide and happy. That'll be a keeper right there.

Being a boudoir photographer isn't my first choice, but desperate times call for desperate measures. At first, I worried I'd be sporting a hard-on all day, but luckily, my clients are clients and that's all I see them as. I've come to enjoy watching their confidence grow during our sessions.

I rarely want to nail any of them. I say rarely because hello, I'm a man. A single man, I'll add. I'd be lying if I said never and lying's never been my thing. My brother does it enough for the both of us.

But as my client, Lizzy, sticks her tits into the air, I'm not even slightly aroused. Mostly because my mind is preoccupied by a certain brunette who I've been told repeatedly—by my parents since I was nine—that I should hate.

"Let's have you roll over now. Stick your ass in the air a bit."

Who else gets to say this shit at work? Other than a porn director.

My assistant changes the lighting, knowing exactly what I'm looking for. I'd never photograph a client without someone else in the room, preferably another woman. Having witnesses fends off any potential lawsuits or having someone misconstruing things. It keeps everything professional, not to mention easier.

A knock on the door stops me as I'm about to step up on a ladder to shoot Lizzy from above.

"Can you see who that is, Madison?" I ask my assistant.

It's a small boudoir photography studio, so only Madison and I are here. We tell our clients if the red light is on outside the door, just have a seat and we'll be with them soon. If someone knocks, I might duck out during a change break—you wouldn't believe some of the outfits these women bring to fulfill their loved ones' fantasies.

Madison opens the curtain that conceals the area I'm shooting in before she opens the door. She only gets it open a crack before someone pushes it forward and she falls to her ass.

"Oh sorry, dear," my mom says.

"Mom! I'm in a session." I pull the curtain shut to fully enclose Lizzy, but my mom must have started her walking regimen again because she beats me before I get the opportunity to hide my client.

"You're a beauty. Oh no, don't hide on my account. Flaunt what you got going on because thirty years later and you're looking at the aftermath." My mom runs her hands down her body.

"Mom, I'm with a client." My fingers tighten around my camera.

"Why thank you." Lizzy blushes. I'd snap a picture if that wasn't weird.

"Trust me, your husband is going to love this. My son is the best photographer in the world." Mom raises her hand, her finger and thumb ready to pinch my cheeks.

What can I say, I'm a momma's boy. Not the "I live in her basement and she washes and folds my laundry" kind. But her happiness means a lot to me, and she puts me on a pedestal I'm not really deserving of. I think it's just that compared to my brother, I'm a prince. Not a prince like Adrian, but you get what I mean.

"You can stay," Lizzy says, seeming to enjoy having an audience.

My mom takes the invitation and sits in Madison's chair.

I roll my eyes. "Give us a moment, Lizzy." I put my finger in the air and politely nod toward the door for my mom to follow.

She sighs but does stand. "Can I give you some advice from an old lady?" Lizzy has no time to answer before my mom speaks. "Night cream is a must, even when you're exhausted. Stay out of the sun and never smoke. And if you do it right, your sex life is exercise enough."

I gag while Madison laughs.

My mom shakes her head. "My son likes to think he was brought into this world by immaculate conception."

Lizzy and Madison share a humorous look. I'm so happy they find my mom so funny.

"Mom," I say with a bite in my tone.

She waves to Lizzy. "Sorry for interrupting. Remember, you're beautiful and sexy and"—she waves away my impatient sigh—"you can be strong and brave too. Speak your mind and never keep anything inside."

"Maybe we should offer an advice booth for you to man when our clients come in."

My mom rolls her matching-to-mine blue eyes. "My son, the comedian."

"Let's go," I say, holding the door handle.

"Oh fine." My mom walks over and pats my cheek before she walks out.

"Hey, Madison, let's change the backdrop to the black."

She nods. "Got it."

I shut the door to the studio and walk over to where my mom's sitting in a waiting room chair.

"When the red light is on, you can't come in. We've been over this." I point at said light in case she missed it the first hundred times I've shown her over the past five years. If I could move her bagel shop so it wasn't just a block away from the photography studio, I'd do it.

"I gave that girl a morale boost. You tell them they're beautiful when you shoot them, right?"

"Why are you here?" I change the subject because my mom needs to stay out of my business.

She nods as if she forgot what was so urgent she had to bust into my session. She opens her purse—which holds everything from tampons she hasn't used for five years because of menopause to pain medicine and a mini sewing kit. Retrieving a folded piece of paper, she straightens it by laying it across her chest and running a hand down to get the crinkles out.

I hold out my hand and she places it in there once she's satisfied it's as flat as it will get.

Calling all businesses!
Come down to the mercantile mart this Saturday between 9-5 with the one dish your restaurant is known for—and get a chance to be on the Food Channel's series Tastes of Small Towns. *If you're chosen, you head to the semi-finals next week, where our celebrity guests will pick winners for the breakfast, lunch, dinner, and treat segment. If you win, you'll appear on our episode featuring restaurants and shops in Cliffton Heights, New York.*
See you this Saturday!

I HAND the flyer back to my mom. "You want to do this?"

She nods. "But you know your dad. He'll say it's a waste of time."

My dad is more the type of guy who thinks, "I make the bagels and you eat them, or you don't. They're the best and if you don't think so, you can take a hike."

It's why he and Mr. Erickson couldn't keep The Bagel and Schmear Shop going. They'd argue about which mattered more—the bagel or schmear. My dad, Chris Andrews, was the bagel guy, and Mr. Erickson was the schmear guy. But because a stupid fight tore the business and their two families apart, Cliffton Heights residents can now choose Andrews Bagel if they want a better bagel than cream cheese or The Bagel Place if they want great cream cheese with an okay bagel.

"So?" My mom raises her eyebrows. "Will you go with

me? I'll bake them fresh and I've been working on this cream cheese recipe, but…" She doesn't have to say it. It doesn't compare to the Ericksons' recipe.

"I'm sure they'll be there too."

There's no way their daughter Evan, the brunette I just envisioned on that bed five minutes ago, will pass up the opportunity to be advertised on national television. I might not know everything about her like I used to, but she's smart and bold. Hell, she's probably already camped out in front of the mercantile mart to be the first in line.

CHAPTER TWO

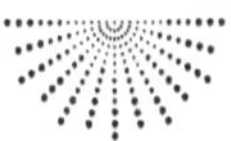

Evan

"Where are you going this early?" My sister, Elsie, plops down on the stool, looking half asleep. "I don't mind the mid-morning shift, but you owe me for this."

I finish the last tray of bagels. "I owe you? Remind me to pay you back that favor tomorrow when I wake up at three a.m. so we have product to sell to pay for your college. All you have to do is unlock the doors and take orders. Mom will be in after she drops off Eli at school."

"But you know she's going to talk to his teacher foreeeever. And last time Mr. Tettlebaum yelled at me because I put too much cream cheese on his poppy seed bagel," she whines because that's what Elsie does. "There was a huge line of witnesses."

"This is one morning. Please, just handle this."

"But why? Tell me what you're keeping from me? Are you

surprising Brock?" Her eyelashes flicker up and down in a dreamy state. "It's like a Cinderella story with you two. One day he's going to come in here and sweep you off your feet, take you to his castle on the hill, and you'll live happily ever after." She rests her chin in her palm as if she's envisioning it all happening right now.

I won't break my sister's naively romantic heart, but Brock isn't the type of guy to put much thought into anything other than his vices—video games, hanging out with his friends, and betting on car races with said friends.

All Elsie sees when it comes to Brock is dollar bills. His fancy sports car and his family's big house on the hill. Sometimes I sit next to him and wonder how we ever started dating. The truth is, it all started here in The Bagel Place.

Brock would come in around noon and ask if we had anything fresh. Eventually he lingered longer and longer, and since business was always slow by then, it was nice to have someone to talk to. Sometimes a friend of his would stop in and he'd make them buy a bagel or a drink. Usually they'd chat for a minute or two then be on their way, but Brock would stay until I closed. One afternoon he asked me out and I said yes even though he's not really my type. If I told that to Elsie, she'd faint like one of the members from BTS just walked in the door.

But Brock surprised me. He's pretty charming and he's been almost sweet on our dates. Except for after a gala we attended, where we ran into Seth Andrews. It was an event for the Testicular Cancer Awareness Group. Brock's dad is a bigwig for some company that bought a table.

All those doubts Seth Andrews keeps trying to bring to my doorstep come to mind—that Brock is a drug dealer and the scum of the earth.

"Hey, have you ever heard any rumors about Brock?" I ask in a light voice, trying to make it sound like no big deal. I shove another tray of everything bagels in the oven because we usually run out of them early and Elsie will be lost if she has to actually prepare anything.

"What kind of rumors?"

I shrug with my back to her. I've dissected Seth's accusations about Brock being his brother Trevor's drug dealer repeatedly. Why would a guy like Brock need to sell drugs? His family is loaded. It makes no sense.

What makes more sense is that Seth has the last name Andrews and anyone with that last name can't be trusted when it comes to us Ericksons.

"You mean other girls? Damn, Evan, you know you're hot, right? He's lucky to get you."

I turn around, wiping my hands clean with a dishcloth. "Yeah, not about other girls."

Although Brock does have a reputation of having no-strings-attached relationships. Even Elsie's sweet compliments can't erase his past.

She tilts her head. "Then what?"

"I don't know. I don't really go out much—"

"Evan, you're dodging the question. What's bothering you?"

I sit on the stool across from her and allow all the nervous energy about what I'm doing as soon as I leave here to disperse from my body. "You know that gala I went to a few weeks ago?"

"The fancy one Brock bought you a gorgeous black dress for? That thing may disappear out of your closet one day, by the way." She laughs and I throw the dishrag at her.

"Yeah, well, Seth Andrews was there too."

Elsie's laugh dies as though someone cut her throat.

"Els," I say.

She shakes her head. "You're thinking of ruining your

chance at a fairy tale romance because of something Seth Andrews said?"

I never expected to see Seth there—in a tuxedo, no less. It was probably his first time wearing one since junior prom when he got crowned as king. Brock was seething after our confrontation with Seth and actually demanded I have nothing to do with him. I'm not sure why Brock's worried. It's common knowledge to anyone who lives in Cliffton Heights that Seth's dad and mine had a falling out years ago. As if that's not cliché enough, I see actual voting polls on our community Facebook group about who has the better bagels: my family, the Ericksons of The Bagel Place or Seth's family with Andrews Bagel Company.

I'm not sure what Brock saw the night of the gala to make him demand I never see Seth again.

"You know Trevor has a—"

"Drug problem? You'd be hard-pressed to find anyone in Cliffton Heights who didn't see that downward spiral."

I nod. Elsie's younger than me by enough that the family feud happened right before she was born. "Well, Seth says Brock was… er… is Trevor's dealer?"

"I thought Trevor was in rehab? Is he back and using again?" The judgment in her tone is clear.

My dad is aware of Trevor Andrews' drug problem and has judged how Seth's dad could ever allow Trevor to become a junkie, saying he'd never let his children get that lost. I don't think it's quite that simple though.

"I have no idea about Trevor. I think Seth was warning me or something."

"Warning?" She rolls her eyes. "That Brock might decorate you in diamonds?"

Oh, my poor sister. Once she graduates high school and finds out what the real world is like, she's going to be devastated that her new reality doesn't come with glitter bombs and streamers.

"I'm serious."

"I thought they were friends? Didn't they play football together? There's a picture of the two of them in the glass case with that trophy when we won state all those years ago."

I was a sophomore when Trevor was a senior. I kind of remember Brock and Trevor hanging around one another, but only because Trevor was actually nice to me. He'd smile and say hi in the hallway while Seth scowled as if I was the reason for our parents' fallout.

"They were, from what I remember. But there's no denying that Trevor lost his battle with addiction." I go to the sink and wash my hands. "Anyway, I have to go if I'm gonna be on time."

"Okay, but tell me… are you showing up naked with only a rain jacket on?"

I shake my head at my little sister. "Stop watching all those romance movies and meet the rest of us down here on Earth."

"I bet Brock would love it if you did," she singsongs, heading toward the front of the store. "I hope you waxed. No one likes a hairy pussy anymore, FYI."

"Elsie!" I scold as though she's my child.

I head out the back door, double-check that it's locked behind me, and head toward the mercantile mart, crossing my fingers I'll be the first one in line.

* * *

SADLY, I have to be satisfied being the fourth in line. Cliffton Heights isn't a small town, but it's not big city either. So I recognize Luiz from Los Tacos, Audrey from Scumptuals, Tony from Pizza Pies, and Meg from Spoon and Fork, which is a soup and salad place. They all tentatively smile and wave as I pass them to walk to the end of the line.

None of them are competition for me, and I breathe a sigh of relief. At least I'm first for the breakfast crowd, I guess.

I glance at my watch. It's only six o'clock, which means we have three hours before the doors open. Since I didn't bring a chair like my other Cliffton Heights hopefuls, I sit on the concrete and pull out my phone.

"How's your dad, sweetie?" Audrey peers over the edge of the romance novel she's reading. I glance at the name —*Lessons from a One-Night Stand*. Sounds interesting.

I smile. "He's good."

"And your mom? She came in the other day with Eli and she looked tired."

I want to ask Audrey how I look. Does she notice the bags under my eyes? I never planned on running the day-to-day operations of The Bagel Place. But my mom has to be hands-on with Eli to assist with his special needs due to his Down Syndrome. Elsie isn't much help and I want her to finish college. "She's good. We're all good."

She nods, but her eyes are soft and kind. "It's hard running a business."

Her gaze bores into my soul as if she sees every piece of the resentment I've buried deep inside.

"Yeah, but rewarding too."

She nods. "Sometimes. Scrumptuals was my dream."

Is Audrey trying to use telepathy to tell me she knows I feel stuck in a life I didn't choose? My dad's health isn't what it once was, and my mom runs ragged after my brother. I'm a good daughter to them for running the store, but stuck in a destiny I never wanted.

"Let's hope this will help increase the tourist population in Cliffton Heights." I change the subject more to strip that pitying look from her face than anything.

"Oh!" She puts her unicorn bookmark between the pages and shuts the book. "It's going to do great things for us. That's why it's pivotal for all of us to be on the show."

I nod and bite my lip.

"Which reminds me, this guy came in the other day." She moves her chair to face me, leaning forward.

Unease wraps around me. She's going to tell me something I don't want to hear.

"It's crazy, right, but you know the ongoing battle this town has with your cream cheese and the Andrews' bagels? He asked me about my cream cheese frosting on my chocolate cupcakes and I said that I buy it in bulk from The Bagel Place. He said he bought a tub of your cream cheese and then went to Andrews Bagel and bought a dozen for a family brunch thing. And everyone raved about the combination."

I nod. What exactly does she want me to say to that?

She pats my leg, then her gaze falls behind me, and her eyes widen in surprise. "Well, well," she says softly.

I glance over my shoulder and spot Seth Andrews and his mother getting in line. Seth's holding a coffee, his hoodie over his head, while his mom talks with Lucy from Porterhouse.

My gut twists. It's not like I didn't think anyone else from the breakfast crowd would show up, but why did it have to be them?

Audrey pats my leg. "No worries. There's no contest when it comes to your cream cheese."

And that's exactly it—the cream cheese. But cream cheese can't stand on its own. A bagel can.

I glance back once more and Seth notices me this time. He nods then smirks. I can almost hear him thinking, "Game on, Erickson."

CHAPTER THREE

Seth

I stare at Evan Erickson's profile for three hours. Okay, I don't stare because I'm not some creeper, but my gaze keeps returning to her direction as she scours her phone or talks to every person in line as if she's their best friend. Her smile is immediate, her warmth radiating to everyone but me.

I sip my now-cold-ass coffee and push the hood of my sweatshirt off my head.

"That's Evan," Mom says—not in a whisper, mind you. We're only five people behind Evan, so she looks at the sound of her name.

I inwardly roll my eyes. "Way to be chill, Mom."

"I didn't know if you'd recognize her."

Sometimes I wonder how my mom thought I attended Cliffton Heights High School without interacting with Evan. The town might not be Pleasantville small, but it's not a major city. Hell, I had to be lab partners with her sophomore year until she flirted her way into a seat change.

But I'm not going to tell off my mom. That's not cool and she's already nervous as hell about this audition thing. My dad's stubborn ass should be standing next to her. I washed my hands of the bagel company as soon as I left for college at eighteen, but it keeps sucking me back in.

So instead I say, "I do."

"She's really grown into a beautiful woman. Her hips are good. Won't have a problem carrying a baby."

I peer down at my mom and blink a few times. "Did you really just check out whether she had child-bearing hips or not?"

Mom slaps me on my stomach and a few local business owners glance back, apparently not surprised to see me buckle over slightly. I toss my coffee in the trash can just to act as if my mom can't give me a beat-down.

"It's important at her age. I saw her last weekend by the lakefront with Brock Floyd."

I roll back on my heels. Why is it that as soon as you hit stardom level or a certain degree of wealth, people refer to you with both your first and last name?

"Jenny's probably over the moon about the possibility of her marrying into that family."

There's a longing in Mom's tone that irritates me. My parents are only getting older. Trevor isn't reliable anymore. Before his stint in rehab, he broke into the business and stole everything in the safe—including my grandma's heirloom diamond necklace. Putting all their valuables in the business safe wasn't my parents' smartest decision, but when your son robs you blind at your own house, it's hard to find new hiding places.

Now I'm the lucky safe holder, including the diamond necklace they had to purchase back from the pawn store at double the cost because they weren't willing to press charges against my brother to prove it was theirs and get it back without having to pay for it. It helps that I'm roommates and friends with a police officer. But my life has gone from smooth and worry-free to "fuck me, they're calling again." My parents are relying on me to solve their problems with the business now that Trevor isn't an option. I feel their pressure beating down on my neck like the hot sun in the desert and it makes me break out in a sweat.

My gaze returns to Evan and I'm reminded of how she took on that role years ago. Maybe I should be thankful I've had some carefree years.

"The Floyds are fake as shit," I say.

My mom lands another smack to my stomach. "Why would you say such a thing?"

"Hell, Brock was the one who started Trevor down the path he's on."

Brock and my older brother were teammates and best friends. Until my brother got the quarterback position senior year. I guess when rich pricks don't get what they want, they resort to sabotage. Not that I'm excusing my brother. He had a choice not to snort white powder up his fucking nose.

"I highly doubt that. They were friends. Addiction runs in my family. That's why I told you boys not to ever tempt yourself. Some can handle and others can't. Trev can't. There's no way Brock ever did such a thing to your brother."

I sigh and drop the conversation. Everyone in this damn line, including Evan, sees another man when they look at Brock Floyd. For a moment, I wonder why he's not here with Evan, supporting her. Especially since she's biting her nails like when she was seven and Kimmy down the street bet Evan she couldn't ride her bike down suicide hill. Then I remember why he's not here. He doesn't gain anything from waking up this early. None of these people are his clients. I scour the crowd—at least I don't think they are. Hard to tell who's a user sometimes.

"So I wrote a pitch," my mom says, gaining my attention again.

"A pitch?"

My mom shoves a piece of paper at me. Her grocery list is on one side and her chicken scratch is on the other. I turn the paper over, and sure enough, she's got every bagel company name on the other side and there's one with a slogan almost identical. I read what she wrote. "Everything is tastier on an Andrews?" The slogan sounds oddly familiar. "Mom. That's plagiarism."

"No." She points at the paper, and I notice her wedding ring is missing. The one she's worn every day since forever. The one that's left an indent in her skin.

Fuck Trevor. Please tell me my mom didn't sell her wedding ring to pay for his rehab?

"I say tastier. They said better. They probably paid millions and their ad agency couldn't use a thesaurus to find a better adjective?"

I chuckle. My mom. She truly is the best and works too damn hard for all of us. That she took the time to look this up says how important it is to her. I feel like this was my dad's dream, but she's the one making it come true.

"Well, we should try to think of something more unique. But it says this round, they just meet with the business owners. We talk about our products and what we have to offer. Then they make a short list and we bring in items to taste." After my mom barged in on my boudoir session, I looked up all the rules. "So just relax and be yourself. Everyone loves you." I put my arm around her shoulders and kiss her temple.

This time, her hand pats my stomach. We stand there for a moment before Evan stands.

"She really is beautiful, huh?" my mom whispers.

I glance down to see her staring at Evan. I should lie and tell her fuck no, but instead I nod without correcting her. What? Evan is fucking gorgeous.

* * *

BUT GORGEOUS EVAN is a pain in my dick. That's how annoying it is to be up against her. As soon as the building opened, we were split into groups—breakfast, lunch, dinner, or treat. So now I'm stuck in a room with her and five café-type owners.

My mom approaches her first. "Evan, how are you?"

I had no idea they were even on speaking terms.

"Hi, Mrs. Andrews. I'm good. Thank you."

Always Miss Polite. It's like Evan went through some transformation. The girl used to have a sharp mouth and snappy wit. She used to be the one convincing me to do shit we shouldn't. And now she's smiling and happy as if she's Cinderella, free of her captors and singing down the streets of Cliffton Heights, in charge of spreading cheer.

"You remember Seth?" My mom pulls the sleeve of my hoodie.

I stumble closer as though I'm five and Mom's taking me to the dentist.

"Hi, Seth." I guess Evan doesn't want to spread her cheer my way because her tone is one of distaste.

"How's the boyfriend?" I raise both eyebrows, annoyed that she didn't take my advice and break up with the douchebag. I never thought she could choose wealth over character.

"He's good. Thanks for asking." She says all the right things, but there's no warm and fuzzy tone in her voice.

"Oh yes, you're dating Brock Floyd, right?" My mom pretends as if she didn't already know.

If I hear the words Brock Floyd one more time, I'm going to puke all over this floor.

Evan's face lights up and my chest hurts as if I just ate a spicy-ass burrito from the gas station. Damn, could she really like a guy like him?

"I am. It's new though."

"Well, he's quite a catch. I'm sure your mom is thrilled."

Evan's smile fades, and for a moment, I care enough to decipher what that look means—before I realize I don't actually give a shit. I warned her, she didn't listen. Not my problem anymore.

"What about you, Seth?" Evan asks.

Her question takes me by surprise. I blink a few times, still shocked that she initiated a conversation with me.

"What about me?" I narrow my eyes.

"Girlfriend?"

My mom slides her hand through my arm, an answer on the tip of her tongue. She'll spout the whole "once he's ready, he'll pick from all his admirers" if I let her.

What? I told you I'm a momma's boy. She knows she's got the best-looking son in all of Cliffton Heights.

"No girl… friends."

Evan huffs at my implication that I have girls but not girlfriends.

"One day he'll choose," my mom says.

Evan smiles politely when I guarantee she wants to flip me off and turn around. Not sure why she would give a shit if I'm sleeping with a ton of women. Although truth is, I'm not. Sad as the truth sounds.

"And she'll be so lucky."

I cough at her sarcastic reply. Maybe I was wrong about her witty side dying.

"You could always get in line," I say.

My mom stares at me for a moment and her eyes widen. But I steady my gaze on Evan, waiting for her to enter our ring of banter. *Come on, girl, you can do it.* But Evan's eyes flicker to my mom before her almost-scowl flips to a smile.

"I have Brock, but thanks for the offer." She touches my mom's arm. "Nice to see you, Mrs. Andrews, but I'm going to practice what I'm going to say."

"Good luck, sweetie," my mom says.

"Seth," Evan deadpans and turns toward the other side of the room.

My mom touches Evan's arm tentatively, and Evan turns around to face her again. "How is your mom doing?"

Evan's eyes bounce to me because she heard it too. I thought it was only my heart that just cracked for my mom. Her voice was longing and yearning and... desperate.

Evan grabs my mom's hand. "She's doing well."

Well is about as good of a word as fine.

We all know Jenny Erickson's life hasn't been the same since Evan's dad had a heart attack one year ago. For a moment, I thought it might patch the feud between our dads. That my dad would reach out after finding out that his ex-best friend had almost died. But sadly, it didn't.

Now, looking at my mom, I see something new when she talks about her ex-best friend. She's still worried about Jenny and wants to know she's doing okay.

"That's good. And your dad?"

Evan's shoulders sink even farther. "He's getting stronger. He comes in to the shop for a few hours every day."

"That's good." My mom nods, a little overenthusiastically.

"I'm sorry to hear about Trevor," Evan says.

I divert my gaze.

"Thank you. He's in rehab. I'm sure he'll be out and healthy in no time. Just like your daddy will be soon."

Evan nods with a tight smile. "Well, good luck, Mrs. Andrews." She pats my mom's hand and tucks her head down, walking away.

"She's still so beautiful and sweet. Jenny and Vic did a good job there."

I put my arm around my mom's shoulders, needing to get rid of the melancholy mood lingering around us. "Hey now, no one did a better job than you and Dad with me."

I beam at her and she swats my stomach, laughing. Even with her smile, her eyes are filled with sorrow.

"Andrews Bagel," a man calls.

I raise my hand. "Time to put on your competitor's hat, Mom."

She nods and we walk toward the man, disappearing through a black curtained-off area, but I can tell that neither of us are as gung ho as we were before we spoke with Evan.

CHAPTER FOUR

Evan

"The Bagel Place!" a woman calls from the opposite side of the room I just saw the Andrews go to.

My stomach clenches as I raise my hand and shove my phone inside my bag.

"Hi," the friendly blonde says and walks steadily past a black curtain. "How are you?"

"I'm good."

That's the extent of our conversation—which I'm thankful for, because I feel as though I might throw up. After Mrs. Andrews gave me those puppy dog eyes and asked about my family, I felt the weight of her grief for losing her best friend. Because although Mrs. Andrews hates us, she still loves us too, and she knows our family has been through the wringer lately. But so has hers. I have no idea what it's been like, but the rumors about Trevor and what he's done to support his habit have been upsetting to hear.

"Here you go." The blonde woman opens a curtain, and there sits the host for the Food Channel's most popular show, *Tastes of Small Towns*, Nick Klein.

He stands. "Miss Erickson from The Bagel Place, right?" His hand is outstretched across the small table and I slide my small hand into his large one.

"Yes. Thank you."

He smiles. It's warm and kind and it puts me a little more at ease. "You're welcome. Please sit down. I'm—"

I laugh. "I know who you are."

He chuckles and leans back, putting his ankle on his opposite knee. "Sorry, I'm surprising a few businesses. A mutual friend called in a favor."

"That's nice of you."

He shrugs and holds his calf in a casual way. "I think you know them. The Floyds. Bruce Floyd. I heard you're Brockie's girl."

My gut twists. I brought this event up to Brock two nights ago at dinner at a fancy five-star place in the city. He didn't act like he was really listening, but I guess he was. I can't decide if I like that he called in this favor or not.

"Yes. We've been dating," I say.

"For how long?"

"Um." I swallow. "Just a couple months."

"I think that's pretty long in Brockie's book, no?" He chuckles as if I should agree that I know I'm dating the town playboy. Some nights I wonder if I did in fact tame him.

But I plaster on my smile. Regardless of how I got here, I need to be here. For Eli, Elsie, my mom, and my dad. And myself, because this move is slightly selfish too. "I suppose so."

He glances at a piece of paper in front of him. "I'm supposed to ask you all these questions. They're boring." He drops the paper back on the table. "Let's talk about you."

I twist my fingers in my lap. "What would you like to know?"

"The Bagel Place? Was it yours originally or did you buy it? You're young."

"It's my parents' actually. I run it though," I quickly add. "But my parents started it almost twenty years ago. Before that—" I stop talking because I don't want anyone involved with the show to know about the feud. Who knows what they'd think of my dad if they did?

"So you were always destined to take the place over?" Nick has got one of those charming smiles like he's listening intently and there's nowhere else he'd rather be.

"Kind of, yes." I thought I was about to make my escape when Eli started school, but then my dad's heart attack sucked me back in like a tornado.

"And you enjoy it?"

"I do. Very much." I sit up straighter in my chair.

His smile fades for a second, but it pops back into place. "You should always do what you love. So what part is your favorite?"

"The business side mostly. I mean, I don't mind the baking and making the cream cheese. Then again, maybe I only enjoy the inventory and numbers side because that's the only time I'm off my feet." I smile and shrug.

He laughs. "Well, I hope Brockie's giving you a good foot rub at the end of the day."

Yeah, right. I suggested once to sit at home and do nothing, and Brock gasped like a schoolgirl who'd just heard she's the topic of a wicked rumor.

I smile rather than tell him the truth.

"You might be the only person I've met who says your favorite part is the business side. That's usually the side restauranteurs hate. They like the creativity in the kitchen. Are you allowed to fiddle?"

"Fiddle?" I ask for clarification.

"Test things. Try new products. Do your parents allow you to mix things up?"

Truth is, I've never really tried. I just stand by what they started because it's easier. I can imagine my dad coming in and asking why I changed something that's working though. Changing things would rock the boat. I don't like to rock the boat.

"Yeah, they allow me to," I lie.

"That's great." He shifts in his seat. "I could see a business like a bagel shop growing boring after a while if you can't try new flavors and products."

Someone lifts the curtain to his right, poking her head in and softly speaking in his ear.

His foot falls to the floor. "That's all the time I've got, I'm afraid. But I'm having dinner at the Floyds' tomorrow night. Maybe I'll see you there." I nod and stand as he does. He extends his hand. "It was great meeting you, Miss Erickson."

"Evan please," I say.

"Evan." His full mouth of straight white teeth gleam. "I have a good feeling about this opportunity for you." He winks.

It's not lost on me that he's pretty much telling me that because I'm dating Brock, he'll make sure I'm in.

"Thank you for meeting with me, Mr. Klein."

He shoves his hands into the pockets of his jeans. "Nick. Please."

"Thank you… Nick."

"Have a great rest of the day," he says and walks away, leaving me standing there feeling a little speechless.

The blonde who brought me to him pokes her head in, startling me. "Ready?"

I nod and follow her back to the big room full of people I

was in before. She rattles directions at me and says if I make the cut, I'll receive a phone call.

When I walk out of the building, the sun is high, but there's a chill in the air signaling the impending winter.

"Babe!" I turn to my left to see Brock standing next to his fancy fast car.

I walk toward Brock and he opens up his arms for a hug. He's usually not an outwardly affectionate guy. Never holds my hand. I hug him and he squeezes me so tightly, my breath catches as he swings me around.

"How did it go?" He places me back down and his finger tucks a section of hair behind my ear. My eyes follow the path of his finger because all of this is odd behavior for him.

"I think you probably know how it went." I raise an eyebrow.

A mischievous smile crosses his lips and he belts out a laugh so loud, it ricochets off every building on the block. "See, good things happen when you date a Floyd. Let's head back to my place and you can thank me." He winks.

I'm not sure if it's the fact that he arranged for me to do well here today or what Seth has told me, but I'm suddenly seeing Brock in a different light. Then again, can I really trust a guy whose family hates me and puts me down every time I see him? Seth must be full of it.

"I have to get back to the shop," I murmur.

He puts his hand on my hip and pulls me toward him as if he can't go a minute without touching me. "I thought Elsie was watching it for you today?"

"Just while I'm here. You could stay and keep me company?"

"You know I'd love to, but my dad's got about a million things he wants me to do."

I nod. "Okay. Call me later."

He chuckles and places a kiss on the tip of my nose.

What the hell is up with him?

"Babe, I'll drive you to work," he says as if that's what he always does.

"Okay… thanks."

I shift my weight to step back, but he grabs my hips, thrusting me into him. He kisses me as though he's going off to war and he'll never have my lips on his again. But it's not lingering and romantic. It's claiming and hard, and I don't feel one ounce of arousal deep in my belly. He closes the kiss and pushes my hips so I'm away from him now.

As my eyes snap open, he takes my hand and leads me to the passenger side of the car. He opens it, and his gaze lands to our right with a cocky smirk.

"Andrews," Brock says with a nod.

Seth is leaning against the brick wall, scowl in place.

How long has he been there? But Brock's arrogance as he bends to kiss me one more time before shutting the door confirms that his performance was all for Seth, not me.

I refrain from looking back at Seth because his expression is already haunting me. He looked almost… jealous?

Seth

$\mathcal{I}$ walk into Ink Envy, my buddy Dylan's tattoo shop, and slump into a chair in the waiting area.

"What's wrong with you?" Dylan asks from the reception table. He walks around and sits across from me.

"Just a shitty day."

"Did you try to hit on one of your clients?" Frankie, another tattooist, asks as she dips her needle into more ink.

"No, I'm a professional." You have no idea how many times I have to tell that to my friends. They think boudoir photography is porn. It's not how I want to use my skill as a photographer, but it's what's paying the bills. My friends Blanca and Ethan threw some freelance work my way a few months ago, but they don't need me on the regular.

"Oh, I think maybe he did hit on a client and they said no," Jax, one of my roommates and also a tattoo artist, calls, dropping his sketchbook on the table in front of him. "It's okay, Seth, just hop back on the horse."

"Yeah, Jax can give you some tips. He's never gotten off the horse," Frankie snips.

Jax rolls his eyes. "You have it all turned around there, Spark Plug. I'm the horse that the women don't want to get off of." He winks at her, which I know pisses her off.

Dylan puts his head in his hands. "They never stop," he mumbles.

Dylan is the owner, Frankie has rented a chair from him for a long time, and Jax is Dylan's high school buddy who returned a few months ago. All Frankie and Jax do is bicker about everything.

"And let me guess, you're referring to yourself as a horse because you're hung like one?" Frankie doesn't look up from where she's working on her client.

"We can go in the back and you can confirm it for yourself." Jax stands with his hands at his sides.

The woman Frankie is tattooing perks up and Frankie forcefully pushes her back down on the table.

"It's not always about the size, big guy," Frankie says.

"And whoever told you that has a micro dick. Believe me, Spark Plug, if you took a ride on me, you'd realize how lame that statement is."

"Give it a rest," Dylan says. "We have a client here."

"Oh, I don't mind. I mean, if he wants to whip it out right here, you'll hear no complaints from me," the woman on Frankie's table says with a smile.

Frankie guffaws and Jax's fingers go to the button on his jeans.

"For Christ's sake, have some self-respect," Frankie yells.

Jax laughs, sitting back down and picking up his sketchbook with a shit-eating grin so wide, it makes me think it makes his day when they go back and forth like this.

"You're such a manwhore," Frankie adds before the sound of the needle drowns out whatever Jax might say back.

Truth is, Frankie's wrong. Jax talks a big game and I'm sure in the past his talk lived up to his actions, but he's never brought a woman back to our apartment. If he isn't working, he's usually home. I thought when he moved in, it'd help with my own game. I had visions of Jax, Knox, and me going out to bars and having parties, a circulation of girls in and out every weekend, but sadly, we play our fucking Xbox more than we actually find chicks to fuck.

"I just… sorry, man, I'm going to Rian's shop." I stand.

"I'll come with." Dylan turns toward the others. "I'll be next door if you need me. Try not to kill each other."

He follows me to the shop next door—his fiancée Rian's baking business, Sweet Infusion. The doorbell chimes when we step in, and the scent of sugar and icing hits us. Dylan flips over the closed sign and locks the doors.

"We've been over this. If it's five o'clock, you're closed. I don't like the door open when you're in the back, washing dishes," Dylan lectures Rian as we walk into the back where she's washing cake pans in the large stainless steel industrial sink.

She's also unaware of our presence because she's dancing to "Dancing Queen" by ABBA. I do all of us a favor and turn off the Bluetooth radio. Rian whips around.

"That's my cleaning up playlist," she says.

I slide up on the counter and scroll through her phone next to the speaker, with what looks like a playlist filled with seventies songs.

"You have to lock the doors," Dylan repeats with a pleading look on his face.

She kisses him. They probably saw each other at lunch. Hell, they probably fucked… I raise my hand.

"What?" Dylan asks.

"Can you tell me the surfaces you guys haven't fucked on in here?" I glance around.

Dylan scans the room and his lips purse. "Rian, you wanna take this one?"

She giggles. "Right where you are is our favorite place."

I jump down as they laugh.

"Jeez, Seth, we don't have sex in my kitchen. Health codes. Now." She tilts her head at Dylan, and he chuckles. "Dylan's office is another story."

"Remind me never to go in there. Damn, Jolie sleeps on that couch."

A huge bang on the glass interrupts us. I peer around the corner and see that it's Blanca and Ethan. I leave the two lovebirds to go open the door for another pair.

"Hey, Seth," Blanca says. "We come bearing good news."

"That you guys canceled your church wedding and we're heading to the Caribbean instead?" Dylan asks, emerging from the back with Rian.

"Funny. No, we're thinking of doing a joint bachelor and bachelorette party," Blanca says.

I scrunch my forehead at Ethan. *Grow a pair of balls, man.*

"Um…" I'm at a loss for words of how to tell them that's the stupidest idea ever. "So you guys will sit side by side while strippers put their tits and dicks in your faces? Is this some kinky fetish? I'm not judging, but I think it's something you should do behind closed doors."

Blanca hits me on the back of the head.

Damn Italian women.

"No, there won't be strippers."

I stare blankly at Ethan.

He shrugs. "I'm not really a stripper kind of guy."

My neck cranes toward Dylan and back to Ethan. "You're not a stripper kind of guy?"

"No. I don't care."

"And I don't want a dick swinging back and forth in front of me." Blanca's face is contorted in disgust.

"Please tell me unless it's Ethan's. Or I might have to stand up at your wedding and protest."

Her jaw cocks. "What the hell is wrong with you?"

"He's cranky," Dylan says matter-of-factly.

"Horny is more like it," Ethan says, and Dylan raises his hand for a high five.

Assholes.

"I'm not horny." Although that would explain why I'm suddenly fantasizing about Evan. Maybe I do need to get laid.

"The fact that you're upset that Ethan doesn't want strippers at his bachelor party says you are. Go down to a strip club if you want to see them so bad." Blanca sounds angry as hell and I step back.

They say I'm cranky? *Look in a damn mirror, Blanca.*

She inhales a deep breath, seemingly calming herself. "Listen"—Blanca puts her palm out in front of us—well, not us, me—"I have done so much for this wedding. A traditional Catholic wedding just like my mom wanted." She glances back at Ethan and he puts his arm around her waist. "I don't need a night of freedom away from Ethan. I want us all to go somewhere together and have fun. Everyone can have a plus one. Maybe we head to Vegas, or a beach, or hell, I'll go to a cabin in Maine. I just want a few days of peace before the wedding. Is that a problem, Andrews?" Her brown eyes narrow.

"Fine. Cool. Whatever the bride wants." I hold up my hands.

"Good. Everyone throw us any ideas you have."

"Are your brothers coming?" Rian asks, and Dylan cocks his head. Even though I'm a dude, I'll admit, Blanca's brothers could grab a spot on *The Bachelor* if they wanted to.

"No, it's just going to be us. You'll have to wait until the wedding to see them." Blanca rolls her eyes at Rian.

"Hey, it's Sierra who drools every time they come over," Rian says, putting her arms around Dylan's neck.

A soft knock lands on the glass and we all turn our heads. My jaw drops when I see Evan. Without looking at anyone else, I open up the door and let her in.

"Are you stalking me?" I ask.

"You wish," she says and beelines past me with a pair of bags in her hands.

"Seriously, she's closed. Why are you here?" I'm fully aware that I sound like a dick.

Blanca huffs at me and Ethan shoots me a look to say *be cool, dude*. But all I envision when I see her is Brock's tongue down her throat. Why did I have to follow her out of the building earlier today? I should've stayed next to my mom as she talked with every business owner in town. What was I really trying to accomplish anyway?

Ask Evan if she saw it? The look on my mom's face that struck us both silent? Even if she did, it's not like either of us are going to do something about it. So my mom feels bad for the Ericksons. How could she not? This past year has sucked for them, and Evan is trying to hold it all on her shoulders.

"She's here for me," Rian says and walks Evan back to the kitchen area.

"For you?" I ask, following.

Dylan puts his hand on my chest to stop me. "Don't be a prick."

"Me? Prick?" I pick up his hand to remove it from me.

"You tend to lose your mind when she's near," he says.

"I do not."

"You do so," Blanca says, laughing. "I'm surprised she didn't knee you in the balls just now. I would have."

I circle around to her. "She's not a short-tempered Italian."

"You better watch it," Ethan warns. "She *will* knee you in the balls."

I disregard all of them and head to the back.

Rian is raving on and on about some mixture. "This is perfect. Thank you so much, Evan. Tell me, how did it go today?"

What? Are they friends? Instead of announcing myself, I eavesdrop further.

"I was so nervous but..." Evan looks over her shoulder and I duck behind the wall.

Dylan shakes his head at me. But thankfully Knox walks in and distracts them from watching me.

"I actually met with Nick Klein," she says.

Fucking A. She got to meet the host. Mom and I were with who I suspect was some intern.

"That's crazy. How do you think it went?" Rian asks.

"That's the thing... you know the Floyds?"

Rian sighs. "Who doesn't. I saw you at the gala with Brock Floyd. Are you dating him?"

Why is Rian acting dumb? She knows Evan is.

I don't hear Evan confirm she is, but she says, "I think Brock pulled some strings for me. Nick Klein knows them."

"Oh," Rian says. "Well, that's okay."

Um... no, it isn't, Rian!

"I mean, things like that happen all the time."

"I know," Evan says. "But it feels wrong."

"I wouldn't worry about it. You have a great product. It deserves to be out there for everyone to know about. I mean, this cinnamon cream cheese you made is going to make my icing taste awesome."

So Rian's buying cream cheese from her?

"Thanks, and if you have any other ideas you want me to try out, just let me know." Evan's voice grows closer.

I step back, but a large hand grabs my neck and pushes me forward through the door to the kitchen.

"Ladies. Seth just wanted to say hi." Knox releases me and shakes his head while grabbing a cookie from the pile Rian set aside to give to the shelter tonight. That's where all her extra baked goods go now that we're all sick of them. Everyone but Knox, I guess.

"Seth." Rian raises her eyebrows, probably assuming correctly that I was eavesdropping.

"How long were you there?" Evan asks, her hands falling to her hips.

"Long enough to hear that your boyfriend is making chess moves for you." Bitterness coats my voice. "Oh, and that you're selling *your* products to *my* friends."

Evan's phone rings and she digs into her purse.

"That must be Romeo now." I stuff my hands into my pockets.

She answers and nods and smiles, turning away from me.

My own phone rings and I silence it when I see it's my mom. I can tell from Evan's end of the conversation that she got a callback. I guess I shouldn't be surprised.

"Yep, tomorrow? Perfect. I'll be there." Evan hangs up.

"You got a callback?" I ask.

"I did." She nods toward my pocket holding my phone.

"Are you even surprised?"

Rian looks as if she's not sure where to go, especially since I'm standing in the doorway.

But Evan ignores my question. "I have to go because… I just have to go." She turns to Rian. "Let me know, okay?"

"Definitely." Rian waves.

I slide a smidgeon out of the way. Evan's shoulder brushes my arm.

"Way to go," Knox says after she's gone.

"What?" I ask.

"Are you under the impression that you get girls by being a dick?" he asks.

I scowl at him. "What are you talking about?"

"The fact that you want to fuck her, not fuck her over." He chomps down on his second cookie. Which seems odd because he's usually a health nut.

"Thank you." Rian raises her hand and Knox smacks it. "Someone finally said it."

"You're both delusional." I leave before they figure out I'm lying through my teeth.

I will not accept that I want to sleep with the woman I've been raised to hate. Not without a fight anyway.

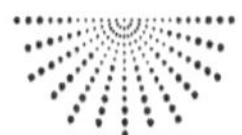

CHAPTER SIX

Evan

I have no choice but to tell someone about this opportunity we have with the Food Channel. I'm due to bring my products in at noon today, which means I had to ask Elsie to come in again. So I chose to tell my mom. She'll eventually be the one to sign the papers since she's one of the rightful owners of the shop.

"Hey, sweetie, how is everything?" Mom rushes in and heads to the back, where she washes her hands.

"Good. A slower-than-normal morning."

"Oh really? I wonder why?" Her dark curly hair, not unlike mine, doesn't look as though it's been brushed and it has a slight frizz today. She cut hers to shoulder-length since she doesn't have the time to actually style it.

As usual, her full attention isn't on anything I'm saying because she believes I have it all under control. That I'm the child she doesn't need to worry about, the one she can rely on if she needs to.

"I'm not sure." I stand in the doorway between the kitchen and the counter, unsure how to bring up what I did. I took a chance and so far it's panning out, but she might think that what I'm doing is wrong because she knows my dad won't agree. He'll be here in an hour or so after he's done his cardio physical therapy. "Can I talk to you for a second?"

She dries her hands and rests her hip on the sink, looking me over. Her wide eyes fill with worry. "What's wrong?"

That's the aftermath of when a horrible thing happens. Your first thought when someone says they want to talk is that it's bad news. First it was my dad's heart attack. Then the surgery. Then the rehab. And he's still not back to where he was. The business stresses him out, so we agreed that I'd take over the day-to-day and he'd help out where he could. Which is why I need to make this place more profitable. Profitable enough to hire outside help so my parents can live off the income it generates without the stress of managing it.

"Nothing's wrong. But… can we sit?"

She huffs. "I have to make the cream cheese for Scrumptuals."

"I did it already," I say.

Her eyes light up. "You did?"

"I told you it was slow."

A soft, gracious smile lands on her lips. "Thank you, sweetie."

"You're welcome."

For a moment, we're not manager and owner—as it often feels these days—we're mother and daughter again.

She grabs a cup and swings her arm around my shoulders, leading us to the front of the shop. "Let's sit."

I sit in the first booth, which is more or less our family's. Eli does his homework here, Elsie whines, my dad reads the newspaper. My mom and I might be the only two in our family who don't sit here actually.

Once she fills her cup with some soda, she sits across from me. "What's up?"

"Did you hear about the Food Channel's auditions at the mercantile mart?"

She shakes her head. I'm not surprised. My mom is busy and doesn't really have time for much outside of the business, my brother, and my dad.

"Well, the Food Channel is filming in Cliffton Heights for Nick Klein's show, *Tastes of Small Towns?*" I wait to see if the show name sparks any recognition.

My mom sips her soda and shakes her head.

"Well, I… um… I went down yesterday to audition."

"That's why you had Elsie come in?"

I nod. "We were chosen to come in today for them to sample our products. If they like them, we'll probably make it onto the show."

She continues to sip her drink for a moment. My anxiety skyrockets, wondering about her reaction. It'll come down on one of two sides—that it's good for the business or that dad won't like a bunch of strangers and a production crew up in our business.

"What happens if we're chosen?" she asks.

I shrug. "I think they come here, film, and say how good our food is. Maybe they choose a specialty item. Then it airs on television."

She thinks it over for a moment. "Okay."

"That's it?"

She smiles. "It sounds like a good opportunity. We'll just wait to tell your dad until it's for sure. No need to put that stress on him until it's certain."

Guilt pinches my chest at the thought of causing my dad undo stress. "You're not mad I went behind your back?"

She pats my hand. "Sweetie, this is your future. I can't be mad for you wanting to make it a success."

My gaze deviates out the window.

My future.

A bagel shop.

Yippee.

"But you know it will be a tough sell to your dad, so hopefully it wasn't all for naught." She slides out of the booth. "But let's make the best batch we can so you can really wow them."

I slide out to follow her. "I already made a few samples."

She stops before venturing into the kitchen. "Pretty soon you won't need me."

I chuckle. "I'll always need you."

Her eyes are kind and sweet when she glances over her shoulder at me. I'm reminded that it's not only me sacrificing something these days.

She takes the containers I already made up out of the fridge and pulls out some plastic spoons. "Did you see the Andrews there by chance?" She pries off the plastic lid, spooning a small taste.

My family doesn't talk about the Andrews very often and never around my dad.

"I did actually." I sit on the stool and she looks at me, waiting for me to continue. "Seth and Mrs. Andrews were there."

"Seth?" She cocks her head. "I didn't think he was part of the business."

"I think because of Trevor…"

She nods, lips pressed together. "Makes sense. He'll have to step up, I suppose."

Will he? Suddenly, I envision the two of us running our parents' bagel shops in twenty years, feud still thriving. One or both of us married and the hatred running down to our children. I straighten to get rid of the pang tugging on my heart.

"She asked about you," I say as she closes the lid on the plain spread and moves to our chive flavor.

"Who did?"

"Debbie. Mrs. Andrews."

She nods but never makes eye contact with me. "Oh really?" She opens the strawberry flavor next.

"She seemed worried."

There's no reaction from her again. I guess that longing I felt from Mrs. Andrews is one-sided.

"We're fine. Did you tell her that? That we're fine?"

I nod. "I did."

"Good." She closes all the containers and pushes them toward me. "They all taste great. You did a wonderful job. If I didn't own this place, I'd be worried you were going to take my job away."

She chuckles and heads to round up the unsold bagels from this morning so she can cut them and bake them into chips.

And we're back to manager and owner again.

Great.

* * *

I ARRIVE at the mercantile mart and the place is running like a well-oiled machine. I head to the breakfast area to turn in my items. The blonde woman who introduced me to Nick Klein is in the background, talking to other workers.

"So you're Bagels 'R Us?" the man who's supposed to clearly mark my items says, jotting it down before I correct him.

"No, we're The Bagel Place," I say.

He nods as though he knew that. "That's right, they

already dropped off. Sorry. All these bagel places. What's up with this city?"

He's right, there are a plethora of bagel places, but where is there not? They're about as popular as cupcake shops were five years ago. But the good part is The Bagel Place is on top of the list. Unfortunately, Andrews is sitting right next to us on said list. No one can ever pick which one of us is better without saying the same old crap about morphing us together. I mean, get over it, people, it will never be again.

The woman from the lunch station comes over and I'm thankful she's going to help this poor confused man, but she swipes the pen out of his hand. "Just one second, mine ran out." She heads back over to her station.

Dan, the man in charge of breakfast, laughs and leans back in his chair as though he's got all the time in the world. "No problem, Nance," he says, whereas I want to say get my cream cheese in the fridge ASAP.

Nance (I'm assuming her name is Nancy, but Dan the man can't be bothered to use the y) talks to the person in front of her, taking down the information on the items they brought in.

I silently look at the paperwork on the table between Dan and myself. I can't help but notice that Seth is listed as a legal part-owner of his family's business. When did that happen? Irritation fills me that after all the time and effort I've put into my family's business, I'm still not an official owner, but Seth, who's just jumping in to help cover while his brother is away, apparently is.

"I think she's done with the pen," I say politely to Dan, who's now rolling his head to stretch out his neck.

"I needed a break. You wouldn't think this work was hard, but you creative types are difficult to deal with."

I glance at Nance jotting down notes on a separate piece

of paper, transcribing what the woman she's talking to is telling her.

"Are you stalking me or something?" Seth comes over and places his bagels and four cream cheeses on the table.

I huff. "Yeah, because I'm a masochist."

Dan has his arms above his head now, pulling on his elbows and sighing in relief. He spots Seth through one barely open eye. "Are you with her?"

Seth laughs. "That's a hard no."

Likewise, buddy.

"I'm Andrews Bagel Company." He pushes the tray closer.

"Here you go, Dan. Sorry," Nance says with a bright smile, returning the pen.

How on Earth do they only have one pen? It's the Food Channel, for Pete's sake.

"Thanks for the break." Dan sits up straighter, poises the pen on the labels in front of him, pointing the back end of the pen toward Seth's items. "So that's The Bagel Place?"

"No!" I screech and Seth's eyebrows scrunch up. Even Nance glances over with concern. "That's Andrews," I say in a much quieter voice.

"Jeez, I knew you hated me, but that reaction is a little dramatic, don't you think?"

I want to punch Seth in the upper arm like I used to do when I was nine and he flirted with Zoey Rekert. Instead, I ignore him and point at my goods. "This is The Bagel Place." I point at Seth's. "That's Andrews Bagel Company."

"That's right. Okay, you're all checked in."

I stare at the containers Dan *hasn't* yet marked. He has the labels written out with times and marked the ones that need refrigeration, but he's yet to place them on the products.

"Here are your numbers." He hands us each a number since the companies have to remain anonymous. "Good luck to you both."

"Thanks," Seth says, stuffing his paper inside his pocket.

"Now, you will remember, right?" I ask.

"Jesus, Erickson, give the guy a break," Seth says, walking away.

Dan laughs. "Don't worry. I've got it handled."

I reluctantly walk away from the table because of the line forming behind me. I blow out a breath. It's out of my hands now.

Hopefully Dan knows what he's doing.

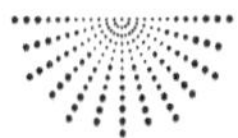

CHAPTER SEVEN

Seth

The breakfast crew, as they call us, is called in to sit in a room where we can watch the judges critique our food. We're stuffed like fucking sardines in this room with a small-ass television so we can watch someone say how delicious or shitty something we made is. It's like signing yourself up to get your ass kicked.

"Why are you here?" Evan asks, sitting in the seat next to me.

"Why are you sitting next to me?"

"Answer my question first."

"My mom begged and pleaded." She was busy at the store, and since we're still keeping this under wraps from my dad, she couldn't escape. Her meeting me in the back alley with a tray of fresh bagels and cream cheese wasn't suspicious at all. No wonder my brother got away with his drug problem for so long under my dad's nose.

"You're such a momma's boy."

I smile proudly. I'm not embarrassed to love my mom and want to take care of her. Besides, Evan's doing the same thing I am. Her reason to be here matches mine.

Other bagel shop owners eye Evan and I because well, we're their biggest competition. Andrews Bagel Company and The Bagel Place run this town as far as bagel shops go. No other place has survived long enough to be a true competitor to us since our dads split the business all those years ago.

The judges come into the room and sit in the three seats side by side.

"So what did you bring?" Evan whispers.

I catch a scent of her perfume. It's nice. Shit, it's more than nice. It's dick-saluting level. I shift in my seat and cross my legs to make sure mine doesn't salute.

"Our best sellers, of course." I'm lying. I don't know what our best sellers are. I just brought what my mom told me to.

"Your everything bagel, right?" Jealousy rings in her tone and I smile from the satisfaction that she knows Andrews Bagel Company bagels are better.

"Probably," I say nonchalantly, like I don't really care what happens today.

"What does your dad put in the dough?"

"Wouldn't know." I crack my neck from side to side.

My dad won't share his recipe with anyone. After what went down with Vic Erickson, he said he trusts no one. Not my mom, not Trevor, and definitely not his son who abandoned the family business to take pictures.

They bring out the first sample and the woman announces the number. I pull mine out of my pocket because I didn't even look at what it was. Seventeen. I glance at Evan, who has the tightest grip on hers. Sixteen.

As they work their way through each number, it's clear

we were some of the last to get our items in because they're going in numerical order.

Evan groans when one judge spits a piece of coffee cake into a napkin, saying it's inedible. A woman two rows up weeps silently and shuffles out of the room. Damn. It's a good thing I didn't bring my mom here. She'd go apeshit on these people if they spit out an Andrews bagel.

I place my hand on Evan's bouncing knee—mostly because it's hitting my chair and making me anxious and annoyed. I don't react when her body heat seeps into my palm and seems to travel up my arm. "Relax."

"Sorry, Mr. Cool." She stops for a moment.

As soon as I move my hand, her knee starts bobbing again as if it's on a fishing line in a windy lake. "What are you, ten?"

She's only half-listening to me. So her confused, narrowed eyes show she doesn't understand my meaning.

"The Mister part—" I let it go because hell, if she doesn't get it, the insult mustn't have been a good one.

"So obviously you were able to take time off from your porn job?" She's still focused on the television as she asks that.

A guy growls when the judges shake their heads and push away their plates. *Damn, number five. Sorry, big guy.*

"Well, as talented as I am, I do get a day off occasionally. Much to my clients' dismay."

I glance over when she doesn't respond and she's staring blankly at me. "You have regulars?"

I nod.

"Like, women ask for you?"

"Have you seen me?" I look down over my body that's folded in the chair.

She huffs and rolls her eyes.

I'm not going to explain what I do to someone who judges me or my clients. I don't want to be a boudoir photographer, but not because I'm embarrassed by what I do. If I loved to take pictures of people, it would probably be a great job, but I like capturing architecture. I like angles and the way the light plays on bricks and metal at different times of the day.

Don't get me wrong, I love candids of people. I enjoy capturing a look that crosses someone's face for a split second. But I love a sunset or sunrise or right before a storm is going to pound us with rain and the sky is going to crackle and boom. I enjoy capturing the feel of a city through one shot. But no one wants to hear that, just like no one wants to hear that the majority of the women who come for boudoir photography want to capture the feeling of being wanted again.

Number ten gets called and the room feels as if it's growing smaller.

One judge actually says it's the worst thing he's ever tasted. This time, the guy kicks a chair and leaves.

"This is horrible. I'm not sure I want to hear what they're going to say," Evan says, her nails now in her mouth.

I ease her hand away from her mouth, locking her wrist over her bouncing knee. "You'd make Deepak Chopra anxious. Calm down. It isn't the end of the world if they don't like your stuff."

Truthfully, they're going to like the Ericksons' cream cheese. Their bagels, eh, I don't know. I haven't eaten one in two decades, so I don't really know. But I'd bet my right nut that they aren't better than ours. I have no idea how my dad makes them, but Evan is right—they're the best this town has to offer. Maybe even the best in all of New York, and that's saying a lot. Me vouching for my father and all.

I'm not sure if we're being so civil to one another just because we're on what feels like the same capsizing boat.

We've seen fifteen people's dreams shatter by the time they call number sixteen, and we're the last two in the room.

Evan stands as a tray gets set in front of the judges.

"Sixteen!" the woman booms through a microphone, staring at the camera as if she can see us.

"I'm so nervous," Evan says, walking up to the television to get a better view.

I sit back in my chair and watch from afar. It's not like I'm going to give her moral support when we're pitching against one another here.

"No!" she yells. "That's not mine!" She actually raises her fist and knocks on the television as if it's a window. "No. No. No." She flips around. "They're serving my cream cheese with your bagels. What did you do?"

"Me?" I point at myself and stand.

She circles back to the television, continuing to yell as though someone will hear her.

"Fantastic. Now this is a New York bagel," one judge says.

"The cream cheese." Nick Klein moans as if a woman just slipped his cock into her hot, wet mouth.

"What a combo. A one-two punch," the third judge says.

"Oh my God," Evan whines. "We have to do something." Her eyes are pleading.

"I'm sure we can clear it up." I don't move because they announce seventeen and that's my number. "Let's see what they say about..." I stop, realizing that if sixteen was Andrews Bagel Company bagels and Erickson cream cheese, then seventeen would be Erickson bagels with Andrews cream cheese.

"Ew," one judge says.

"Meh," Nick Klein says. "Nothing spectacular at all."

"I agree. Mediocre," the third judge says, and they all ask for sixteen to come back.

"I have to do something," Evan says and stomps out of the room.

Their faces light up as they taste more of the perfect combo. I fall into a chair and watch their reactions, dissecting each moan and groan as if they're all in the middle of an orgy.

What the fuck did our dads do twenty years ago? I shake my head and lean forward, resting my forearms on my thighs. Who knows what would've happened if they hadn't let that stupid argument tear them apart. My mom wouldn't be missing her wedding ring. Hell, we could be living like the Floyds up on Society Hill.

Damn their stubbornness and ruining the future for both their families.

Evan comes in with a woman who works on the show, explaining the entire situation and looking to me to back her explanation.

I think Evan might be the one who lost the most because of our dads. Her future irrevocably changed that day. Hell, that shouldn't feel like a pinprick in the heart, but it does.

"Seth!" Evan yells. "Tell her about the mix-up." She holds her hand out to the woman who is waiting for me to agree.

"There was a mix-up. You just presented a combination that doesn't exist and never will," I say dryly.

Of course Evan gets it all straightened out in the end and the woman says not to worry so much, she'll let them know.

As we walk out of the mercantile mart, I'm still stuck on how much we've lost, while Evan is apparently relieved it all got squared away. Didn't she see and hear those judges' reactions? Are we all so brainwashed into hating one another that we can't see that we'd be better together than apart?

"I better go. Crossing my fingers you make the list." But Evan uncrosses her fingers in the air.

"I could show you a better finger to use, but I'm a gentleman." I smirk.

"That's not what I hear." She turns and stalks down the sidewalk toward their shop.

"That's because women don't want a gentleman in bed," I holler back.

She shakes her head and turns the corner.

I turn right to head toward my parents' shop and almost plow over an elderly woman. Not just any elderly woman—my old kindergarten teacher, Mrs. Reindorf.

"Hey, Mrs. Reindorf," I say, hoping she didn't hear me just now.

"Seth. I see not much has changed."

She continues walking the direction Evan did and I ignore her jab. I mean, isn't every six-year-old boy curious about what's under a girl's dress? In my defense, it was Evan's dress and she wanted to show me her new underwear. How were we to know it was inappropriate?

I wonder what kind of undergarments she wears now? Damn it. I need my brain to give my dick a stern talking-to, just like Mrs. Reindorf used to. Otherwise my life will surely be a disaster.

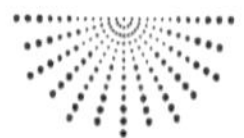

CHAPTER EIGHT

Evan

Brock honks his horn and I walk down the outside steps of my apartment that's above my parents' garage. Yes, I'm the loser who lives rent-free at her parents'. But I do run their business for a measly wage, so there's that.

"Seriously, he can't even pull in the driveway?" my dad says, throwing a ball with Eli.

"I love his car. Will he take me on a ride?" Eli asks, dropping the ball and meeting me on the driveway.

"Never," my dad answers for me.

Dad looks older than he should. I hope once his health is back to where it should be, he'll go back to being full of life. He's always been my idol. He's the one who taught me the business—thankfully before he gripped his chest and fell down in the kitchen. I blink to push back that memory.

I always felt there was time. Time to tell him I didn't want to run the bagel shop. Time to pour out my heart. But when I lacked any true desire to do anything else, I fell short of being my own advocate. Then after the incident (as my mom refers to it), placing all that in his lap felt selfish.

"I don't like him." Dad pushes back his longish brown hair because he doesn't get it cut on a routine schedule anymore.

He no longer has a minute-by-minute schedule for his day either. The doctors say he was too stressed, too busy, and not taking care of himself properly. So my mom banded the Ericksons together and we now carry that stress for my dad. Though with the wrinkles prominent on his forehead right now, I don't think he's in any Zen-like state.

My mom comes out with a drink and bowl of popcorn. "Leave her alone. She needs a life. And it's Brock Floyd."

My dad rolls his eyes. "A Floyd. Then, by all means, he can go by his own rules."

Brock honks again, and I raise my finger at him. We had a discussion last time he picked me up about him honking.

"I don't get boys these days." Dad's gaze steadies on my mom. "I went to your house even though your dad said he was going to come after me with a machete. I stood up to him and asked for your hand in marriage even though he hated me."

I swallow a lump. "No one said anything about marriage."

I balk at the thought. I mean, I like Brock, but we're just dating. We haven't even classified ourselves as exclusive.

"Look at her, she's pale just thinking about marriage." My mom points and laughs, patting my dad's arm.

"Good. No need to get married for a long time."

"Oh, Vic, you wish she'd become a nun," my mom says.

My dad nods and we all fall silent. I really hope we're not all recollecting a time when he didn't wish I'd become a nun. When he had a boy picked out for me and thought the plans were almost written in the stars for us.

Ever since I made Seth dress up and act out a wedding,

our families were on the Seth and Evan bandwagon. They imagined us married and spending every holiday with all of them, giving them grandchild after grandchild—which they'd happily watch while retired because Seth and I would be running The Bagel and Schmear Shop.

Oh, how wrong they were… except for the fact that I'm the one running the bagel shop.

Eli sits in a patio chair and takes a fistful of popcorn. My mom tells him he should go inside and get a hat because it's getting colder, while my dad heads to the side of the garage to grab wood for the fire pit.

My dad picks up a log as Brock honks again, longer this time. "You can tell your boyfriend that next time, he'd better park in the street and walk his sorry ass up here. We not good enough for him? He can't step foot on common people's grass?"

"Vic," my mom sighs and shoos me with her hand because we both know if I stay, my dad will continue to argue with me. "Go, Evan." Mom winks.

"Okay. Bye, guys."

Eli rushes over and wraps his arms around my waist. "Bye-bye."

I hug him back and kiss his temple. "See you tomorrow, Eli."

After walking down my driveway past my dad's beat-up truck and my mom's minivan that's in its last days, I climb into a car that probably costs the same as both of my parents' vehicles brand new.

"Hey, gorgeous," Brock says, his hand instantly landing on my bare thigh. "Love the dress."

"Next time you pick me up, my dad would really like to meet you," I say.

He puts the car in gear and pulls away from the corner. "For sure. Next time."

We drive through Cliffton Heights up to his parents' neighborhood, Society Hill. They live on a hill that overlooks the town, as though they're royalty and we're the common folk below. Sometimes I get the impression that Brock believes he truly is a prince and above all things.

We pass some other driveways, all with black iron-rod fences with a monogram welded into the artful design. Some have security outside, and others have lines of tall trees so the view from the street is obstructed as though they're movie stars in Bel Air. Every time I drive up here, my hands itch because even before my dad's incident, we didn't have a ton of money. We're lower middle class, middle class on a good year. The shop keeps a roof over our heads and food on the table, but with my dad and Eli's doctors and Elsie's college, we make do with what we have.

It's still hard not to gasp when Brock pulls into the main entrance of the Floyds' house. It's a huge white brick mansion that sits more prominent and higher than all the others, as though they planned it. There are concrete statues and a giant F manicured into their lawn while a huge circular brick driveway is in front of the entrance. Lights glow in every window. I have to think Brock was never told, "We don't own the electric company." Hell, he probably keeps the water on while he's brushing his teeth.

We come from such different worlds. I hate myself for wondering why out of the girls he could have, he picked me. Like it comes straight from some fairy tale shit and a small part of me doesn't want to play the part.

"Relax, it's just my parents," he says, shaking my knee. He probably thinks I'm anxious about the dinner.

I don't want to be the poor girl a man like Brock saves. I'm not lucky to have him—he's lucky to have me. For the first time I ask myself, why do I want to date Brock Floyd? A question I should've answered well before attending a dinner party at his house.

I've met both of his parents before because when you live on top of your parents' garage and your boyfriend has an entire pool house to himself, you tend to spend your time at his place. But all the meetings have been brief, and never as long as a dinner.

Brock parks his car, pocketing his keys and holding my hand as we walk into the house. We follow the sound of chatter into a formal parlor.

"Evan Erickson," Nick says and waves. The blonde next to him is the woman who ushered me to him that first day. So they're dating? "You remember Renee?"

I smile and wave. Then I go and say hi to Mr. Floyd, who nods and shakes my hand. Mrs. Floyd kisses my cheek as she sweetly embraces me.

Brock must've picked me up just in time for dinner because we're all seated immediately at the dinner table. Brock fills my wine glass while the butler brings him a dark amber drink.

It doesn't take long before the conversation shifts my way. I guess I'm not surprised that Nick moves it that way.

"So we tasted you today," Nick says.

"Rephrase that, Nick," Brock says and laughs.

My cheeks heat.

"Good one, Brockie," Nick says and steadies his eyes on me. "Your family recipe?"

"The bagels or cream cheese?" I ask.

"I have a feeling you know."

I can't get a read on Nick Klein. Sometimes I think he's flirting with me, and other times he seems like just a friendly guy who wants me to succeed. But is my success important to him only because I'm dating Brock?

"Yes, the cream cheeses are my mother's recipe. She

tweaked it a little, and I've been fiddling a little bit here and there."

He nods.

"Can we please not talk about bagels and cream cheese?" Brock whines. "I have to hear enough about it from Evan all day long."

I turn my head toward him. I'm shocked by Brock's melodramatic, teenage-boy reaction. Plus, I never talk to him about work. But it's probably smart to stay away from the topic in case Seth's name comes up.

"After-dinner drinks. Me and you in a corner," Nick says.

"Remember, she's mine," Brock warns.

I snap my head back in his direction.

He laughs as if he's joking, and slides his hand over my bare thigh. "You know what I mean, babe." He winks.

It doesn't make me feel better though. Lately, not much of what Brock says does.

Evan

The dinner conversation consists of politics, the economy, and other boring topics. And while I wish I could ask Nick more questions about the show and what happened at the tasting, because of Brock, I'm restricted until we're excused.

Brock wraps his arms around me and whispers in my ear, "You've got about ten minutes, then we're hiding out at my place. Skinny-dip later?"

I kiss his lips and step back, wiggling out of his hold. "I won't be long."

Nick's waiting for me in the study when I walk in. Renee's across from him in one of the four leather seats huddled together with a table between them.

"Evan, please come in." He waves me in. "I asked the Floyds if we could have a moment with you. They'll be in shortly."

"I was told by Brock that I had ten minutes."

Nick rolls his eyes. It's the first time I've seen any sign that maybe he's not so keen on that particular Floyd. I sit down and he pours me some liquor in a fancy crystal glass.

"You have as long as you want," Nick says, handing me my drink. "Renee is here with me tonight because we knew you'd be here."

She smiles in a sweet manner at me.

"It was decided today to do something a little different in Cliffton Heights. The producers want to test out a new concept." Nick leans back and rests his ankle on his knee, much like he did during our first meeting. "We're going to put two companies together."

I frown and sink back into the leather seat taking a large sip to calm my nerves. I welcome the burning feeling down my throat because I know exactly where he's going with this.

He must see the look of dread on my face because he raises his free hand. "Now wait until you hear me out. We've done our research… we know that you and Andrews Bagel Company have a history, but we also know it's your parents' history, correct?"

Renee pulls a file from a messenger bag I hadn't noticed tucked at the side of her chair. Nick signals to her.

"It's fair to tell you, we researched the Cliffton Heights area before we decided to do a show. I mean, we have to." She shrugs.

I nod because I can understand that. Then I take another sip of my drink. I should probably stop since I had some alcohol with dinner but I think I could use the liquid courage for where this conversation is headed.

She continues, "Most of the other companies we're putting together are all complementary of one another. We'll admit it's a little different for you and Andrews Bagel because your items can't stand on their own. They have to be together. For example, we have Los Tacos steak tacos and the Red Penguin's margaritas. We have Spoon and Fork supplying a salad to go with Pizza Pies."

"And we can't have just a tub of cream cheese out there," Nick says, laughing.

Renee joins him.

"Aren't there any other bagel companies I can partner with?"

Nick drops his foot and leans forward. "I'm going to be straight with you. I've been in this business a long time. We've read the reviews from fans of both of your companies, and we agree with them. Your cream cheese was the best thing we tasted. But their bagels are better. I know that probably pains you to hear."

I refrain from admitting that I know he's speaking the truth. Mr. Andrews sprays some kind of magic on them, I swear. I've tried to mimic it so many times, and each time, the result was worse.

"But your cream cheese was the best. The only one we would entertain spotlighting. I'm urging you not to make a bad business decision due to personal problems."

"But—"

Nick holds up his hand. "This is your shot." He glances at Renee and back at me. "Can you excuse us for a moment, Renee?"

She nods and stands, leaving the manila folder on the small table between us.

Once the door is shut, Nick moves to the seat across from me instead of beside me. "I can tell that this isn't your dream."

"What?" I pull my head back as though he's slapped me. Why doesn't he think I came out of the womb wanting to bake bagels and be elbow deep in cheese every day? He holds my gaze, and I crumble. My shoulders fall and I shake my head. "Yeah."

"This is your shot. You've got a great product. A product that could potentially be bought for mass production."

"Oh, you don't know my dad—"

"If your dad is a smart businessman, he'll see the possibilities."

"Even if I agree, there's still the Andrews. They hate us just as much."

"I noticed in the notes that it says two people originally came in for them." He grabs the folder and fingers through it. "Shit, I need my reading glasses." He shoves me a piece of paper. "Who are the names on there?"

I swallow the lump in my throat at seeing Seth's signature. He's obviously going to be involved in this whole process then. "Seth and his mom, Debbie."

"Maybe since the blood is bad with the older generations, I can go to Seth. Are selling bagels his dream?"

I shake my head. "He's a photographer." I take a sip of my drink and the alcohol no longer burns going down.

"There's your opening then. Sell it to him, Evan."

My eyes widen and I sputter for a second. "Me?" I point at myself as though he might not know who I mean.

"We've had some push back from a few companies, but mostly people see this as a win-win. I think you might have better luck with him than me or anyone in production. You going to him shows that you're willing to work with him and let bygones be bygones."

I chew on my lip, still unsure.

"You want to be on television? You want us to showcase you, right?"

I nod.

"Then convince Seth that this is a good idea. The show

will make people come out here just to try your stuff. You never know what the future holds."

I bite my lip. I have no idea if Seth will agree, but I think I need him more than he needs me at this point. A bagel can stand on its own or be paired with coffee, but cream cheese?

"I'll try," I say.

He leans back in his chair and pulls out his wallet and removes a business card. Grabbing a pen Renee left behind, he scribbles down his phone number. "Call me if you think he's a no? We'll brainstorm ways to convince him."

My shoulders fall. I have nothing to say but so many questions I want to ask.

Nick tilts his head. "What?"

"Why do you care so much?" He's a successful chef. Why does he care that this isn't my dream?

He chuckles and stands. "Let's just say I didn't want to own a hardware store." He winks.

* * *

I WALK OUT of Bruce Floyd's study to find Brock pacing in the hall.

"What the hell?" His gaze falls over me, eyes narrowing.

I stop in my tracks. "What?"

"Just seeing if anything is amiss. Why would you be in there alone with him?"

I shake my head. "We were just talking out the whole *Taste of Small Towns* thing. It was business."

"Business," Brock huffs.

"Yes, business. What's your problem?" My heart rate picks up.

Where is the guy who was sweet and endearing and waited for me every day while I closed the store? Ever since the gala, it's like he's morphing into someone else. *Or are you just seeing him in a different light?*

"Maybe it's that I keep finding you alone with men."

I cross my arms. "Men?"

"First Andrews and now Klein. Who else am I competing with?" Brock spreads his arms and circles as if I should bow at his feet.

I let my arms drop to my sides. "I think I should go home now."

"Oh, babe, I'm only kidding," he says, his voice more jovial, but I'm not sure I buy it.

"I still think I should go home." I walk past him to leave, but he whips me back around by grabbing my upper arm. And he's not gentle about it.

"Where are you going? You gotta see my point. What if I had a girl in my room? How would you feel?"

At this point, I wouldn't care. "If it had to do with business, I'd be fine with it."

"Then I guess you don't feel nearly as strong about me as I do you."

"I'm sorry?"

"What if it was Andrews and another girl?"

I throw my hands in the air. "Why on Earth are you bringing Seth into this?"

He doesn't respond right away.

"Why do you think you're in competition with him?" I can't hide my exasperation.

"The hell I'm in competition. He's a fucking photographer for middle-aged women who have shitty sex lives. I'll run Floyd Steel one day. I just find it funny."

"What exactly is funny?" I'm realizing that I have to ask Brock that an awful lot.

"That you look at him like his dick is nine inches long and you want to fall to your fucking knees and suck him off."

I blink, stunned and silent. Holy shit, we have really spun off course. I have no idea what the hell he's talking about.

"You're crazy and I'm calling an Uber now." I turn around to walk out.

Mr. Floyd comes out of a nearby room and stops before I reach the door. "Brock?" he asks with an edge to suggest he heard everything. "I think you should volunteer to drive Evan home now. And after you do that, I'd like to have a word with you."

I swallow past the dryness in my throat. At this point, I just want to leave.

"I can request an Uber. He doesn't have to go," I say, avoiding looking at Mr. Floyd.

"No, Evan, that's not necessary."

"Really. It's fine."

Mr. Floyd pulls out his phone. "At least let it be on me." He taps his phone. "They're ten minutes away. Brock will keep you company until it arrives." Before I can answer, he nods at Brock and walks away. "In my study after Evan leaves, son."

Brock blows out an annoyed breath. "Let's go, high maintenance."

He walks ahead of me and yep, time just expired on this relationship.

We venture outside and the air is a little chilly. It's growing colder by the day. He sits on the cement stairs while I stand, searching out the headlights of the Uber.

"Brock, I think this thing between us has reached its end."

He blows out a breath and huffs. "Whatever."

"I don't understand. Why are you so mad? I've done nothing."

"Do you know how embarrassing it is when my girlfriend—"

I hold up my hand. "I was never your girlfriend. We've been dating, but—"

"You're Evan Erickson. It's not like you're the type to sleep around. I never thought you'd play games either." He pulls out a vile of white powder and dumps some in the lid before snorting it.

Holy shit.

My mouth drops open. I guess there's no longer any need to pretend he's something he's not in front of me anymore. Was I really this stupid and naïve?

"So you and Andrews then?"

"You're delusional. I was dating you. Happily until you jumped off the deep end tonight."

Thankfully, two headlights rise above the hill and I blow out a relieved breath. I just want to go home, get in my pajamas, and lose myself in some shitty TV, forgetting this night ever happened.

"Here's your chariot, ready to take you back to Loserville," he snips.

I decide to take the high road by not responding and I walk toward the car that's driving toward me, but Brock's footsteps fall behind me.

"Goddamn it, Evan." He grips my upper arm so hard, I cry out and crumple to the ground.

The Uber abruptly stops, and I hear the car door open.

"Motherfucker, get your hands off of her."

The driver punches Brock and he falls into the perfectly manicured hedge, but the guy jumps on him, pummeling fist after fist into Brock's face.

"Get in the car," the driver yells, and a flicker of light catches the most stunning pair of blue eyes. The eyes of the first boy to ever earn my trust.

What the hell is Seth doing here?

Seth throws another punch at Brock, but I grab his arm to pry him off. "He's not worth it."

"He hurt you." I can't see Seth's face, but it's clear from his voice that he's seething.

"Come on." I tug enough that he stops.

Brock stumbles to his feet, but his equilibrium is off and he wobbles. "So you are fucking him."

I step in front of Seth and give Brock a punch of my own. He might not fall into the hedge like from Seth's punch, but blood spurts from his nose onto the concrete and that's enough satisfaction for me.

Seth sees me to the car and climbs in, flipping Brock off as we head down his driveway past the cement lion statues and the manicured F in the front yard. I swear I don't breathe until we're off Society Hill.

"You okay?" Seth asks and places his hand on my knee.

I nod a little frantically, shaken by what just happened. "What are you doing here?"

"I came to warn Brock to stay away from my brother once he's back from rehab. Good thing I showed up when I did."

Our eyes catch in the light from the streetlights—then a rush of nausea hits me as the adrenaline leaves my system and the alcohol I drank with Nick swirls in my stomach. I have no time to open the door, so I end up throwing up on the floorboard.

"I guess it's true what they say," Seth says with a sigh.

"What?" I groan, still leaning down over my seat.

"No good deed goes unpunished."

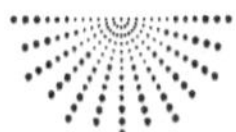

CHAPTER TEN

Seth

*E*van continues apologizing as I drive us to the car wash to clean up my car. I park and dig through my center console for quarters.

"I'm so sorry," she says.

"It's okay. Brock Floyd makes me want to puke too. I just would've preferred you'd done it on him." I climb out and help her out of the car.

"I got this, Seth. Honestly, you just sit there."

I chuckle. "I'm not letting your drunk ass clean my car." Thankfully, most of it is on the floor mat, so I carry it over to the trash can and gag as it drips in.

"I'm not drunk. I'm just not used to sipping hard liquor, then everything went down with Brock… I don't know."

"How were you getting home?" I ask.

"Oh shit." Her hand flies to her mouth. "His dad called me an Uber."

I shrug. "Serves him right to explain why you left before it arrived."

"True enough." Evan heads to the vending area and buys some cleaning cloths with her array of quarters.

"Did you rob a grandma or something?" I yell because it's only us here. No one else is washing their car at nine o'clock at night.

"Funny. Maybe I just come prepared."

"Or you have your store deposit in that purse of yours."

She doesn't respond and I shake my hand, feeling the throbbing in my knuckles setting in now that the adrenaline is leaving my system. I clench and unclench my hand a few times, my knuckles red and angry.

"Shit, Seth, you need to get some ice on that." Evan's standing over me at the side of the car, her long dark hair like a veil so I can't see her face.

"I could say the same thing to you." I raise an eyebrow at her and she rolls her eyes. "It would've been easier if you would've believed me when I said he was a douchebag from the get-go."

She sighs. "He was sweet at first, but something changed. He changed. Tonight was just the last straw."

"What was with the 'you fucking me' comment?"

I had to bite my lip to keep from smirking when he mentioned Evan fucking me. Does Brock not pay attention to the gossip in this town? Evan hates me and I hate her. Kind of. Not really. But no one needs to know that. I'm happy he thought I was fucking his girlfriend. I'd say it's nothing compared to what he did to Trevor. He ruined him.

She steps away from me and over to the other side of the car. "He said I eye-fuck you." She bends over, tucking her hair behind her ears, and uses a rag to puddle up the vomit as she chokes back more from erupting out of her mouth.

I take another rag she purchased and lean across to help clean up the mess. "Take a load off."

"No. I did this. I'll clean it."

I meet her gaze. "Use your one free pass."

She huffs but steps back, so I go over to the passenger side and throw out my soiled cloth. I grab a clean one and bend down on my haunches while she stands behind me.

For a moment, I debate asking her more questions. The whys and hows of how she came to be running The Bagel Place. But sadly, I understand family responsibility. It's the reason I'm now on the owner paperwork for Andrews Bagel Company. My parents have to protect themselves from their own son. How fucking sad is that?

"Let's get back to why it looked like Brock was about to hit you when I pulled up."

Brock is a safer subject than our families.

"I thought we could discuss why *you* were there," she says coyly.

"You first."

"I confronted him about getting all jealous. Nick Klein was at their house tonight and he asked to speak to me privately about the show."

Jealousy pricks my veins, and not because the host of the show is giving her special treatment. I want to make sure he's not trying to persuade her to spend some time on the casting couch. "And?"

"Brock accused me of liking other guys. You in particular. What's the deal with you two?"

Jeez, nothing that I can think of. I mean, Trevor and Brock were competitive their whole friendship, but I was just Trev's younger brother. "I don't like him for obvious reasons. No idea what his issue is with me."

"Well, he definitely sees you as some sort of competition."

I stand and throw out another cloth. "I am better-looking than him. Maybe that's it."

She smiles. It shouldn't make me happy as shit that I pulled a smile out of her, but it does.

"It's okay to agree," I say.

This time I'm rewarded with a giggle and an even bigger smile.

Fuck. What is happening? I'm in so much trouble.

"Should we go to the store and get some cleaning supplies?" She changes the subject, for which I'm thankful.

"Nah, I'll drop you off and do it in the morning."

"Um… no. We're going." Then she climbs into the car, putting her feet on either side of the mat so she doesn't step in the wet spot that smells like puke.

We ride to the store with the windows down and our heads as far out as possible, as though we're two dogs on a joy ride. She makes me stop at a drug store so she can buy a toothbrush and toothpaste and brush her teeth in the bathroom. When we finally walk into the big box store, she grabs a cart.

"We're not buying cleaning supplies in bulk," I say.

She ignores me and detours down the chip aisle. "I didn't each much dinner. They had Cornish hens and—"

"I'm surprised you didn't say foie gras." I toss a bag of cheese balls into the cart.

"Thank God no. I'm not sure what I would've done."

"I would've raised my hand and asked for a cheeseburger."

She laughs and puts a bag of pretzels in the cart. I swipe a bag of white cheddar popcorn. At this rate, we'll be throwing up again from overeating.

"Knowing you, I don't doubt it," she says.

"Is that a knock on me? I've been awfully polite tonight, even after I saved your ass—again."

"Again?" She cops an attitude and stops the cart.

"Don't act like you don't know what I'm talking about. Do you want me to name all the times?" I chuckle and pretend my bag of beef jerky is a basketball. When it drops in the cart, I put up two fingers. "Two points."

"First of all, I saved you plenty too, and second of all, why are men so annoying and act like everything is a basketball and a net?"

"It makes life a lot more fun. You should try it." I pick up a random item and toss it in just for fun. "Two more points."

She blows out a breath.

I can't believe I'm walking the aisles of a store with Evan Erickson, and our hands aren't around each other's throats.

"So tell me what Nick Klein is offering you," I ask because it's clear that although we're being cool with one another, she's holding something back. I've caught her staring at me as if she wanted to ask me something a few times, but then she doesn't.

"They're changing the format of the show."

My footsteps halt on the concrete floor and I stop her from walking by gripping the end of the shopping cart. "What does that mean? Changing the format?"

She sighs. "They want us to work together." Her voice is soft like she can't believe she said that.

"Together? Us?"

"Well, The Bagel Place and Andrews Bagel Company, yeah."

I shake my head. Of course. There's no *us*, no Evan and Seth. I'm only doing this for my parents anyway.

"Well fuck. Our dads would never agree to that." I take my hands off the cart and we stroll through the aisles until we hit the cleaning supplies. I grab some vinegar and a bucket and cloths.

"It's a great opportunity. Klein was impressed with both of our items... individually. They're trying something different with this episode. For each segment, two businesses will have items that complement the other. We'd be fools not to do it."

I huff. "You act like I have the final say. My dad isn't going to agree to working with yours." I shake my head.

The show was a nice way to get my parents clear of the mess my brother put them in and get me out of ever having to run the shop. But my dad would never sign off on working with The Bagel Place.

"But you do." Her voice is back to that low whisper as though we're in a crowded store and she doesn't want anyone to overhear. "I saw the paperwork. I know you're a legal owner of the shop now."

I run my hand through my hair. "Are you sure Nick Klein didn't want to screw you? He let you see that I'm part owner?"

"He's really invested in us. I think he's on our side."

"Our side? What the hell? There's no *our* side." I walk away, unable to process what she's asking me to do. She's asking me to bring all that shit from the past into the present. Make our lives more turmoil-ridden than they already are.

"Come on, don't act like I'm some stranger to what's happening. I know you think I'm weak for taking responsibility for my parents' store, but you're in the same position now that Trevor is in rehab."

I never thought she was weak. I might have teased her, but I always felt bad because I saw her as stuck.

She tugs on my arm. "This is our chance, Seth. To make their businesses thrive and allow our parents the financial freedom to hire outside help. It'll let us do what we love."

I whip my head in her direction and meet her gaze. "And what do you love, Evan?"

She lets go of my arm and her eyes widen in surprise. "Um…"

"See? You don't even know. I know my answer. But what will you do when The Bagel Place doesn't need you?"

Her gaze narrows on me. "All I know is I don't want to wake up every morning at three and open up a bagel shop. That's at the top of my 'what I don't want to do' list. So anything else is better than that at this point."

I nod. I can't blame her. "Let's say I somehow go behind my dad's back. What about you? Your dad isn't going to agree to this either."

"Well, one idea popped into my head." Her voice is tentative, almost like she's resistant to her own idea.

"What?" I groan.

"If we become friends again, maybe it will spur them to be friends."

I scrunch up my forehead in confusion. Has she met either of our fathers? They're two of the most prideful and stubborn men on the planet. The whole reason we're not friends is because they cast one another as an enemy.

I shake my head. "It's not enough to sway them." I stand there thinking, hands on my hips. "We need something a lot stronger than that. What if we work on our moms? I saw my mom's face when she was asking about your mom. She misses her still after all these years."

I can't believe I'm going along with this, but Evan's right. The last thing I want for my life is to be locked into running the bagel shop. And I know if it came down to it, I would do it for my family if I had to.

She shakes her head. "No way my mom would cause my dad more stress when he's not fully recovered from the heart attack yet."

We walk aimlessly now when we should be having this conversation while cleaning my damn car. We end up in the party planning aisle, surrounded by balloons and streamers and cake toppers. I'm reminded of all the birthdays our families celebrated together, all the times our moms would ooh and ahh over us.

We come to the white and black script items with caricatures of a bride and groom on them.

"We could…"

As though the idea pops in Evan's head at the same time, she says, "Say we're dating?"

"Dare you to say we're engaged."

She blinks. "You dare me? You didn't even want to do this."

"You know me. I'm go big or go home. Dating is usually temporary and can be fixed with a breakup. And since I'm not actually going to *marry* you just to get on some television show, engagement is the only option. Engagement is semi-permanent. It's a commitment."

Her face drops, but she knows I have a point. "They won't believe it. I was just dating Brock until moments ago."

"Yeah, you're gonna have to be the hussy in this scenario. You had to have been dating me and Brock at the same time."

She guffaws. "No way."

"Yes way. This is your bright idea, and you dated Floyd even after I warned you what he was really like." I shrug like 'what are you gonna do?'

She worries her bottom lip for a moment. "I have no idea if we can pull this off."

"With me? We're golden. Now, we're going to have to plan this to make it believable."

She groans like it wasn't her idea to do this in the first place.

"Seth?" Just as I rub my hands together, the sound of my dad calling my name at the end of the aisle alarms me. "Evan?"

My eyes widen since my back is to my dad. Evan smiles since she's facing him. I mouth "game on" to her and turn around.

"Dad?" I pretend to be shocked and alarmed that he found us here together.

Seriously, someone call the Actors Guild because I'm about to win Best Actor.

CHAPTER ELEVEN

Evan

I haven't seen Mr. Andrews close up for a few years. He no longer attends the Chamber of Commerce meetings—Mrs. Andrews does. I'm not sure how my parents are with Seth if and when they run into him, but his parents are usually cordial to me.

Seth steps back to meet me on my side of the cart. We're shoulder to shoulder and all the nausea from an hour ago stirs in my stomach like a witch's brew.

"Dad?" Seth says.

Mr. Andrews watches his son put his arm around my shoulders. Seth's smooth movements make it seem as though he's done this a million times, while I remain stiff and uncomfortable.

"Can I have a word, Seth?" His dad doesn't wait for a response but heads past us down the aisle and turns.

Seth looks at me and winks before following his dad.

While I slide the cart inch by inch down the aisle, his dad's deep voice is clear—meaning he hasn't changed much over the years. He's still the guy who says what he wants in front of whoever without apology. I'm surprised he even asked to speak alone and we aren't all hashing this out right in the middle of the decorating aisle.

"What are you doing with Evan Erickson?"

"Listen, this is going to come as a surprise because we haven't been ready to tell anyone, but we've been sneaking around. I've been dating Evan."

"Dating?" I mouth to myself. I thought we were going to pretend to be engaged?

I'm not going to examine why I feel slightly disappointed.

"Your mother told me this evening that she's dating Brock Floyd?"

Damn the gossip in this town.

"As a cover-up," Seth says. "They broke up tonight. I'm convincing her to go public."

"Public? Who do you think you are? Brad Pitt?"

Seth chuckles but stops because I'm sure his dad doesn't find this funny. "You're the first to know. I get that you have to tell Mom, but can you keep it to yourselves until Evan has time to tell Mr. and Mrs. Erickson?"

I shake my head at Seth's forwardness. I'd probably be pleading with my parents for permission, but he just lays it out there with a "deal with it" attitude. But then again, the apple doesn't fall far from the tree. I imagine if Mr. Andrews found himself in our position, he'd do the same thing.

"You do understand the trouble this is going to cause?" Mr. Andrews says.

I honestly thought the entire greeting card section would be destroyed by Mr. Andrews by now. His son dating his ex-best-friend-slash-business-partner's daughter cannot be on his list of favorite things.

"I do."

"And she's that important to you?"

Seth doesn't say anything, but his dad releases a long, anguished breath.

"How have I never heard anything about this?"

"I told you, we were keeping it a secret."

"This is Cliffton Heights, and I might live like a hermit, but your mother does not. Have you been hiding out in your apartment? People would talk the minute they saw you two out together."

He has a point. That's something neither of us thought about.

"We go into the city most times."

This is where we're going to have problems. Seth lives on his own, so his parents really don't know his comings and goings. But I live above my parents' garage. Sure, it's a detached garage and I could be gone without them knowing, but I'm at the shop most days.

"And you know, we just have quickies."

My mouth falls open and my head lands in my hands.

"At The Bagel Place. My apartment. My car if there's nowhere else."

I clench my teeth before I scream that he's making me sound like a hussy.

"I don't need to know that." Mr. Andrew's voice is pained.

"You asked." Seth's voice is steady as though lying comes easily to him. Not a comforting thought.

"About how I hadn't heard that you're dating her, not about where the two of you are having… just." He never finishes his sentence, seemingly annoyed. "Come by the house tomorrow so we can talk about this."

"With Evan?"

"No, Seth. Not with Evan. We need to discuss this as a family."

There's a beat of silence and I wait for Seth to round the end of the aisle back to me, but he drops a bomb instead.

"I'm asking her to marry me."

"What?" His dad's voice rises. "Marriage?"

"She's important to me. I want to show her my commitment to the rest of our lives."

Another bout of silence and I suck in as much air as I can. It's one thing to be tossing this idea around and another completely to be waist-deep in the plan minutes later. Seth's bold bravery is something I haven't witnessed in ages.

"Do not propose to her until we talk as a family. Do you hear me?" His dad's threatening response squeezes the air from my lungs. The hatred he has for my family is present in every syllable.

"I'm sorry, Dad, I can't."

I place my hands over my face and close my eyes. Why is he being so adamant about this in the middle of a big box store?

"Seth, I can't handle this right now. I have your brother in rehab. I'm already shopping at nine o'clock at night so that I don't have to face people after your brother stole from us and the entire town knows I raised a druggie. Now my other son is going to propose to an Erickson? I can't have it."

"I'm not asking your permission, Dad."

My stomach drops. I wondered why Mr. Andrews was here so late. I guess maybe I'm not surprised. Why do parents hold so much of the blame when their kid doesn't turn out perfect?

"Seth," he warns.

I want to run over and tell Seth to chill out. His parents are in pain and we're only making it worse. Speak the truth and hope that Mr. Andrews still allows us to work together for the show.

"Sorry." Seth's voice grows closer. "We'll plan a dinner

with you, Mom, and the Ericksons. We can all talk about it, but nothing is going to change. We're getting engaged."

"Seth."

Seth appears at the end of the aisle, but he stops and turns toward his dad, waiting for him to say something.

"Just think about what you're doing."

Seth's shoulders falter, and for a moment, he's not that strong guy who does what he wants. "Believe me, this is good for all of us."

* * *

Seth's dad takes his cart toward the checkout lanes and we watch him leave through the front door, still shaking his head to himself.

"Maybe this is a mistake," I say.

Seth throws his arm around my shoulders as I push the cart. "No way, this is brilliant. We're both going to get out of the bagel business once and for all. But one thing is clear, we need to get our stories straight because I could tell my dad doesn't believe me. So since his intuition is spot-on, we're going to really have to sell him on it."

I nod. But now I'm thinking that although I'm the one who suggested this, there's a great possibility that it's going to blow up in our faces. "I don't know if I can lie."

He chuckles and steals the cart from me, hopping on it and riding it until he hits the jewelry counter. "Sure, you can. You've been *acting* like you hated me all these years." He presses his finger on the bell to call an associate.

"What are you doing?" I ask.

He peers through the glass as though he's seriously considering a purchase.

A woman comes over and slides her spiral plastic bracelet with a key off her wrist. "Can I help you?"

"No. I'm sorry." I tug on Seth's sweatshirt, but he doesn't budge.

"I'd like to see that one. First row, third in from the left."

I peer over his shoulder. It's a modest carat made out of moissanite. Oval on a silver band. Simple and nothing elaborate. Something I would probably wear if this were for real.

"What size are you?" He grabs some paper sizing thing they have sitting around.

His fingers wrap the paper around my finger, and with every brush of our skin, my heart rate kicks up a notch. He smells crisp and fresh while I probably reek of puke.

"Perfect fit." He takes the paper and slides on the ring. "What do you think? I don't think they'll be able to tell the difference."

"I think we could tell them that we're going to shop for the ring." I slide it off my hand and place it on the black velvet in front of the lady. "Thank you for your time."

"Yeah, I hate to break this to you because you prefer to put me in the douchebag category, but I would never propose without a ring." He snatches it back before the lady can put it away.

Her forehead scrunches and we both freeze. I don't recognize her, but that doesn't mean anything.

"She's so concerned about money," Seth says, another perfect lie falling from his lips. "But we only do this once. Am I right?"

She smiles. "Definitely. Accept the ring, honey."

I bore my gaze into Seth. We are not going to spend almost two hundred dollars on a fake ring. He tilts his head as though he's saying accept the ring and let's go.

Our nonverbal tug of war ends when he falls to one knee in front of me. Gasps echo from the two checkout cashiers. Seth smiles wide at them, winning them over.

"Evan," he says, and I stop looking around to look down

at him. His hand holds mine and his fingers rest on the bottom of my left hand ring finger. "What can I say except that I think we've been destined to be together since the womb. All those years we listened to our families and allowed our friendship to grow apart, I never stopped thinking of you. Dare I admit, I missed you. And now that we're finding common ground"—he winks and it pulls a smile from me—"I think we're a perfect pair. Come on this journey with me and I promise you—I'll get you exactly what you want."

I shake my head, but I lose my fight with my smile and he doesn't even wait for me to answer before sliding the ring on my finger.

"Yeah, we both know this is what you want," he says.

"OHHH…" The two cashiers hug and I swear one wipes a tear from her eye.

Did they actually listen to the proposal?

"Kiss!" the jewelry worker says, clinking on the glass case with the rings on the underside of her finger.

I freeze, but I should've predicted Seth being prepared. He wraps his arm around my waist and dips me slowly. My eyes widen the closer he comes, but as soon as our lips meet, a tingling sensation runs through my body. I slide my hand to the back of his head, my fingers weaving through his thick hair.

He licks the seam of my lips and I open, allowing him in. His body heat seems to seep into me and spread through my veins as a tingling sensation starts between my thighs.

I've never felt this much from one kiss. Thank goodness he has me because my body practically weakens from how great this kiss is. His tongue tangles with mine and his taste is divine. I can't help but want more of it. My body pulses with a need I know will never be fulfilled. But in this moment, I don't care, because seriously how did Seth learn to kiss like that?

I hear a whimper when he closes the kiss and I'm embarrassed to realize it came from me.

Seth laughs and sets me upright. "Damn, babe, your kisses always make me hot."

All the women bystanders stare at his crotch. Sure enough, he's fixing his hard-on.

My cheeks heat and I say, "Time to get you home."

On our way to the cashier, he slaps my ass and I whip my head in his direction. With a chuckle, he shoots me a look to say, "hey, we're just acting." And I better remember that because damn, that kiss.

We check out as the cashiers all ask if they'll be invited to our wedding. Little do they know that they're as likely to be there as I am. Because there's no way this thing between us could ever be real.

CHAPTER TWELVE

Seth

I stop in the bagel store before meeting Evan at mercantile mart because my dad told me he's not going to tell my mother—I am. They don't keep secrets, so I better get my ass down to the shop and tell her this morning.

I'm distracted when I walk into the shop, thinking about the kiss I shared with Evan. I've never thought so much about a kiss in my life. I keep replaying it over and over in my mind, wishing I could do it again.

It takes me a second to spot Ethan and Blanca sitting in a booth by the window, both their laptops open, typing away and eating bagels. They're both workaholics.

"Seth," Blanca says, glancing up from her computer screen when the bell over the door rings. "Oh, I have some news for you." She slides out of the booth and walks over to me.

"Let me guess, no alcohol at the bachelor/bachelorette party?"

She hits me in the shoulder, and I rub it. Man, her brothers taught her how to hit. "No, and we're having a vote in two days about where to go, so I expect you to be there." She points at me with authority.

"When did you become so bossy?" I ask.

"The moment I came out of my mother. I have three older brothers. I had to learn fast."

Blanca's brothers are all professionals who make bank in Manhattan, but they're cool guys. Not douchey at all.

"Anyway, I was going to call you about something else today." She steps back and grabs her coffee as though this will be a long conversation.

I instinctively look at the clock over my mom's head at the cash register. Ethan's got his headphones in, so we give one another a nod.

"Those pictures you did for us?" Blanca says.

"Yeah?" I can't help the eagerness in my tone. Their blog doesn't need a lot of what I like to photograph, but if I can get another gig from them, it'd help me not to have to Uber anymore.

"A woman reached out to me after she saw the pictures and wanted to contact you. Her email signature says she owns a gallery in the city." She clenches her teeth and widens her eyes like she really wants to squeal.

I raise my eyebrows. "Really?"

"Yep, and I gave her your phone number so…" She does this little dance with only her upper body. Her shoulders move up and down and her hands move in circles. I'm sure Ethan finds it cute as hell, but I'm wondering if she's having a seizure.

"Great, thanks." Not what I was expecting when I came in here today, but I'm excited. I'm just more nervous about talking to my mom than anything right now.

"I hope something comes out of it. We're planning out

our next six months today, so I'll let you know if we need anything."

"I'm curious, do you two ever fuck anymore?"

The smile strips from her face. "Don't be vulgar." She backtracks to the booth.

"I'm just saying five minutes doesn't really count. Keep that in mind."

She discreetly flips me off by placing her middle finger along the bridge of her nose as she sits back down—beside Ethan this time. Blanca smacks a kiss on his lips, surprising him. At least the guy grabs her by the back of her head and deepens their kiss.

"Close your eyes," I whisper to a little girl standing in line before I walk to the head of the line. "Mom."

She's talking to a customer, so I head to the back and grab a coffee. I don't know how Evan takes hers, so I make my best guess, snagging an everything bagel from the bin and shoving it in a bag.

Once everyone is either waiting for their bagels or are sitting down, my mom looks to me to start talking as she takes inventory of what they still need. I'm used to the multi-tasking my mom does while I try to hold a conversation with her.

"So I ran into Dad at the store last night," I say.

She rolls her eyes. "I've told him a million times, it is what it is. It's a disease and he doesn't need to be embarrassed that our son succumbed to it, but he feels as though all the blame rests on our shoulders. Well, I'm not down with that. Look at you." She steps forward and pinches my cheeks.

"Mom," I say like I did when I was twelve and we were outside the school.

"But still he insists on going late, usually when I'm asleep." She shrugs. "What can I do? Nothing. He'll figure it out on his own."

"Yeah, so that's not what I came to tell you."

She glances up from her pad of paper. "No?" I shake my head and she drops the pen, turning toward me. "What is it?"

"He saw me with Evan Erickson," I admit, trying like hell not to allow one ounce of nerves into my tone. She can spot me lying without a word leaving my lips.

"Oh?"

"Yeah. We've been dating."

Her eyes peer into me as though she's scrutinizing the thoughts in my brain. I can practically see the checklist in her head. Eyes, doubtful. Heartbeat, rapid. Limbs, shaky.

"I thought she was with Brock?" She sips the coffee she left off to the side.

"Oh, that was just a front." I wave as if it's no big deal. "We made it official. Actually, I asked her to marry me last night."

Her coffee comes out of her mouth in one sputtering stream. "You what?"

"I proposed and she said yes."

"Proposed?" Her voice grows louder.

My dad emerges from the back, his hands on his hips, nodding like, "Can you believe it, Deb? Our second son is screwing us over now too."

"Did you ask her father first?" Mom asks.

My forehead creases. "What?"

She looks at my dad and her shoulders fall. "Seth, you cannot ask a girl to marry you without her father's permission. Have we not taught you anything?"

That's what she's disappointed about? "Well, he would've said no."

My parents exchange looks.

"Hey, Mrs. Andrews." Blanca comes up to the counter, oblivious to the fact that we're having a private conversation.

"Yes, he probably would have, but that doesn't mean you

don't ask." She turns to Blanca. "Did Ethan ask your dad before he proposed to you?"

Blanca nods with a big smile. She's so far gone, she practically has hearts in her eyes.

Mom points at Blanca. "See!"

"Wait, what? Who's engaged?" Blanca asks, a line forming at the bridge of her nose.

"You haven't even told your friends yet?" My mom's head cocks back. She's searching for the truth now. Slowly, millimeter by millimeter, her head straightens but her eyes never leave mine. "Seth?"

It's all in her tone. The one that says what are you hiding?

"Well, we were going to tell our parents first," I lie and my voice hitches. *Damn it.*

"Blanca, have you seen a girl around Seth's apartment at all?"

"Which one?" she says.

I narrow my eyes. I'm not a manwhore and she knows it.

Blanca laughs and says, "Just kidding. Not really, but we usually hang at Rian and Dylan's place."

My mom nods, but I can tell she's not convinced.

"See, it's crazy, right, Deb? I mean, this all comes out and you haven't heard anything around town. How do they keep it such a secret for this long and now they're engaged?" my dad says.

"Wait, Seth's engaged?" Blanca points at me. "You?"

"Do you know another Seth?" I deadpan.

She turns to Ethan, and he looks up as though he can sense when she needs something. Fucking happy couples.

She waves him over and he abandons their little workaholic nest. "Seth's engaged."

"Really?" Ethan says. "Congratulations, man."

"What? How are you not surprised?" Blanca asks Ethan, whose answer is a shrug.

"Seth Andrews, if you are keeping something from me…" my mom says.

I hate this, but I have to remember this is what's best for everyone. "We're engaged."

"Then you march your ass over to Vic Erickson and ask for her hand in marriage." Mom points at the door.

"There's more to it than that," my dad says.

"I'm fully aware, but he'll show respect to her father no matter how much I hate the man."

Ethan tugs Blanca away from eavesdropping. I'm thankful, because she's only going to add to my mom's suspicion.

"Fine." I raise my hands. "I'm going."

"And while you're there, please set up a dinner date with all of us."

"Hell no," my dad says.

My mom doesn't respond—she only conveys with her eyes that I'm to do what she said.

So as if I'm back to being nine, I walk out of my parents' bagel shop without the bravado I walked in with.

* * *

"So I have to go to your dad," I tell Evan when we meet inside the mercantile mart to have our meeting with Nick Klein and the bigwigs.

Panic coats all her features. "What? No, you don't."

"My mom is demanding that I ask for your hand in marriage. I've been searching for a coat of armor all afternoon."

She smiles at my joke because I am joking. Kind of. Her dad could very well kill me.

"If your parents know, then I have to tell mine. If the news travels to them…" She sits down in the waiting room and I find her left hand bare of the ring I gave her last night.

89

"Hey, wifey, where's the bling?"

"I couldn't wear it and have my mom ask questions. You didn't think I'd keep it on all the time, did you?"

I'm not even sure what I expected. I certainly didn't expect it to feel like a blow to my ego that she isn't wearing it, but there you go. "Once we talk to your parents, you better make sure you wear it and keep it sparkly."

"Sparkly? Why?"

"Because it's a symbol of our love, and the shinier it is, the purer our love," I say with sarcasm.

She steadies her gaze on me. "You're insane. You do know that, right?"

I shrug. "I believe your mom always told you to do a job is to do a job right."

She shakes her head with a smirk. I love when she doesn't want to smile or laugh at something I said but she can't stop herself. Her hair is half down today. For a moment, I imagine her curly hair sprawled out on my pillow while she's under me.

Fuck, that kiss messed me up last night. I actually beat off to Evan afterward, which shouldn't be a problem because she's technically my fiancée, but it's messing with my mind this morning. A half chub starts in my pants and I shift to get rid of it.

"Anyway, so after this little powwow, I'm going to gird my balls and head over to your parents'. Be prepared for the fallout."

She sighs. "I'm not sure we should go through with this. I mean, all of this just so our businesses can be spotlighted?"

I turn toward her. She's the one who convinced me. "No. All of this so we can be free. If we're spotlighted and business soars, you can move on and your parents can hire an actual manager. Same with mine. If they can hire employees or franchise or hell maybe a food company wants their recipe? We're doing this for our future."

She nods. "Okay, yeah. For us, not just the companies."

"And our parents. We're going to mend those relationships too while we're at it. It killed me seeing how much my mom misses your mom."

She frowns. "You really think that's possible?"

"Yep." I pop the p.

Thankfully, Nick Klein comes into the room and beelines it over to Evan. He holds out his hand to her. Jeans, Converse, and a V-neck T-shirt. He pulls off that "I purposely have this scruff although I look like I rolled out of bed" look. A man after my own heart.

"Evan, I'm so happy you agreed to the terms." He shakes her hand and moves over to me. "Seth Andrews, right? So glad to have you on board. This is going to be great for both of you."

He leads us across the room and through a door.

There's no turning back now. Come what may, we're committed—in more ways than one.

CHAPTER THIRTEEN

Evan

I thankfully convinced Seth to wait a couple days before asking my dad for my hand in marriage. But he trumped me by asking me to come to his apartment for a get-to-know-each-other session—in the name of being able to convince everyone that this engagement is legit.

I'm a little on edge as I walk up to his building. Will he want to have a repeat of that kiss we shared? I already know I want to. It left me wanting more in the moment, and still, I feel as though there's so much more we could explore if we had time and some privacy.

I press the buzzer and he allows me in. I take the elevator up and realize how weird it is not to know where your fiancé lives. My phone vibrates in my pocket and I pull it out for something to do.

Brock: *I'm sorry. We need to talk.*

I click the screen to make it go black. The fact that he waited until right now to text me means he doesn't care about me. Which is fine because I don't think I was ever really that into him. He hasn't crossed my mind since we split. Then again, my life's been crazy recently, what with me agreeing to a fake engagement and landing a spot on a TV show.

I knock on the apartment door and it opens a crack.

"Come in," says a guy with a much deeper voice than Seth.

The door inches open as I push on it and in front of me stands a huge guy. Wide shoulders, bulging biceps, and although he's wearing a T-shirt, I'm sure there's a set of abs underneath.

"Evan, right?" He puts out his hand. "I'm Knox."

"Hey, Knox." Now that I'm closer, I see the shirt is a plain gray one and his pants are police uniform pants.

He's barefoot and heads over to a chair, where he picks up a gaming controller. "Do you play?"

I look at the screen and see characters running around with weapons. Fake splatters of blood hit the screen. "Not that game."

"She's more a Zelda fan, right, honey?" Seth comes out of the door to my right with a towel wrapped around his waist. His hair is damp, and a few drops of water cascade down his chest.

Jeez, my husband-to-be has a hot body. I didn't even know he worked out. He's not the size of Knox, but he's cut, and the towel is so low that my mouth waters when I see the two indents in his hipbones.

"I know. You're marrying one hot guy, am I right?" Seth winks and heads across the room. "Let me just change really quick." He stops and turns around at the door that must be his bedroom. "Unless you want to practice your wifely duties. I mean, if I must, I'll take one for the team."

Knox's lips tip up and he glances at me. Good thing his friend finds him funny because I don't.

"Babe, I know your mom must have taught you that the woman always gets hers first, otherwise it's not worth doing." I take a seat on the couch and lean back, crossing my legs.

Knox actually stifles a laugh and coughs out, "Damn."

Seth opens his door. "I'm all about equal partnerships, so we could call it even and sixty-nine?" He waggles his eyebrows and walks into his room, shutting his door.

"So I heard you've agreed to marry my boy," Knox says, his thumbs moving across the controller. "What are your intentions with him?"

"I can tell you he probably has a lot more intentions than I do. None of mine are sexual."

He laughs. "No shit." He drops the controller and turns his chair to face me. "You seem like a sane person. Explain this to me. I mean, this has Seth written all over it."

I shrug. Truth is, I was the one who brought it up. Seth just upped the game by making it an engagement.

Seth walks out of his room in a pair of low-slung jeans, still pulling a T-shirt over his head. I stifle the urge to press my thighs together. Just like Knox, Seth's feet are bare, and he heads to their kitchen and grabs three beers before joining us.

He hands Knox his beer then opens mine before passing it to me. Falling onto the seat cushion next to me, Seth downs a big gulp of his beer. "What are we talking about?"

"The fact that you're insane," Knox says.

Seth doesn't refute him. In fact, he nods.

"So how long is the engagement?" Knox asks before sipping his beer.

"We signed the paperwork for the show two days ago. Technically, my baby over here forged her mom's signature."

"Rebel," Knox says and stares at me while he sips his beer.

I wonder if he feels protective over Seth. I mean, the only ones from this group who used to come to The Bagel Place are Blanca—because she didn't know better—and Adrian—worked for me briefly before it all came out that he was a prince.

"In one month, the marketing is going to hit, and we film in two months. So we have to get our parents to agree to it before marketing starts."

"You have one month to get your parents behind this idea, and you thought acting like you were engaged was the best way to make that happen?" Knox asks.

"Save the interrogation for work, Whelan. We already made our decision." Seth shifts in his seat.

"Do you even know anything about each other?" Knox asks.

"Yeah. I just told you she played Zelda when we were younger. I know plenty about my girl." Seth puts his arm around my shoulders and the scent of whatever he uses in the shower washes over me. God, he smells good. "And she knows everything about me."

I cringe. I didn't know he had ripped abs or a treasure trail that would show me exactly how to get to the pot of gold. "We could probably learn more. I mean, we haven't really talked in almost twenty years."

Seth studies me and I shift uncomfortably. He looks as if he took it as an insult that he doesn't know me anymore. "Okay. I still think I know you."

Knox shifts his gaze between us—waiting for us to do what, I have no idea. "I have a great idea. Why don't we do something like the *Newlywed Game?*"

"What?" I croak out because seriously, I think a simple questionnaire from Google we can each fill out and memorize will be fine. It's just our parents. We're not trying to get a green card.

"That's an awesome idea." Of course Seth thinks it is.

The door opens and in walk Rian and Dylan and a guy I don't know.

"Evan," Rian says, heading right to me, and sits on the arm of the couch. "I didn't know you were here. Do you watch *Blue Bloods?*"

"*Blue Bloods?*"

Seth stands and holds out his hands. "I'm out tonight. We've got some getting to know each other to do." His tone and his body language suggest we're going to his room to make out.

"We could go to a coffee shop?" I suggest.

"What am I missing?" Rian asks, sliding into the spot I just vacated.

Dylan doesn't take long to take Seth's spot, placing his hand on Rian's thigh. They make a cute couple.

"You didn't hear?" Knox finishes off his beer and stands. "Ol' Sethy boy popped the question. These two kids are gettin' hitched." Knox puts his hand on Seth's shoulder and Seth shrugs it off.

"And another one gone and another one gone," the guy I don't know sings like the Queen song.

"What the hell?" Rian says, clearly shocked.

Knox laughs and lifts a beer at the fridge toward his friends. Dylan and the other guy accept, but Rian declines.

"One day, Jax, one day," Rian says.

I guess his name is Jax.

He leans back in his seat. "One day I'll be the envy of all of you."

"Not happening. I've got no complaints here. Regular sex without trying," Dylan says.

"I don't try either, man," Jax says with a smirk.

Rian groans, then she leans forward. "So wait, explain this. You two are getting married? Are you living here?" she asks me.

"Then I'm back in your apartment," Jax says to Rian. "The bathroom here is already like a subway during rush hour."

"No." I laugh. "It's a fake engagement but you can't tell anyone that. We're just… it's a long story."

"The show's about to start," Jax says, grabbing the remote.

"Pause it," Rian says, her attention still on me. "We've got time."

I glance at Seth because these are his friends. He needs to be the one to explain.

"It's really none of your business," Seth says.

"You told Knox!" I can tell that she's offended.

Seth sits in Knox's recliner. "Fine."

Seth tells them the entire story about the contest, and I'm surprised to find that none of them think it's a good idea. Not even Rian, who I thought would see my side of things.

"You're dumber than I thought." Dylan shakes his head and goes to the kitchen for another beer.

Rian's gaze digs into me as she wraps her head around the news. "I'm shocked you two agreed on anything. I thought you hated each other."

Seth puts his hand over mine, entwining our fingers. "Turns out I like my soon-to-be wife." But he picks up my hand and looks at my left ring finger, his gaze moving up to meet mine. "Jax?"

"No, I won't be the best man in your pretend wedding." He rolls his eyes.

"I need a favor," Seth says, his gaze never leaving mine.

"What? I'll admit this to you guys, but it better not leave this room. Your mom scares me, Andrews. So don't ask me to lie to her."

"No. I need you to tattoo a ring on my fiancée's finger because she keeps taking off her ring."

I slide my hand from his and roll my eyes. "I'm gonna go. We'll do this another time."

"Wait!" Rian calls. "Even though I am not on board with this because I think that something will go very wrong and someone will end up getting hurt…" She glances at me. "You have to be prepared, right? I mean, we didn't believe it, so I'm sure your parents will be skeptical. If you're going to sell it, you have to really sell it."

She has a point. We can't do this half-assed. We have to play our roles with conviction.

"Rian's got a point. Because right now, Seth is coming off as a protective prick who's bullied you into marrying him when you'd rather be thrown into a ring with UFC fighters," Knox adds.

"Let's add in some Jell-O so I can get a visual," Jax says and chuckles.

Seth whips his head around to narrow his eyes at his friend. "Don't imagine my fiancée Jell-O wrestling, man. Not cool."

Jax holds up his hands in defense.

"I told them we should do a *Newlywed Game*," Knox says to Rian because even though I'm not part of this group, I could pick her to be the one who's on his side.

"Yes!" She jumps up, clapping.

See? I knew it.

"Let's see, how should we do this?" Rian leaves a groaning Dylan on the couch and she and Knox go sit at the kitchen table.

Knox pulls out paper and a pen and they brainstorm.

"Great. Thanks, Andrews," Jax says. He stretches out with his feet on their coffee table and leans his head back.

"Rian, I thought we were gonna…" Dylan stops talking when she holds up her hand to silence him.

"Please tell me you aren't scheduling sex now." Jax cocks one eyebrow at him.

But I never hear the answer because Rian comes over and pulls us up, pushing Seth and me toward his bedroom. "Okay, you guys have to go in there and talk to one another for a bit while we figure this out."

"What? I was gonna order pizza," Seth whines, turning away from the bedroom.

"Stop complaining. What's your motto? 'Go big or go home'?" Rian deepens her voice as if she's Seth. "You're not doing this half-assed. Dylan will order the pizza."

"I will?" Dylan says.

"You go get to know your darling fiancée." She shoves us into Seth's bedroom and shuts the door.

The first thing I notice is that the room smells like him, and the second is that he lives like a bachelor. No headboard. A dresser with receipts scattered across the surface. His shoes poking out of his closet so the doors can't shut. The towel that was wrapped around him when I arrived is slung over a hamper in the corner.

He falls back on his mattress, putting his hands behind his head and making his shirt rise so that I can just glimpse his tempting treasure trail. "Should we find out what makes us tick sexually first? Any fetishes I should know about, baby?"

My shoulders sink and I wonder for the thousandth time why I put myself in this situation. It's clear that there's lots that can go wrong, but is it even possible that something could go right?

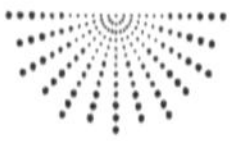

CHAPTER FOURTEEN

Seth

Evan Erickson stands in my bedroom as though she's a virgin on prom night and I'm some sleazy guy pushing her to be here.

"Relax, Evan, it's me. I'm kidding."

"I know." She nods. "I know. It's just…" She sits on the edge of my bed. "Why are we the only ones who think this is the best way to accomplish our goal?"

I can't argue that I haven't had my doubts. We're toying with our parents' emotions. My mom could get really attached, then it will all be over within two months. They'll still just be getting used to one another at that point. But my hope is that our fake engagement will bridge the gap between our families enough by that point that they'll stay in each other's lives. That, and make our businesses even more successful.

"It's two months. We'll have a fight and agree to part ways

amicably. Hopefully if our parents are friendly with one another through this process, they'll stay that way, and if not, then nothing will have changed from how it is now."

She nods. "I'm worried about Eli. He can attach easily and if we're spending time at my parents'…"

"Are you asking me to be an asshole to your brother?"

She pushes me and I fall back on the bed. "No. Just… promise me one thing."

"You know I make no promises." I laugh and she doesn't, which means I need to be serious for a moment. "What?"

"After all this is over and if we hate one another again, don't ignore him if you see him."

"Jesus, Evan, do you think I'm a total asshole? I would never do that. I say hi to him now as it is."

She tilts her head.

"Do you think I've gone twenty years without seeing your family at all?"

"No, but he wasn't even born when it all went down, so he didn't know you, didn't have to lose you."

"Elsie either, but she's got no problem telling me off every chance she gets." The girl has a mouth that needs soap and water on the regular.

"Yeah, I know. I'll work on her. She's not going to understand why things ended with Brock."

I grit my teeth at the mention of that asshole's name. "She liked him, did she?"

The girl gives me death glares that could make an entire Navy SEAL team shake in their boots, but Brock she likes. Money, it always comes down to the money.

Evan shakes her head. "Elsie likes what he offers. She likes that he drives a fancy sports car and takes me to expensive places."

Her dress from the gala comes to mind, how mind-blowingly sexy she looked. I'd guessed that Brock bought her that dress and the diamonds around her neck. Good thing this thing is fake because I can never compete with that.

Not that I'm not a catch, and one day I plan on being a successful photographer, but I can't imagine ever building some mansion on a hill to make everyone below me feel inferior.

"Anyway, we're wasting time. Want to start with our favorite color?" She unzips and toes out of her boots before sitting cross-legged on the bed. "Can I just ask one question first?"

I lean on the bed with my head resting on my palm.

"Are these sheets clean? I mean, the last time you slept with someone wasn't—"

"No. My mom made my bed today when she dropped off my laundry," I say.

She balks.

"I'm kidding. You're gonna have to get used to my jokes and pretend you like them if you're going to be my fiancée." I lean forward and touch her nose with my finger. Ugh. Why can't I seem to stop finding excuses to touch her? "Sheets are clean."

"Just asking. Okay, so, favorite color?"

"You are aware that's not going to be a question my friends ask, right?"

"Why? That's a typical first-date question." She pulls her hair back and secures it with a ponytail holder she had around her wrist.

God, she's so beautiful, sitting here all fresh-faced and relaxed on my bed, and I bet she has no idea. Whatever. I pull my mind away from how tempting she is and focus on the task at hand. "Yeah, it might be a first-date question but not an engaged-to-be-married one."

She hems and haws, but I know she sees my point. "Then you ask the first question."

"Sure, favorite sexual position?" She picks up a pillow and throws it at me, which I catch and put behind my head, sliding up my bed. "Okay, okay. Favorite movie?"

"Well, what kind? Like favorite action, favorite rom-com, favorite sci-fi…"

I pretend to yawn. "Let's just say *The Notebook*. It sounds like a chick thing and I'll remember it."

"We can't just make shit up. Elsie knows my favorite movie is not *The Notebook*." I quirk an eyebrow, and she huffs. "I mean, I like it, but it's not my favorite."

I chuckle. "Okay then…" I wave my hand at her.

"It's *P.S. I Love You*."

"What? That movie is sad as shit."

Her eyes widen a bit. "You've seen it?"

"The guy dies, right?"

She nods.

"I thought for sure you'd say *When Harry Met Sally* or *Notting Hill*."

"It's a great movie. She found herself, and he loved her and knew her so well that he knew what she'd need after he died. That's romantic."

I shake my head. "Okay, give me your best action flick then." I cross my fingers that she has better taste in this department.

"*Avengers*. Any of them," she says.

"And not just because of the hot guys in tight costumes, right?"

She shakes her head and a flush rises in her cheeks. I'd love to see it cover her entire body. "I like the action and Eli loves them, so we usually watch them together."

I pause, soaking in what life is like for her. "What do you do for fun?"

Her gaze flies to mine, and there's trepidation there. "I don't have much of a social life. I talk to some of my friends from high school, but most went to college and got married and live far away now. By the time I'm done at the shop, I'm going to bed to do it all over again. It's a little like *Groundhog Day*."

"Why did you ever agree to do it?" Her dad had just had his heart attack last year. Before then, I imagine they could've managed.

"I was supposed to go to community college like Elsie, but…"

I lean forward and dip my head, so our eyes meet. "You can tell me. I won't judge you."

"Eli," she rushes. "I love him so much, but he needs attention and care. More than I do. Someone had to help my dad so my mom could be hands-on with him."

A tear slips down her cheek and she quickly wipes it away. I'm shocked at the way seeing her upset like this constricts the air in my chest.

"Every time I talked myself into saying something to them, thinking we were in a good spot, something horrible would happen. Like the oven going out and we'd need to replace it or the rent going up. It's like before I knew it, I blinked and I was twenty-nine." Another tear falls and hits my bedspread, and that pain spreads in my chest. "God, I'm gonna be thirty." She climbs off the bed and paces my room. "Thirty, Seth, and I'm living above my parents' garage, with barely any friends, no life. It's like my biggest fear is coming true."

"What fear is that?"

"That I'm going to die alone. They'll find me in that bagel shop, slumped over one day. And no one will be at my funeral because I never had time for friends or lovers or anything else."

"Hey, you have a fiancé. A great one, I might add." I try to lighten the mood, sliding to the end of the bed.

She laughs and huffs at the same time. "You're fake."

I pinch myself. "Ouch. Nope, not fake."

"You know what I mean."

"Come here." I pat the spot next to me.

I never expected her to come sit, but she does. I put my arm around her shoulders and kiss her temple as though we're the best of friends. Maybe because I understand the pressure she's under. I ran away from mine until Trevor couldn't handle it. Now I'm the son they're calling on and look what I do—arrange a fake engagement so they won't need me.

"We're going to get you out of this obligation," I say. "And by the time people are singing 'Happy Birthday' to you on your thirtieth, you're going to have a whole new life in front of you."

"I don't even know what I want to do. I've never allowed myself to explore any options."

"I think you do know, but maybe it's buried deep down. Give it some thought. Take these next two months to figure it out."

She nods, but I'm not sure whether she'll do it. "God, I'm sorry. I'm a mess. You didn't sign up to be a therapist."

"Technically I think that's exactly what you sign up for when you're in a relationship. This is just, like, practice for when I am a husband."

She laughs. "You probably don't even want to get married."

Do I? I think so. I just haven't found anyone yet. "I think I will when I know I'm with the right person."

"Kids?" she asks.

I'm not sure if she's asking for the game or to satisfy her own curiosity. "Ten too many?"

"I think you need to disclose that to your future wife. She might be game."

"I want four, I think. Then again, I'm almost thirty and I don't want to be an old dad. So I guess I do want kids, but I'll take it as is."

Truth is, with a lot of my friends moving ahead with marriage and kids, I'm starting to feel like I might be the bachelor friend. The fun uncle who has a different woman at every birthday party.

"At least you can have babies up until you die," she says. "My eggs are shriveling up every day."

"Thirty is not fifty, calm down. Plus, you're smokin' hot. Some guy is gonna snatch you up. Just make sure it's not Brock Floyd."

"Man, you got the compliments down."

"I only speak the truth, you know that."

"I don't know… you lied pretty well to your dad the other night."

I can see from the look in her eyes that this is a legitimate concern for her. I let my arm drop and turn away from her for the first time during this conversation.

"Seth?" Her voice is quiet and unsure.

"I'm not a liar," I say. "I hate lying."

"Okay."

I swivel to face her. "I'm serious. I'll always tell you the truth. I fucking hate liars and fake people." My voice comes out with a bite I didn't intend.

"Okay. I believe you."

I nod. "Sorry. It's just Trev. The lies and deceit, it just shattered everything. Even now when he comes home, I won't believe a word out of his mouth. I hope he gets his life together, but I'll never trust another word he says."

She places her hand on my knee and runs it up and down. "I know you guys were close."

And we were until high school. Growing up, I looked up to Trevor. He was my idol, the coolest guy around, and to see him now is just depressing as fuck. I haven't called him since he went to rehab this time.

But I'm not going to sit here and cry all my feelings out. "Let's do a fast question round. We'll go back and forth to get ready for this damn game."

Evan takes my change of topic, probably agreeing with me that things were getting too heavy. She swivels so she's facing me with one leg bent and resting on the bed, the other one stretched out toward the floor. "You first."

"Favorite color?" I ask.

She laughs. "Purple. You?"

"Orange. Favorite food?"

And we go back and forth with questions and answers until there's a bang on the door.

"Ready, lovebirds?" Knox says through the door.

I stand and take her hand. "This means nothing. It's just my friends' dumb way of finding fun in their life."

"I'm excited. It's been a long time, Seth Andrews. I'm sure there's a lot I don't know about you."

"And me you. But just between us, what is your favorite sexual position?"

"There are some things you just have to find out on your own."

I stop as she walks out the door. Was that an invitation? Would I entertain sleeping with her?

Hell yeah, I would.

But that's just asking for trouble, so it's never going to happen.

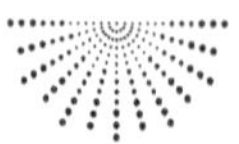

CHAPTER FIFTEEN

Evan

Where did that come from? Now he probably thinks I want to sleep with him.

I really need a best friend I can confess things to. I love Elsie, but with nine years between us, there's a lot I keep to myself.

We walk out of Seth's room, and though I'm embarrassed by the words that came out of my mouth, I'm even more embarrassed that I broke down in there. At least he didn't try to wipe my tears away. I must have sounded pathetic.

There's pizza on the counter, more beer bottles lying around, and we're joined by Ethan, Blanca, Sierra, and Adrian.

"We figured you'd need some other couples to play against, and since I'm the host"—Rian points at herself and smiles—"Dylan and I are out."

"Which sucks. Knox can be the host or let Jax," Dylan says.

"Yeah, if I didn't live here, I wouldn't be here," Jax says.

"I'll do it if you want to play so bad, Phillips," Knox says and takes the notecards from Rian.

She doesn't look very happy, but she pulls over two more chairs and adds them to the contestant line.

"Congratulations, boss," Adrian says to me.

Adrian doesn't work for me anymore, but I realize when I see him that he was the first person I admitted my disdain for what I do for a living to.

"They're not really engaged," Sierra tells him. "It's fake."

"I can still say congratulations." He nods at me with a great big smile. It's weird seeing him dressed up, since he was always in uniform at the shop. "Not to mention I just returned from Sandsal and you know how much I don't like to socialize on my first night back." He waggles his eyebrows at Sierra.

She pats his leg. "Relax. We'll be home in no time. And you're home for good, right?"

Everyone claps and says "finally." Envy hits me at how invested they all are in each other's lives. Seth is lucky. I'm not sure he knows *how* lucky he is to have this group of friends.

"Okay, you new lovebirds have a seat." Knox signals to the two vacant chairs. "You each have a whiteboard. We'll ask a question, and whoever has the whiteboard will write the answer and keep it covered. After that, their partner will answer. If you get it right, Jax will score you."

"No, I won't." Jax tips back a water bottle before chewing on a bite of pizza.

"You have to, man, Dylan is a contestant now," Knox says.

Blanca raises her hand.

"Blanc, just ask. This isn't grade school," Knox says.

"What are we playing for? Just bragging rights?" Her face is screwed up as if that's not enough.

"Welcome to my fiancée's life, where everything is a competition. Another thing to thank her three brothers for." Ethan rolls his eyes and grabs his beer off the table.

"I'm game. What did you have in mind?" Dylan leans forward, rubbing his hands together.

"We do have the bachelor/bachelorette trip coming up and we haven't picked the destination yet," Ethan says.

"That should be your decision," Rian says.

Blanca and Ethan share a look and shrug.

"We really don't care. We just want to get out of town. I mean, not to mention, we've been together the longest," Blanca says.

Ethan laughs as though none of us have a chance of beating them.

"Then it's settled. Winner picks where the bachelor/bachelorette getaway will be. So if someone chooses Vegas…" Seth says, and I'm fairly sure I'm missing something.

"You want to play that way? You and your fake fiancée think you're going to beat me and my real fiancé?" Blanca stands.

Ethan tugs her back down by pulling her sweatshirt. "It's just a fun game to help our friends out."

"Let's go, Mancini," Seth says.

I turn and face him. He's got conviction, and I kind of want to lean in and say that he might want to tone down the bravado. We might feel like we know one another, but we really don't.

"We're going to wipe the floor with your ass, Andrews," Blanca says. Ethan blows out a breath, but Blanca smacks his leg. "It's go-time."

Ethan sits up straighter, but there's no enthusiasm in his movements or his face. I stifle a chuckle.

"Things are getting exciting here at *Lovebirds Uncovered,*" Knox says in a voice like a game show host might use.

"You titled it like a police show," Jax says.

Knox ignores him and continues. "This one is for the men to guess."

Seth stretches out his fingers then cracks his knuckles.

"Women, please write down on your boards what you wear to bed," Knox says.

Blanca bends over laughing, pointing her dry erase marker at Seth. "You're screwed."

Seth glances at me, worry in his features. He's never going to guess this one. I write down my answer and tip my board so he can't see.

Once we're all done, Knox says, "Dylan, let's hear your answer first."

"A silk shorts and tank top set." He's confident.

Rian blushes as she turns her board over.

"And that's one point for you guys," Knox says, looking toward Jax—who blows out a breath but picks up the pen and marks a slash under Dylan and Rian. "Next up is Sierra and Adrian."

Adrian looks at Sierra. "Nothing."

And sure enough, Sierra turns her board around and it says 'nothing.' Adrian winks at her.

"Okay, Blanca and Ethan." Knox points.

The longer we have to wait to answer, the more worried I feel. I mean, if we lose, will Seth blame me? Whatever this trip is, it sounds like there have been disagreements already.

"Easy. My boxers and T-shirts," Ethan says.

Blanca turns her board around with a smug expression at Seth.

"So far everyone's got it right," Knox says. "Let's see if our new couple, who have never spent the night together, can at least make an educated guess."

Seth looks at me one more time and I bite my lip because he's never going to get this.

"I'm going with pants and a T-shirt combo." He looks at me. "It's either that or nothing, but I'm good with my answer."

I slowly turn my board around. Seth jumps up, putting his fist in the air.

"Lucky guess," Blanca says. "Ask some harder questions, Whelan," she says to Knox.

Man, she's feisty and competitive.

"I'm not sure my parents are going to ask me what Seth wears to bed. I think they might actually think I'm a virgin."

Everyone laughs and I find myself laughing too.

Seth kisses my cheek and whispers, "That's one, baby."

His scent wafts my way, and I'm reminded of the kiss we shared when he picked out my fake engagement ring. A part of me wants to turn my head to feel the press of his lips to mine again and enjoy the way he tastes—but that's not going to happen, so I push those thoughts from my mind and concentrate on the game.

The rest of the questions consist of favorite places to eat in Cliffton Heights, which I somehow get right with Seth. Knox digs deeper with questions focusing on childhood. I thought we'd be a slam dunk for the category, but Seth was bragging before we'd even answered one question. We did clean up pretty good in the "favorites when you were little" area.

"What was the first meal your lovebird ever made for you?" Knox asks.

Seth claims victory while my cheeks grow hot. Seth is clearly confident, and I have no idea.

"They haven't even had a meal together!" Blanca yells.

"Wrong!" Seth makes a buzzer sound.

He jots his answer on the whiteboard and covers it up so I

can't see it. I wrack my brain to figure out which of the disasters was our first. I remember a pizza burning in the oven once. Mac and cheese spilling over. Times when we should not have been left alone to cook lunch, but our parents were working. Was it a peanut butter and jelly sandwich? Fuck. He's so sure of the answer. I see it on his cocky face.

Knox goes around the room. Rian gets it wrong, and so does Sierra. Blanca nails it of course, which leaves me.

"You know this," Seth says, seeing the look on my face.

"No hints," Blanca says.

"I'm going with…" Then it dawns on me. Seth loved SpaghettiOs. I asked my mom to get them special for him and it was my first time trying them. "SpaghettiOs."

Seth turns over his board and he's written "burned SpaghettiOs," but Knox accepts the answer.

"They weren't burned," I mumble into Seth's chest because he's pulled me into a bear hug.

"They were, but it's okay. It was the thought that counted." He lifts my feet off the floor, and I inhale the scent of him, my eyes drifting closed. I love the moment way more than I should.

"You didn't win yet, jackass," Blanca says.

I thought she was a sweet girl, but she's so competitive.

"Yes please, contestants, sit down," Knox says in an official-sounding voice.

We continue the game and end up in a lightning round with Blanca and Ethan. I'm fairly sure Dylan and Rian gave up, and Adrian couldn't stop touching Sierra, so I think she was distracted. But they're all couples and have nothing to prove.

Knox hands Blanca, Ethan, Seth, and me a page of questions and a pen. We each go into separate corners and fill out questions about the last movie we saw, which physical feature our lovebird likes the most, the least, etc.

Seth and I exchange a look across the room because we both know we're sunk. We could call it now and just give it to Ethan and Blanca, but we're into it now too. We'll give it our best shot, even if defeat is headed our way.

After we've all filled it out, each of us takes our turn in the hot seat. Blanca goes five for five, Ethan four for five, so we'd have to be perfect to win.

Seth does this pretend punching in the air thing like he's a boxer. "Give it to me, Knox."

"Favorite physical feature?" Knox asks.

Seth's eyes fall over me for only a moment because we're being timed. "Um… lips."

My cheeks heat. Is he thinking about the kiss we shared too?

"Least?"

"Hair." He looks at me quickly. "Only because it blocks your face."

Blanca looks at me and I can't decipher her look—curiosity maybe.

Knox asks my favorite color and favorite movie, which thankfully, we did discuss in Seth's bedroom.

"Last one, what frightens your lovebird the most?"

Seth looks at me, searching and I hold my breath. He'll be five for five if he tells them what I said in his room when I was a crying mess. We can win this if he wants. I wrote the real answer on my sheet, as hard as it was, but the idea of hearing it spoken aloud in a room full of people I just met makes me feel entirely too vulnerable.

Seth's eyes remain on me when he speaks. "Spiders."

Knox makes the noise that Seth got it wrong.

Blanca jumps up and down in victory. "We won! Which means no strippers, no Vegas, we're going to a cabin in Maine!" She turns to me. "I do hope you join us, Evan."

"Oh no." I shake my head.

"Yes, you're his plus one," Sierra says. "I mean, you guys can't screw anyone else while this arrangement is going on anyway."

Of course her mind went there. Adrian's mouth rarely leaves her neck.

Everyone starts cleaning up the game and talking about how surprised they are that we did so well for not knowing each other. My gaze searches out Seth. As though he feels my eyes on him, he looks in my direction.

I mouth thank you and he nods. Because he could have won and gone on whatever trip he wanted to, but he didn't out me to a room of strangers.

And just like that, the trust I had when we were nine years old returns. It's almost as if no time passed and the twenty years apart was just a blink. Except that the small boy with long skinny legs and big feet has grown into a sexy man.

Maybe the feud was the best thing that could have happened to us, because it would've been a travesty if I'd never fully appreciated the man in front of me and only thought of him as my best friend.

I'm not sure what to think of him in this moment.

CHAPTER SIXTEEN

Seth

After twenty years of absence from this home, I pull my car up along the curb of the Ericksons' house. It's only three blocks from where I grew up, but after I turned nine, it might as well have been a thousand miles. The easiest way to get to the grocery store means going past their house, but my mom quickly learned to go a few blocks out of the way to keep everyone's mood as chipper as she could.

Knox pulls up behind me in his cop car.

Can you blame me? Of course I called my cop roommate to be my protector in case Evan's dad pulls a gun on me.

I walk up to his driver's side door and Knox rolls down the window. His partner, Lucas, sits at his side.

Knox smirks. "You have us until we get a call."

"Do you really think he's going to go after you?" Lucas asks.

My heart beats as though I snorted a line of coke five

minutes ago, confirming that I am in fact scared shitless that Mr. Erickson might have a weapon with my name on it. I wouldn't even put it past him to tackle me. His picture still lines the wall of Cliffton Heights High for his stellar linebacker skills.

"Yeah, I do," I say. "The man hates our family, hates me, and I'm about to surprise him by asking him for his daughter's hand in marriage when he doesn't even know we're dating."

Knox glances at his partner. "Seth's family owns Andrews Bagel Company, but the man in that house owns The Bagel Place."

"Oh, shit. Let's call in a break, I wanna see this." Lucas moves to press on his radio, but Knox shakes his head.

"Nah, Seth here is a big boy. Aren't you?" Knox looks at me.

A lesser man would say hell no. But if I'm going to be the person Mr. Erickson would want his daughter to marry, I better man up. "I'm cool. Just stick around for, like, five minutes."

Knox chuckles. "Sure thing."

I nod, wishing I looked as intimidating as Knox does.

Knox and Lucas laugh while I round the back of their squad car and up the Ericksons' walkway. Maybe no one is home and I'll get to live to see another day. Sadly though, I hear people inside after I ring the doorbell.

"No, Eli!" a deep voice booms with authority.

I clench my hands to stop them from shaking. As my stomach grows more twisted and bile rises up my throat, the door creaks open little by little, feeling as though it happens in slow motion, until Vic Erickson's large frame takes up the entire space. I gulp down the dry lump lodged in my throat.

"Who are you?" Eli asks, peeking around his dad.

"Hi, Eli," I say.

"He knows my name," he says to his dad, who has yet to actually say anything.

But Mr. Erickson's eyes say a lot. Like "get off my fucking porch."

"I know this is unexpected, Mr. Erickson," I croak out. "May I come in?"

He widens his stance, crossing his arms. "What do you want?"

"I recognize him. Who is he?" Eli asks.

"I'd really like to come in and talk to you. It's important and has to do with Evan."

Mr. Erickson's head tilts and he studies me for a moment. The only thing I have on my side is that Mr. and Mrs. Erickson have never been outright mean to me—and I imagine neither have my parents to their children—but what I'm about to do might be the end of that.

He steps aside and opens the door wider. "Eli, this is Seth. Seth Andrews."

Eli's only twelve, so he came along eight years after the epic feud. He might have no idea that the last name Andrews is most likely treated like a curse word in the house I'm now standing in.

It might sound weird, but the house smells the same as it did when I was young. The further I venture into the Ericksons' house, the more the memories swarm me and pull me back to when I was young. When Mr. Erickson would ask me about my peewee football team and try to explain the game of football to me when all I wanted to do was go on a bike ride with Evan. He used to treat me like a son. It isn't until this moment that I realize I miss it.

When I reach their living room and sit on the couch, I feel as if I'm nine years old and making polite conversation, waiting for Evan to barrel down the stairs with her eyes wide and tell me our adventure for the day. Usually something she read in a book or a magazine. Our summer days when we had the freedom to travel around town on our bikes and explore Cliffton Heights, discovering places that felt like our own secret hideouts.

"Sit," Mr. Erickson says.

Eli sits next to me, looking at me as if he's memorizing my face. "Your parents own Andrews Bagel?"

I nod.

"How do you know my name?"

I'm not sure how to answer, so I say simply, "Evan told me."

His eyes widen. "Evan? You're her friend?"

I nod again.

"Eli, go on upstairs. This will only take a moment." Mr. Erickson sits across from me in one of the same chairs they owned twenty years ago.

As Eli whines and Mr. Erickson's voice grows sterner with his son, I case the surroundings. Sure enough, other than new pictures of the family, everything here is almost identical as it was all those years ago. Even her grandmother's urn still sits prominently on the mantel of the fireplace. Evan confided in me how horribly creepy it felt to her to sleep in the house the first night it was here.

At that point, I hadn't lost my grandparents and I had no idea how to console her or comfort her.

Eli eventually heads upstairs, but I catch his feet stop just out of sight at the top of the stairs, eavesdropping on our conversation.

"What do you want, Seth?"

Just then, a squawking of police sirens goes off and Knox yells through the radio, "We're out. Way to grow a pair, Andrews."

I tense up and freeze.

"Friends of yours?" he asks.

"Yeah." I sit on the edge of the worn-out brown sofa and run a hand through my hair. "Roommate actually."

"Good to know those are the people sworn to serve and protect us."

"Honestly, they're good—"

He holds up his hand to stop me and I shut up. Amazing how similar he and my father are in their mannerisms and general intimidation factor.

"Okay, I'll just get to the reason I'm here." I swallow hard and fist my hands on my lap. My stomach feels light and tingly, and sweat forms on my hairline. "You don't know this, but I've been dating Evan."

He quirks an eyebrow and his lips press into a firm line.

"I know it comes as a surprise, but I'm sure you can imagine why we kept it a secret. You know, due to the family dynamics."

He says nothing.

"Things have grown more serious, and I'm here to ask you for her hand in marriage."

There, I said it. I feel relieved that it's out, yet somehow also guilty knowing it isn't real.

His face blanches white, still expressionless. This is it—I'm going to be the cause of his second heart attack. And then the families will never ever get back to where they were. Then again, that isn't our end game. We just need to get them to agree on this business venture for the show.

Then Evan and I will go our separate ways and… but damn, playing that game with my friends and being teammates felt good. Even though we lost and aren't a real couple, it was pretty damn awesome.

"You're dating my daughter?"

I blink and come back to the moment. "I am."

"I thought she was dating that asshole Brock Floyd?"

I smile inside at his classification of Brock as an asshole. At least we're on a level playing field, I guess.

He sits back in his chair and props his ankle on his knee. "Just the other night he showed up here in his fancy sports car. From what she was wearing, I'm fairly sure it was a date."

I nod. "Well, we…"

Shit, this part sucks. Lying to Mr. Erickson more than I already am puts me close to Trevor's territory—where one lie starts it off and you allow them to pile up until before you know it, you start to believe the lies yourself.

I wonder how Knox would handle him. Mr. Erickson's like a police officer—the deafening silence, the eyes boring into mine as though he knows he's got me right where he wants me.

Fuck it. This is for our futures.

"We kept our relationship a secret," I say. "However, I will say she's probably going to be shocked when I propose. It's a little early, but I need her in my life."

His eyebrows rise.

"I should clarify that. Um…"

Again he doesn't fill the silence, like he's watching me tie my own noose around my neck.

"I love your daughter." It's a lie, but in some messed up way, there's a bit of truth there. I'll always love Evan. Not as a fiancée or a wife, but as a friend. Even if I haven't had a lot of contact with her in twenty years. I tried to warn her about Brock, that's proof enough.

"You do?"

"I do."

He examines me further, letting time draw out between us. "And she loves you?"

"I believe so."

"And she was dating that Floyd guy as a cover?"

I bite my lip and nod. "Yeah."

He sits up and places his forearms on the arms of the chair, linking his massive hands together. "Why do I find this whole thing odd?"

"Um… I don't know." I swallow and gulp like a kid being asked questions after he accidentally broke a window. Okay, so that happened once before. When I was six, I broke Evan's window by throwing a ball at it.

"So you love my daughter and you want to marry her?"

"Yes, sir," I say.

He smiles, but it doesn't reach his eyes. There's something cynical and conniving in the creases of his eyes. "We'll plan a family dinner then, with both families. You and Evan can come over and you can propose to her here."

Shit. I'll never be able to pull it off in front of both families.

"I had a private proposal planned," I say.

"Nah, an engagement is a family thing. Since you love my daughter so damn much and you want to marry her, we should all be part of the moment."

I nod. "Okay."

Okay, what? I'm going to fall on bended knee in front of the people who know me best and try to pull off this lie?

"Great. Tell your parents this Saturday at five-thirty. We'll meet here and Jenny will make dinner for everyone." He stands and puts out his hand.

I nod and rise to my feet, which feel numb at this point. Fuck. I'm so screwed. "Sounds great."

He walks to the door and opens it for me. As I walk over the threshold, I'm thankful I still have my life, but that might change come Saturday.

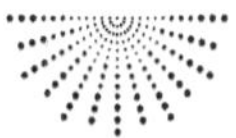

CHAPTER SEVENTEEN

Evan

I'm hurrying to fill a large order that's supposed to be picked up in ten minutes. My mom was supposed to be here helping, but she called and said something came up. Then she wouldn't give me any details when I pressed her.

I know it has nothing to do with Eli because he texted me from my dad's phone a half an hour ago to say that a friend of mine came by the house and was talking to Dad downstairs. When I called to pry more information out of Eli, he told me it was Andrew. It only took me about five seconds to figure out that Seth went to my house.

Eli said he tried to hear what was said, but he heard Brock's name and then he started thinking about his sports car. Then Eli asked me if he could go for a ride in the sports car, to which I had to say I didn't think so. He of course asked why, and everything just trickled down from there.

Now I'm jittery and nervous, wondering how it went with my dad. Not to mention concerned about how he took the news because of his heart.

My phone dings, but I don't answer it. I'm sure it's Eli wanting to ask a million questions about Seth. He's always inquisitive. Normally I'm happy to answer his questions, but not about this. Not right now anyway.

The door chimes and my head falls back so I'm looking at the ceiling, letting out an exasperated breath. I can't catch a break today. Taking off my plastic gloves, I toss them in the trash and walk to the front.

There's a guy with a ball cap pulled low over his eyes which are covered by dark sunglasses. Hair sticks out of the back like a mullet, and he's wearing a trench coat that covers most of his clothes except for his classic Vans.

Seth.

"Is anyone else here?" He disguises his voice.

"No, it's just little ol' me," I play along.

"Alone? No one in the back?" He nods.

I suck in my lips to stop from smiling. "Hey, buddy, I gotta gun under the register," I say, my hand moving to grab a stapler.

"Whoa, hold up. It's me." Seth throws off his sunglasses.

I burst out laughing. "Yeah, I know. What are you doing?"

"I didn't want your mom to recognize me if she was here." He takes off the baseball cap with fake hair glued to the back.

He's such a weirdo sometimes. I smile at him anyway.

There's my handsome guy.

My mind takes a mental pause. I didn't really just think that, did I? He's not mine. But unfortunately, I can't deny the handsome part.

"She's not, but I gotta finish this order. I'm assuming this has something to do with you visiting my dad today?" I raise my eyebrows.

He chuckles. "I forgot how intimidating he is." Seth rounds the counter and walks into the back.

"What are you doing?" I follow him and find that he's already putting on plastic gloves.

"What is this, tuna or chicken salad?" he asks.

"Chicken," I say, watching him scoop little dollops onto the bagels.

"Come on, you put on the lettuce and tomato." He continues as though this could be an everyday routine for us.

I glance at the clock and find that I can't really turn down his help. Mr. Tettlebaum will not be happy if he has to wait even one minute when he arrives. This order is for the book club he holds at the community center. He originally asked me to bake the title of the book on the bagels and I said no, so he'll be cranky already.

"Are you sure? This isn't your job." I put on a fresh pair of plastic gloves.

"This is a husband's duty."

Jeez, he never stops. "You're not my husband."

"Same thing. Fiancé is just a husband-in-waiting."

How can the man who I thought disposed of women like a monthly magazine subscription step into the role that's not even his reality?

"Okay, well, thanks."

He looks up and our eyes catch for a moment. "You don't have to thank me."

I say nothing.

"When I go down on you, then you can thank me." He winks.

I throw a tomato at him and he laughs.

"Are you ever serious?" I ask. I wonder if he'd notice if I stuck my head in the freezer right now to cool down from the thoughts of his face between my thighs.

"I find humor to be the most effective icebreaker." Once he finishes scooping, he picks up the onions.

"Oh, and how did you figure that out?"

He shrugs and concentrates on the task at hand. Seth always had a comedic personality, but never to the extent it is now. Now it almost seems like a defense mechanism.

When I've given up on him answering and I'm about to ask about him going to visit my dad, but he says, "I think it was back when Trevor started using. It helped my parents. They didn't laugh for a long time and things with him got progressively worse until they just looked depressed all the time."

"Where is he now?"

"He's in Florida. Another rehab place that will hopefully help him get his shit together. He says he's serious this time, that he hit rock bottom."

I nod, placing a piece of lettuce then tomato on the bagels. He puts on the tops of the bagels and cuts them in half before wrapping them and placing them in the box. He's obviously done it numerous times at his parents' bagel place.

"You don't sound so sure?" I look at him.

He glances at me. "Yeah, I know. I'm his brother and I should believe he'll beat this disease, but we've been here before. Last time, my parents went to family counseling. I watched him like a hawk when he returned. Once I let up, he disappeared like usual, holed up in a cheap hotel for days, just getting high. My mom was freaking out and I was scouring every hotel parking lot, searching for his car."

I hear the struggle in his voice. The anger mixed with sympathy. Like he judges himself for not fixing his brother.

"Maybe he'll get better this time. There's a lot of people who don't recover the first time around." I'm basing this on my slight obsession with *The Dr. Phil Show* and *Addiction*.

"I hope so. But the first time, you go in thinking this is

an easy fix. That the doctors will fix him, and he'll go back to the Trevor we knew. We were lucky because he didn't overdose before we got him help. But the second time, you go in eyes wide open. This isn't a disease that gets cured with doctor visits and medicine. Trevor has to do the work, and if he doesn't, we could end up on this rollercoaster for the rest of our lives. I'm not sure my parents will survive it."

My heart solidifies and falls from my chest, shattering on the floor for the pain his family has had to deal with. Mr. and Mrs. Andrews are like my parents—family problems stay within the family. So although they couldn't hide that Trevor was stealing for his drug use, they've kept most of this to themselves.

No wonder Seth cracks so many jokes if it's his coping mechanism.

"I'm sorry," I say in a quiet voice.

He cuts it in half and then wraps another bagel. "Please don't."

"Don't what?"

"Give me that pitying look. I'm fine. I have no control over Trev, and my parents have to learn that too. But getting that look from you, the same one I get from every other person in this damn town who knows about him, sucks."

"They just feel sympathy for you."

"All I see is them asking why couldn't you fix him? Or worse, what did your parents do to bring up a boy like that?"

"No. Not the people around here. They've known your family for a long time. They understand—"

He shakes his head. "No, they don't, Evan. It's sweet that you think that, but they don't. People judge until they find themselves in the same shoes."

I hate that he has such a cynical view of this town. He's lived here his entire life, and the fact that he puts on a smile and wave for everyone while thinking they're rooting against him makes me sad.

"Anyway, enough of that. We have bigger problems," he says.

"Like your visit with my dad?" I say.

"Yeah, how did you know?"

"Eli," I say. "He took my dad's phone and said Andrew came by."

He laughs, then his mood grows somber. "Does he know? About—"

"The feud? Not really. He knows there's another bagel place that competes with us. But I'm not sure he understands what happened in the past. To him, you're just my new friend."

He huffs. "I wish I had that bright of an outlook."

"What happened?" I box up the bagels as the door chime rings. I hold up my finger. "Give me a minute."

I head to the front with the box. Mr. Tettlebaum is here. Usually he's dressed in costume, but today, the only thing different than his suit jacket and gray hair sneaking out of his tweed flat cap is the stuffed cat on a leash that's tucked under his arm.

"We read 'A Man Called Ove' by Fredrik Backman," he says, as though that should make sense to me. I wish I had time to kick my feet up and read a book so I did know what he was talking about.

"Oh, nice." I push the box toward him on the counter. My phone dings from the kitchen and I glance back before taking Mr. Tettlebaum's money and giving him change. "Thank you."

Seth comes out of the back room and Mr. Tettlebaum steps back, his beady eyes widening and alarm striking his face. "Seth?"

"Hi, Mr. Tettlebaum. I'll get that for you." He swoops up

the box. "See you later, Evan. FYI, your mom just pulled up in the alley."

I nod, realizing why he's getting the hell outta Dodge. He makes a motion behind the old man's back that he'll call me later.

Mr. Tettlebaum asks Seth point-blank what he's doing here, and I find myself holding my breath, waiting for the answer.

"Evan and I are friends. Didn't you know that?"

Mr. Tettlebaum glances back at me as though he wants confirmation. "Huh, I didn't know that."

Seth winks at me, and my stomach reacts as though there's a tiny gymnast in it. "Remember when everyone thought we were going to be married, what with our parents being best friends?"

"That was twenty years ago," Mr. Tettlebaum says like that's obviously not the case now.

"A lot can change in twenty years. Then a lot stays the same too." Seth smirks as though we're sharing a secret.

I haven't shared a secret with Seth since we were nine years old, and I'm ashamed to admit, I missed it. I missed our friendship so much, but my body is yearning for more than friendship and that's only going to cause me trouble and heartache.

"Evan?" my mom says. "I'm sorry—"

I gather myself and say goodbye, then I walk into the backroom to find my mom with the plastic supplies.

"Can you believe they said they couldn't deliver it? I had to pick up some knives," she says.

"But they delivered plasticware last week. We still have plenty."

I pick up my phone to see who was texting me. There's a voicemail, which I'm sure is probably Eli, and a text message from someone named Mack Daddy.

Mack Daddy: *We have a situation. Meet me at my work after you close. If the red light is on, just wait in a chair.*

I text back as my mom goes on and on about the plastic cutlery situation.

Me: *Mack Daddy?*

Mack Daddy: *I think it's a cute pet name? No?*

Me: *No.*

Mack Daddy: *Wait until you see what I saved you under.*

Me: *I probably don't even want to know.*

Mack Daddy: *The reward comes to those who wait.*

"What are you smiling at? Who's that?" my mom asks with a happy tone.

She probably thinks it's Brock. I can tell that my dad hasn't told her about Seth's visit this morning. I'm surprised my dad would keep that to himself, but then again, he might think he can stop our engagement before it comes out to everyone in our lives.

I think he's mistaken though. Lately, I feel as though Seth and I are on a train with no brakes, heading down a steep hill. I can only hope we don't crash and burn at the end of the track.

CHAPTER EIGHTEEN

Seth

*H*eidi isn't the usual client someone thinks of when I mention boudoir photography. In fact, she might be the most attractive woman who's ever stepped foot in my studio. And she's not even here for bridal boudoir —she's here for herself.

"I'm just off a breakup and I thought this would make me feel desirable again."

To get some overhead pictures, I step up the ladder Madison put up for me. Heidi's outfits have all been red, black, and dark purple, which is a nice change from white lace and soft pink satin I usually see.

"We get a lot of clients like that," Madison says.

I tilt my head when I come down a rung on the ladder. She's lying, we don't really, but there's something to be said for doing this for you and not for someone else. Although I think that the women get a lot from the sessions, even if the pictures go to their boyfriends or husbands.

"You do? I figured most were bored housewives trying to get their husbands to sleep with them again." Heidi rolls onto her stomach and shoots her feet up in the air. She's obviously researched things before coming here because I've barely had to direct to her positioning in any way.

"More bridal than housewives," I say, snapping her arching her back, her long brown hair lying against her back to the top of her ass.

"Really? That's a cool idea."

"Why did you and your boyfriend break up?" Madison asks.

I send her a "shut the fuck up" look. I don't want Heidi to break down in tears.

"He cheated," Heidi says. "With my boss."

"Shut up!" Madison screeches.

"Yep, I lost my boyfriend and my job all in one day. But it was a blessing."

I want to ask how long ago all this happened because she seems to have a good head on her shoulders. But I'm not willing to encourage this line of conversation.

"How so?" Madison asks.

She and I are going to have to have a conversation about her nosiness.

"Because it finally got me to go out on my own. I'd been working in real estate under my boss for ages because I dragged my feet to get my broker license. So I finally did it and I'm the broker now. I just opened a small boutique brokerage and now I get a cut of every deal I hire under me."

"Good for you," I say, taking a few more shots now that she's not talking anymore.

"Yeah, I'm happy. And the boyfriend thing. Eh, I never want a guy who I have to check his phone or worry when he's out with his friends. I'm not gonna lie, the next guy will probably pay the price, but I try to remind myself I can't stop some guy if he's gonna cheat. There's nothing I can do."

"Good for you," Madison says and prepares to change the backdrop. We've worked together so long, she anticipates the changes I want before I even ask.

"Yeah, but it messes you up in the head too, which isn't much fun at the time."

"That's why Seth likes his life vanilla," Madison says.

"Vanilla?" Heidi peers up at me with questions in her eyes, and I snap a picture. "As in—"

"Not in the sex department."

She giggles and her eyes get a little heated. I've noticed her eye-fucking me a few times.

"I just don't want the stress in my life," I say. "Which means any woman I invite into my life has to be drama-free."

Heidi balks. "That's not a fun way to live. What do you want? A woman to bow down to you? Agree to everything you want?"

"No, I just don't want drama. You know. Phone calls all the time. The questions and interrogation of where I've been."

"Hmm… I hope you like the bachelor life because you'll never find that." Heidi looks over her shoulder at the new backdrop. "I'll be back. I have the perfect outfit for this one."

I nod and she disappears into the backroom. My phone vibrates in my pocket, and I pull it out to see Evan—or shall I say Juliet, as I've named her in my phone.

Juliet: *I'm here. Waiting since the red light is on.*

I hand my camera to Madison. "I'll be right back. Download what I have so far, and we'll start fresh."

She nods and walks over to the table.

Evan is waiting outside the room. She's still in her jeans and T-shirt that says The Bagel Shop. She's not wearing makeup but still manages to look cute as hell. Even with a little bit of flour in her hairline.

"You're early," I say.

"Sorry, my mom said she'd close, and I didn't want to argue. You really need to tell me what happened this morning with my dad, because my mom is acting like I'm still dating Brock."

I sit in the chair next to her. "Seriously? Your dad didn't tell your mom?"

She shakes her head.

"I asked for your hand in marriage."

She blanches and blinks a few times. "And?"

"He doesn't believe us. I mean, he questioned me about you dating Brock and I said that we were secretly dating and that it's still early, but I really want to lock you down."

"You said that?"

I laugh and place my hand on her leg to stop it from shaking. "In a manner of speaking. I did say I love you."

Her gaze moves up and locks with mine. It's filled with questions. Maybe because I take pictures of women all day long, but I can often read what a woman is thinking.

"I had to. We wouldn't get married if we didn't love one another."

She nods. "Yeah. Totally. Yeah." But she still seems shaken.

"He wants a family dinner this Saturday. And he wants me to propose to you then. Is it possible your mom does know but she's trying to act surprised?"

She shakes her head. "That's not my mom's style. She'd question me for sure. Why does my dad think it's not real?"

I shrug. I've been trying to figure that out all day. What did I do to give off that vibe? "I think maybe it's because he thinks we would've come to them sooner with the fact we were dating. Or that they would've heard it from someone who saw us around town together."

Her head falls into her hands. "We should've done the dating thing first and then gone into the engagement. We went too big too soon."

I squat in front of her and take her hands. "We did not. We had to go big. And they'll believe us as long as we *make* it believable on Saturday."

"Okay. That's the whole reason we did the game thing, right?"

"Exactly. We got this. They'll believe us," I try to assure her, but she still covers her face with her hands.

The door squeaks open and Madison stares at the scene in front of her as though she doesn't understand what she's looking at.

"We're doing so much lying," Evan murmurs.

I shoo Madison away with my hand and she closes the door.

"It'll be worth it. I hate lying too, but this is for our future and theirs. They just don't know it." I place a finger under her chin and guide it up so she's looking into my eyes. "I know you haven't had to put this much trust in me since that time I held the rope so you could climb out of the Bruggers' backyard before Hercules got you."

She smiles and shakes her head. Seems she remembers when we were eight and made the stupid decision to antagonize the Bruggers' mutt because of a bet from the Hinkle twins. We put pieces of steak in our pockets and jumped into the backyard and whoever lasted the longest won. Won nothing but the bragging rights of being the winner. Which was me, FYI.

"But." I wait for her to look at me and our eyes lock. "I've got us. Just let me take the lead and we'll come through this okay. I promise you."

She nods, and I suck in a breath in the hope that I'm promising something I can actually deliver.

"I gotta go finish up this shoot. I'll be back."

"Okay." She nods.

I stand and my hand is on the door when Evan calls my name. I turn to face her.

"Thank you, Seth."

"You're welcome," I say and cross my fingers hoping this all works out.

* * *

A HALF AN HOUR LATER, Heidi leaves and I send Madison home, since that was our last session of the day. Evan joins me in the studio, looking around with surprise on her face.

"It's nice in here."

"Did you expect a dungeon?" I ask, sitting to download the shots from today.

"I'm not sure what I expected, but not something so beautiful." She thumbs through the backdrops that hang from the wall. "The bed is a little unnerving. How many naked women do you see a day?"

"Not many." Which is true. "A boob here and there when they switch positions, but honestly, I try to act like I didn't see anything so they're not embarrassed." I thumb toward the door. "That client was pretty open though. I'm not sure she would've cared."

"She was really pretty," Evan says and sits in the giant black velvet chair.

I take my camera off the dock. "Want me to shoot you?"

"No!" she screeches and stands.

"Okay." I hold the camera pointing toward the floor.

"Are they all that pretty? I mean, now that I'm your

fiancée, I feel like I need to keep better tabs on you." Evan laughs, but it's hollow.

There's a part of our arrangement that Blanca brought up the other night that we haven't even discussed. Neither one of us can date while we're fake engaged. Which means, no sex.

"Are you going to put a tracker device on me?" I slide my wheeled chair closer to her.

"No. You're not really mine. You can do what you want." She looks at her fingers, entwining them in her lap.

"I'm not going to do anything though."

She rolls her eyes. "Please. You can continue to live your life as long as no one finds out."

Seeing her so unsure of herself makes my chest tight. I scoot the chair across the floor until I'm directly in front of her. "Do you know how beautiful you are?"

Maybe it's a habit of being in this room and wanting every woman here to have the feeling of being wanted and desired. Or maybe it's just that the woman in front of me is so damn perfect, and she has no idea.

"Oh my God, stop. I am not having this conversation with you." She moves to stand, but I lightly grasp her wrist.

"Tell me Floyd knew what he had?" The voice in my head is telling me to abort this mission, but I can't.

"Seth. We're pretend, remember?" Her voice is barely above a whisper.

I shake my head. "I might be pretending that I'm your fiancé, but I'm not pretending to notice how hot you are."

With her foot, she pushes the edge of my chair so I slide across the room. When I stop, I lift the camera and snap a picture of her. Her blush jumps off the tiny screen on the camera, and her shy and embarrassed look is sexy as hell.

"Evan Erickson, one day you're gonna be under me naked in a sheet."

Her eyes widen. "What?"

"I'm going to photograph you," I say.

She swallows and nods. "Oh yeah, of course. Photograph." She stands. "I better get home."

Is it just wishful thinking or did she really not object when she thought she'd be naked underneath me in a different context? I don't know whether to hope I'm right or not. Is it possible that Evan doesn't want to go back to being enemies after this is over? What would that even mean?

CHAPTER NINETEEN

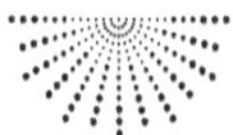

Seth

I offered to pick up my parents to take them to the Ericksons' for dinner, because I figured my dad would either refuse to go or drag his feet. So I was surprised when my mom said they'd see me over there.

Could my parents be over the feud and want to move on? Doubtful.

Me: *I'm on my way. How's your parents' mood?*

Juliet: *They're playing music in the kitchen while they finish up dinner. My dad is actually smiling.*

Me: *I'm worried.*

Juliet: *Yeah, it's creepy. Come and get me before they force me to join a cult.*

Me: *Don't worry, I'll never let them take you away from me.*

Juliet: *Romeo, Romeo! Wherefore art thou Romeo? Oh Romeo, wherefore art thou?*

I laugh as I head to my car, surprised that she came up with that without knowing what I named her in my phone. I only programmed her number under that name as a reminder that she's off-limits—like Juliet was to Romeo. When they ignored that fact, they both ended up dead. It's a perfect reminder that I need to keep my hands off of Evan. No matter how much I replay our kiss in my mind and what it would feel like to do it again and again and again.

Me: *Lock yourself in your room and fight them off. I'm on my way.*

My last message goes unanswered and I start my car to head over to the Ericksons' house. On the short ride over, I run over in my head why my parents would willingly go over there without me having to put them in straitjackets and drag them. Why are they so eager?

Then my mind wanders to Evan and how even though we've only been in this charade for a short time, I feel as if I can hardly remember a time when she wasn't in my life. It's as though the twenty years apart doesn't even exist anymore. All the memories of us together keep replaying in my head, refreshed as if I stored them in a "never forget these" box in my brain.

Pulling up to the curb of the Ericksons', I see that my parents' car is parked right in front and they're not in it. They must have gone inside without me. What the hell is going on?

I told my parents that Mr. Erickson insisted I propose to

Evan in front of everyone tonight and not to tell Evan's parents that I'd already proposed. My mom felt as though she was keeping secrets, but my dad said he didn't give a shit and the whole thing is ridiculous.

I climb out of my car, and Evan walks out of her apartment above the garage as I walk up the driveway. Her curly hair is down and styled, along with a fresh face of makeup and a dress. Damn, I'm wearing slacks and a button-down, but maybe I should've worn a suit.

She jogs to meet me and presses her body to mine, her arms wrapping tight around my neck. "Seth," she coos.

I hold her, unsure where this affection is coming from.

She whispers in my ear, "Our dads are in the backyard. I'm going to slide the ring inside your front pocket, so act like you wish you could sweep me upstairs and make love to me instead of having dinner with all of them."

Finally something I don't have to lie about. So I kiss her neck, and her one hand slides down my side, then I feel a tug on my pocket.

"We're all good," she says.

"Son, you don't kiss your girlfriend on the lips when you see her?" my dad yells from the backyard where he's standing next to Mr. Erickson. My dad has a beer in hand but I notice that Mr. Erickson doesn't.

"They're cordial," I say in a low voice to Evan.

"More than cordial, they're actually talking," she says.

"Don't be shy, Seth, kiss her," my dad says.

I place my hands on Evan's face. "Ready?"

She nods and I place my lips on hers, not adding my tongue into the mix.

"Sad, son, just sad," my dad says, shaking his head.

I step back and release Evan. "Well, I don't like PDA."

"Come on," Evan says and leads me to the kitchen, where our moms are talking over cutting vegetables.

My mom beams at me, and for the first time in I don't know how long, nothing about it looks forced.

"Hey, Mom." I kiss her cheek.

"Hey, sweetheart. Say hello to Mrs. Erickson."

Evan's mom wipes her hand on her apron. "Please, call me Jenny. We're all adults now."

Her arms open wide and I glance at Evan, who shakes her head like she doesn't know what's going on either. It's like nothing happened and if they'd remained friends, this is exactly where they would've ended up.

"Where are Eli and Elsie?" Evan asks, stealing a cucumber from the salad.

"Oh, Elsie took Eli to Los Tacos and for some ice cream. It's just the six of us tonight." Mrs. Erickson glances over her shoulder at my mom with a grin that isn't even close to sly. "Why don't you two set the table?"

I move to follow Evan into the dining room.

"Hey, Seth," my mom calls. "Have you heard from the Food Channel yet? I haven't and wondered if they reached out to you?"

My gaze goes to Mrs. Erickson, but she's not where she was a second ago. Where the hell did she go? "Nothing yet."

"Are you sure you didn't miss a call or anything? I was at the grocery store today and saw Lucy from Porterhouse. She was upset because they weren't chosen."

I shrug. "Maybe they're waiting to notify the winners." *Please accept my answer. Please let this go until I'm ready to tell you what I signed off on.*

"Maybe."

Mrs. Erickson walks back into the kitchen from the garage with a roll of paper towels. She smiles sweetly at me.

"I'm gonna go help Evan." I point with my thumb behind me, then bolt. Evan is putting the plates on the table. "Something is going on. They know."

She scoffs. "How on Earth would they know?"

"I don't know, but they must. Something weird is going on."

"Well, I agree with you there, so make the proposal fast, okay? If you wait, everyone will know you're hiding something."

"Hey, I'll propose how I want to," I tell her.

"I'm just saying that if you drag it out or get all gushy about it, that's not you."

"Not me? How do you know what I'd be like if I was actually going to propose to you for real?"

She stops placing the napkins next to the plates and stares at me with an expression that says, "I know you."

"I'm going to be so convincing even you will think it's real."

She laughs and continues setting the table.

I shove my hand in my pocket, feeling for the ring. "Try me."

As normal as it feels to be with Evan, our parents' attitudes toward one another aren't normal and I can't help but think they know we're pretending. But there's no way they could've found out. Nothing has been announced. Sure, maybe the other paired restaurants know the situation with the show and the pairings, but no one would ever think that we'd collaborate.

Our dads come in smelling of cigar smoke, talking about football and who will win the Super Bowl. Evan and I keep exchanging looks, and I know in my gut that I'm missing something.

"Can we have a word with you two?" Mr. Erickson calls to us.

I take Evan's hand like a good boyfriend, and we walk through the archway into the living room. Our fathers are seated in the two chairs, leaving the couch I sat on just days ago free.

"So, can we hear the story of how you two came to be?" Mr. Erickson says.

My dad sits back, glances at Mr. Erickson, and smirks my way.

They know. They fucking know what we're doing.

"Um…" Evan begins, but I'm not going to play into their hands.

I grab Evan's hand and entwine our fingers. "I can't tell you how happy we are seeing you two mending your feud in support of us together."

Evan squeezes my hand.

The smile strips from my dad's face. "We both believe family comes first and we wouldn't put our crap on you two. Right, Vic?"

"Sure. I mean, if you two love one another, who are we to stand in the way?" Mr. Erickson says. "Though, Seth, I'm upset to hear that you came to ask me for Evan's hand after you'd already proposed."

I look at my dad. Damn it. What doesn't he understand about not saying anything?

"It was an in-the-moment thing. I'm sure back when you fell in love with Mrs. Erickson, you lost all rational thought when she was around. I do apologize."

"There's no ring though?" My dad glances at Evan's hand.

"I have a ring." I pull it out of my pocket and grab Evan's hand—probably with a little too much force—to prove to the two smug men across from me that they're wrong.

"Your mother has your grandmother's ring. Evan will wear that one." My dad raises his eyebrows at me to see if I'll refute his wishes.

Nice touch, Dad, but I'm playing to win here, so I'll give Evan the ring and she'll give it back after this is all over. "Great. That would be wonderful. I didn't want to ask because I didn't know how you'd feel, but since we're all one big happy family now..."

Both dads glance at one another.

"Dinner!" Mrs. Erickson calls from the kitchen.

"Come on, honey, you can tell us all about how you fell in love with Seth during dinner." Mr. Erickson waves Evan to her feet.

We walk to the table, but there's no dinner waiting. The salad my mom was cutting up isn't even on the table. We slide into our seats anyway, giving each other questioning looks.

My dad plops a newspaper down in front of me. "Care to explain this?"

I read the announcement from the Food Channel congratulating all the local businesses that made the cut and will be spotlighted. Each eatery is announced, along with their counterpart, and sure enough, halfway down it reads, "The Bagel Place and Andrews Bagel Company." I pass the newspaper to Evan and she sighs.

As my mind spins to figure out what to say, Evan opens her mouth and beats me to the punch. "I'm sorry we went behind your backs, but we did it so you guys would have to finally end this feud. And then we were going to tell you that we were dating, but well..." She looks at me and her face morphs into an expression filled with admiration and love. "Seth proposed and everything just spiraled out of control. Here we are."

Good job, Evan.

Our parents all sit at the table, staring us down.

"So you guys really are together?" My mom's hopeful expression says that smile on her face when I walked in was genuine.

My father's scowl is as predicted. He and Mr. Erickson thought they could get one over on us.

Lord, please forgive me for what I'm about to do. "We are."

Another wide smile creases my mom's lips and she peers at Mrs. Erickson, who is smiling just as wide.

"Then we need to start planning the engagement party," my mom says.

Evan chokes on her water, spitting it on the newspaper and wetting our names. "What?"

My dad's scowl turns victorious. "An engagement party. You know, it's a celebration that of the love you two share."

"But—"

"Yes, great idea," I cut Evan off.

"Grab a pad of paper, let's start with the guest list," Mr. Erickson says to his wife, who gets up and returns with a pad and pen.

And before I can think of how to spin this, our parents are rambling out a bunch of names to add to the list.

Okay, we can handle this. I mean, an engagement party is fine. It's not like they're asking us to elope.

"Oh, and you two?" my dad says, looking to Mr. Erickson for confirmation. "There will be no joint venture for the show. We can accept you two as a couple, but that's it. So whichever one of you organized that with the Food Channel will have to tell them no."

Evan sighs and her shoulders show her disappointment as they slump. I grip her hand and squeeze.

Parents one, kids zero. But we will come out on top. I promised her she'll get out of her current situation, and I will make that happen one way or another. I just hope we don't end up pretend married in the process.

Evan

"Mom, I don't have to go away this weekend," I say, filling the bagel boxes and cream cheese tubs for our Friday morning orders.

"Nonsense, you two need to go and have fun. You're only young once." Her smile conveys that she means what she's saying, whereas my dad always has some snide remark and a look like I'm about to confess that Seth and I are faking it after all.

Since they cornered us two weeks ago and called our bluff, we've portrayed ourselves like a real couple. Which usually consists of Seth coming to my house to pick me up, then we either head to his place, go to dinner, or a movie. It feels a little like we're dating, but as soon as we're out of anyone's vision, the handholding and the little pecks on the cheek stop.

"But you'll have to run the store—"

"Evan," my mom says, squaring her vision on me. "Relax, we're good. Elsie can come in, and your dad wants to work a bit. I think he got scared when he saw that newspaper article that things were moving out of his control. I mean, did you really think you two could do that Food Channel thing and get away with it?"

"It's a good opportunity for all of us."

Mom turns away from the boxes of bagels and grabs a few containers of cream cheese, adding them to the boxes.

I should let this go. Confess the truth. But that small sliver of hope I had that maybe I can get out of running this place has been sparked, and I can't douse the flame yet. "Mom—"

She shakes her head like a toddler who doesn't want to hear what I have to say. "I know, Evan. I know what you were doing."

"You do?" My heart nearly sputters to a stop. Fear rips me up and guilt consumes me. Guilt that I didn't have the backbone to just confront my parents.

"You and Seth thought if you could mend fences where the businesses are concerned that we'd accept you two. You were so young when it all went down, there are things you don't understand. Your fathers cannot work together. It was a disaster from the beginning. Competitiveness and pettiness about whose whatever was better. Your dad wanted to fiddle with the bagel recipe and Chris the cream cheese. We really are better off this way."

"But are we? The people at the Food Channel raved about the combination."

Maybe had our parents seen the judges' faces, they'd have a different feeling about the entire thing.

She shakes her head. "Believe me, if you and Seth want to be together, it's best to keep business out of it."

I want to scream that we're not a real couple, that we just

want the businesses to collaborate this one time and then we can all go back to hating one another. "Not even just for the show?"

A hollow laugh escapes her. "I can just see it… national television, your dad and Chris at each other's throats about which product makes the other better. It's a lose-lose situation, honey."

I take a handful of the boxes and bring them to the front for pick up. Looking up at the chime of the door, I assume I'll find Seth—since he's supposed to be here to pick me up—but it's Brock. Panic flares and my breath hitches. He's called me a few times since he texted me after we broke up, but I've ignored him.

He casually walks up to the register, staring at the menu as though he doesn't know every item already from all the time he used to spend here, waiting for me.

"Can I help you?" I ask.

"Yeah, I'll get an asiago with vegetable cream cheese. For here."

My shoulders sink. "Brock, why are you really here?"

"Can't a guy get a bagel? Or should I go to your fiancé Andrews' place now?"

The phone rings and I hear my mom answer it in the back.

I inhale a deep breath before I speak. I guess we're doing this. "We were already over before anything started with Seth."

"Do I look like a fucking idiot? You embarrassed me. My friends and family think you broke up with me for that piece of shit, Andrews. Either that, or you were already screwing him behind my back."

"I guarantee you, our breakup had nothing to do with him." I narrow my eyes. "That was all you."

I turn to busy myself making the bagel with the hope that

the sooner he gets it, the sooner he'll leave. If he's here when Seth gets here, I can't imagine what might happen.

"It's like going down memory lane being in here again. Reminds me of when I used to sit here and admire you from the booth. You took so long to warm up and finally accept a date with me."

I keep my back to him, not wanting to stroll down memory lane with him, but since he brought it up, I do anyway. And it's like a mental block opens. I reflect on the days he spent here, as though he'd wait a lifetime for me to say yes. The stream of friends coming and going. How he'd make them buy a bagel or a drink and then—

It all clicks together.

How was I so fucking naïve?

I whip around, pulse hammering in anger, and shove his bagel in a bag before tossing it on the counter. "You were selling drugs here."

"What?" His forehead scrunches, but I know I'm right. "You're listening to your boy toy too much."

I shake my head. "No, you were. That's why you hung around here. Not for me, but for a place to sell your drugs on the sly. You asshole!" My voice raises. "You put my family's business in jeopardy."

"You're crazy! Why would I sell drugs? I'm the next in line to run Floyd Steel."

That's the only thing that doesn't make any sense and the entire reason I had a hard time believing Seth when he accused him. "I don't know, but I trust Seth."

A cackling laugh escapes him. "You trust a guy whose family screwed yours over? A guy you've hated for two decades?"

I shove the bag across the counter. "It's on the house. Now go. And don't ever come back."

He scoffs and shakes his head. "You've fooled this town,

you know that? You think you're above everyone? Got them all fooled into thinking you're so sweet and endearing when you're no better than any other girl." He walks backward, a condescending smile on his lips the entire time.

My gut clenches when Seth rounds the corner, and I watch him through the window, walking closer to the shop. He opens the door.

I've missed what Brock was saying, but I do hear him when he says, "You'll spread your legs for anyone."

Brock turns to leave and Seth's fist cocks back and punches him in the jaw. Brock stumbles, the bag with the bagel fumbling from his hands.

"Fucking hell," Brock says, wiping the blood from his mouth.

I'm half surprised they're not wrestling on the floor right now. I can only assume Brock doesn't want me to call the cops. Maybe he has drugs on him.

"I'm going to have to call you back," my mom says from behind me on the cordless phone. She walks up to my side, her hand on my forearm as if she's afraid for me.

"Get the hell out of here and never come back!" Seth grabs two fistfuls of Brock's shirt, pushing him against the glass. "If you ever speak about Evan like that again, I swear to God, Floyd, you'll be in a body bag."

Seth releases him and Brock tries to straighten his shirt. "Then stop spreading rumors about me. I didn't hook your fucking brother on drugs—he did it to himself." He walks out of the bagel shop.

I'm too awestruck to say anything.

"Oh my," my mom says. "Are you okay, Seth?"

"Hi, Mrs. Erickson. Yeah, I'm fine." He leans over the counter and places his lips on mine as though it's the most natural thing in the world. And maybe it is now, at least in front of others. It's when we're alone that things get awkward.

"Jenny," my mom says, correcting him.

"Maybe I should just call you Mom," Seth jokes.

"One day soon, and after what I just witnessed, I look forward to having you as a son-in-law." She puts her hand over his. "Thank you for that."

"Don't thank me." His gaze shoots to me. "I'll always protect her."

I swallow past the dryness in my throat because his blue eyes say he means what he's saying. But I tell myself that this is all part of the act. "How are your knuckles?"

He shakes his hand. "I'll be okay."

"Good, now you two, go. You don't want to be late." My mom grabs my bag and places it on the counter.

Seth picks it up for me. "FYI, we're with Knox, Jax, and Frankie."

I don't mind because at least they're not couples. The last place I want to be is with couples who can't stop touching one another, reminding me of what it's like when Seth's hands are on me.

Seth rounds the counter and kisses my mom on the cheek. "Bye, Mrs. Erickson. Thanks for letting Evan have the time off."

I hug and kiss my mom's cheek. "Thanks, Mom."

"Stop thanking me, just go." She waves us off.

We walk out of the shop and I glance back at my mom once more. I'm struck speechless when I notice the hopeful look on her face. Her smile is wide, her eyes sparkling. My gut clenches when I think about how disappointed she'll be when we announce this was all a hoax, that we're not really together and we're doing it for the business so that I can abandon her to figure out my own dreams for myself.

Seth throws my bag into the back of an SUV. Frankie is in

the third row. Knox is in the driver's seat with Jax acting as navigator. I say my hellos to everyone.

As we pull away from the curb and head toward Maine, Seth grabs my hand. "You okay?"

I nod, unwilling to admit the guilt that's overtaking me over our stupid plan. I fear I'm hurting everyone around us, and it dawns on me now—what if I end up hurting the most?

"Fuck, Owens, you have to tell me where to go. Otherwise, I'm calling Frankie up here," Knox yells when we miss a turn.

"Excuse me, I thought being a cop, you'd know your way around fucking town. How do you not know how to go north on the highway?"

"Because I always go south."

Jax glances back and smirks. "So are you two doing it already?"

"What?" I look at Seth.

"My dumbass friends think that we're doing it because we can't date anyone else right now."

Frankie leans in. "They only think that because those two can't go two days without getting their dicks wet."

"Not true!" Knox raises his hand.

Seth laughs and puts up his hand to Frankie for a high five.

"You've completely ruined my game since I started at Ink Envy," Jax says, turning in his seat to look at Frankie. "So sadly, I have to go longer than two days now. Talk about a cockblocker."

Frankie puts up her middle finger and slides it along the bridge of her nose. "You're a bunch of idiots."

"Yeah, they are," Seth agrees.

I've never gotten the impression Seth is interested in a relationship, but then again, we weren't exactly besties confiding in each other.

"I don't know about you, but I can't wait to sit by that fire and do nothing," Frankie says, pulling me from my thoughts.

She's right. I haven't had a weekend that didn't include The Bagel Place in years, so I'm going to take this weekend for myself. Because if Seth and I aren't successful with our plan, this just might be my last chance for a long, long time.

CHAPTER TWENTY-ONE

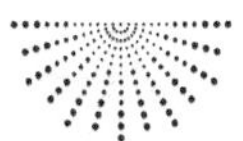

Seth

If someone would've asked me what to expect from this bachelor/bachelorette trip, I never would've said that Evan would let loose. But she's been drinking wine all night, dancing around and laughing. Hell, she and Frankie have been attached at the fucking hip.

And since my friends know that our relationship is fake, I have no reason to touch Evan. There's no handholding or short kisses. I can't put my arm around her shoulders or feel her thigh pressed to mine as we sit on the couch.

Right now she's on the floor with Frankie, painting each other's nails, and I'm at the table with the guys because they want to play poker. I can't concentrate on the game.

"Andrews," Knox calls me out for my lingering stare at Evan.

Jax groans. "This is painful. It's like we're witnessing a

sleepover and they're about to strip down to their underwear and have a pillow fight."

"I think you're hoping for it." Dylan throws a peanut at Jax to get his attention back on the game.

"I haven't gotten laid in weeks," Jax grumbles.

Just then, all the girls coo and squeal as though they *are* at a sleepover.

"That's the great thing about being in a relationship," Adrian says before popping a few peanuts into his mouth. "Regular sex."

Dylan and Ethan nod and smile.

Knox and Jax raise their eyebrows.

"You also have to spend all your non-sex time talking about feelings, watching chick flicks, and fetching anything she wants." Knox sighs, but he's not fooling me. Back when Leilani was around, he was all in. I know he's still bitter that she wasn't.

"Andrews has the shit end of that stick right now," Ethan says.

I glance up from my cards to see all their eyes on me. "What?"

"You have to do all of the other shit with none of the benefits," Ethan says, upping the bet by tossing chips into the pot.

"He went to see that new chick flick with Evan the other night," Knox says.

Jax narrows his eyes. "Why? I thought it was just an act for the parents?"

I shrug. "We have to be believable. Our parents, or at least our dads, are on to us. I wouldn't put it past them to follow us, so we have to act like a real couple."

"Except there's no fucking," Knox says.

They all shake their heads at me in disappointment.

"You guys should make a pact," Jax says.

"Definitely. I mean, if it's all truly an act, then why not just have a friends-with-benefits situation?" Knox asks.

It's not like the thought hasn't crossed my mind. Especially after I kissed her. We have a chemistry that doesn't seem to want to disappear. If anything, it just keeps growing. Like right now, I wish I could walk over there and kiss her, but I can't. Not without raising a few eyebrows.

"I don't think she's the type," I say.

The conversation shifts to football, but my mind won't stop circling back to what Evan would say if I propositioned her with the idea of being friends with benefits.

I know she feels the tension between us. When I place a chaste kiss on her lips for the sake of our act, she rarely pulls away first and we always share a look after that reads to me like maybe she wishes I'd kissed her like I did that night in the store. But screwing one another exclusively until this is over would be like dropping a kid in a toy store and telling them they can have anything they want only to take all the toys away a few weeks later. Sometimes it's better not to know what you're missing.

But damn, it would be so satisfying to finally get her out of my system. Maybe just once. We could have sex one time then go back to being friends.

A peanut hits my forehead. I glance up and all the guys are looking at me.

"Bet's to you," Knox says. "And just go pull her aside and convince her."

I shake my head and fold my hand because I haven't been paying enough attention to decide whether to bet or not anyway.

"I'm sure she's just as horny as you," Jax says.

"Hey, guys"—Blanca comes over to the table—"we need to figure out the sleeping arrangements."

"Obviously the couples are together. And I think Frankie and Evan are rooming together," Ethan says, eyeing me.

My movements stop. How did I not think of this? We don't have to share a room because these people know the truth.

"So I'm thinking Jax, Knox, and Seth rock, paper, scissors to figure out who gets the single and who's sharing a bed," Blanca says.

"Fuck that. I'll take the couch," Jax says.

"Why don't we just do Evan and Seth, then Jax and Frankie, and I'll stay in the single," Knox says, wiggling his eyebrows as though his plan is brilliant.

I'm totally game to go along with it.

"I'm not sleeping in the same bed as a horny toad," Frankie says.

"Are you actually calling me a horny toad?" Jax asks, pointing at himself.

We all laugh.

"I'm pretty sure I can sleep next to you and not put one hand on you," Jax says.

"Ha! Never."

"Let's put a wager on it." Jax stands.

We all share looks as though we're wondering what the hell is going on. I lean back and don't argue because I want to stay with Evan, as messed up as it is.

"Winner gets the next five walk-ins." Frankie puts out her hand.

"Ten," Jax says as though he's positive he's going to be successful. That makes one person.

Sierra raises her hand. "What if neither of you cross the line? And how will we be privy to the information about what happens?"

Jax laughs. "Oh believe me, if we fuck, you'll hear Frankie screaming my name."

"Oh, Jax, if we screw, you'll be the one swearing up a storm because you'll have no idea how to handle a real woman."

Everyone laughs as Jax and Frankie shake on the deal. Now I'm all kinds of turned on, and my vision shifts to Evan, who's just as flushed as Jax is. Her heavy-lidded gaze moves to me. Maybe she would agree to the idea of friends with benefits.

What's the worst that can happen? She says no. It's worth the rejection to try.

* * *

SLOWLY THE COUPLES say good night and head to bed. Knox says he's exhausted and disappears into the room with the single bed.

"I'll sleep on the couch," I offer.

Evan shakes her head, but she's quiet now that her sidekick Frankie went to the bathroom to get ready for bed. "No. It's fine. I think I'm gonna go to bed. Maybe read a little bit before."

"I'll go too."

Jax sits in front of the television, watching the *Fast and the Furious* whatever number—there are too many and I can't keep up. We say good night, and he raises his beer bottle at us. After Evan heads down the hall, Jax waggles his eyebrows at me. I flip him off.

"You guys aren't going to bed, are you?" Frankie whines as she comes out of the bathroom in a pair of boxers and a tight tank top. Good luck to Jax.

"Yeah, the wine made me tired," Evan says, yawning.

"Okay, have a good night," she singsongs and bites her lip, watching us like a creep until I shut the door.

Once we're behind the closed door, Evan goes to her suitcase.

"What was that about?" I ask.

Evan looks at me from over her shoulder. "What?"

"Frankie acting like we're playing seven minutes in heaven." I sit on the bed, tugging off my sweatshirt.

"Oh, I don't know." But there's a hitch in her voice.

"I think you do."

She turns and scoffs, holding her pajamas. "Why would I?"

"Because you two were like best friends today."

She shrugs. "She was just thinking—or was saying, I guess… I mean, it's a horrible idea."

And my mind blows up because maybe for once I was right. Evan wouldn't mind exploring a sexual side of our agreement.

"What was she saying?" I lean back on the mattress, holding myself up with my elbows.

Evan looks hard and long at me. "You already know!" she accuses.

I shake my head, a grin on my face.

"You do so. If you could see your smug face right now." She heads to the bathroom. "I'm going to change."

"We're still discussing this."

She peeks around the corner without her pajamas in her arms. "What are we discussing? Was that your plan to get Frankie to put the thought in my head?"

"Hell no. The guys said something to me about it tonight. I had no idea Frankie was as brilliant as she is."

"Seth," she says with that tone to suggest whatever I'm thinking isn't going to work.

"Let's think about this rationally, okay?"

She stares at me blankly, apparently waiting for me to plead my case.

"First of all—I'm horny, okay? All the teases of touching you, kissing you, and being near you but never going further is leaving me with blue balls most nights."

A beautiful pink blush rushes up her neck and into her cheeks.

"It's like I'm fifteen and dating. I need more but…"

"Do you want to see other people? I mean, I was thinking earlier and maybe we should just be honest with our parents. They still haven't come around and said we can do the Food Channel thing and—"

"What the hell are you talking about? We're seeing this damn thing through. And I don't wanna fuck anyone else. I only wanna fuck you." The words rush out before my brain processes the meaning of the words. "I meant that kiss, Evan. That kiss was so unreal, and it's all I've been able to think about since. Do you know how hard it is for me not to slide my fingers under your shirt when I put my arm around you? Or for my hand to stop idling on your thigh? It's a struggle not to let my hand drift between your thighs when we're seated beside each other and see if you're wet and wanting like I am."

"God, Seth," she says, a whimper falling out of her. "You make it all sound so…"

"What?"

She shrugs. "I don't know."

"Do you not feel the same way? Do you not think about how it could be? At night, don't you lie awake and wonder how I fuck?" She exhales a deep breath and closes her eyes, so I climb off the bed and stalk across the room to her. "Do you imagine whether I would be slow or fast? How much I'd stretch and fill you, and the orgasm that would shatter you from the inside out as I drilled in and out of your wet pussy?"

I run my thumb along her bottom lip, and her eyes slowly open with a hooded gaze. "But…"

I shake my head. "I'm only going to ask this once. I want you, Evan, and if you want me too, then I'm going to ask you to kiss me. We're doing this crazy thing already. Why not have even more fun while we're doing it? Meet me halfway and I promise you, you won't regret it."

I press my body flush to hers and wait. Her soft curves meet my hard chest and my erection pushes against her stomach. Her eyes shift up to me, and for a moment, I feel like I was wrong. Maybe I misunderstood her body language. Then she rises on her tiptoes, her arms slide around my neck, and her lips press to mine.

And it's game on.

CHAPTER TWENTY-TWO

Evan

Someone else has taken control of my body. That's the only reason I would set myself up for heartbreak as I press my lips to Seth's.

A moan slips from my lips the minute he coaxes my mouth open with his tongue. His hands slip around my waist, fingers moving under my shirt until he touches bare skin. He groans as if he was telling the truth, that he's wanted to feel me all these weeks we've been playing pretend.

His lips are hot and firm as his tongue swirls and strokes my acquiescence out of me. I step closer, clinging to his body because this kiss is so much more than the one we shared at the store and that one was a lot.

His lips venture down my jaw, scattering across to my ear. "Jesus, Evan, you're so damn…" He doesn't finish, as though that would take too much effort and he can only concentrate on having me in his arms. "I promise you won't regret this."

I have my doubts about that, but in this moment, having his full attention on me, I don't care. An ache forms between my thighs and my breasts grow heavy the longer I taste him and feel him pressed against me. His hands venture up my back, unhooking my bra with ease.

I feel him through every inch of my body when his fingers graze my skin as though he's an expert on what I want and need. He grabs the hem of my shirt and we break apart to get rid of the thin fabric barrier. My bra goes next and with it, all the confidence I'd been feeling thus far. Now I'm standing before him, bare from the waist up and vulnerable. But his words set me at ease right away.

"Your tits are perfect." He molds his hands to my breasts, his thumbs running across my peaked nipples.

I sigh, arching my back. He bends down, pushing my right tit up, and his mouth covers the rounded flesh, his tongue swirling over my nipple. I step back from the overwhelming sensation of his mouth, and his hands and my back hit the dresser.

His mouth pops off my breast. "Are you okay?"

"I'm good." I nod rapidly.

He chuckles and his hands push up both my breasts, his mouth sliding from one nipple to the other. He stops much too soon for my liking, but when his fingers fiddle with the button of my jeans and zipper, I have no arguments except that he's wearing far too many clothes.

"You too." I pull the hem of his T-shirt over his head. Now both of our hands are in a frenzy, racing to see who can get the other's pants off first.

When mine falls to the floor, he looks at me with a devilish grin. "I win."

"I think we both win." His pants fall next, and I place his

hand over my wet satin panties. "I think you've been wondering how wet I am."

His finger runs the length of my core, over the paper-thin fabric. "Damn, if I'd known you were this soaked, I might've nailed you on your parents' dining room table."

"That would have proven we're in love."

"Or that I'm a horny bastard," he says, circling us so the backs of my knees hit the bed and I fall onto the plush mattress. He bites his lip, staring at me. "Take them off," he says in a husky and authoritative tone.

I grab the edges of my panties and slide them down my legs before tossing the flimsy fabric to the floor.

He takes off his socks one at a time and crawls up the bed. I elbow my way up toward the headboard as he stalks me. "Believe me, you want to stay still because I'm about to rock your world."

I roll my eyes at him, but from the first swipe of his tongue along my slit, I'm transported into the best wet dream of my life. His finger teases my entrance while his teeth, tongue, and sucking mouth accost my clit. I writhe under him, but he grabs my hips to keep me in place. He devours me with my legs spread wide for him.

"Watch me," he whispers.

I use all my energy to open my eyes and watch the tip of his tongue stroke my slit up to my clit, which he sucks. It's been so long for me that I don't last.

"I'm gonna come." I wiggle under his hold, but he grips me harder to keep me in place, forcing me where he wants me.

"Watch me, Evan."

It's nearly impossible to watch him because his face is so expressive. Like he's tasting ice cream for the first time and he wants to eat it for breakfast, lunch, and dinner. His groans drive me to my impending orgasm much faster than I ever have before from having a man between my legs.

I clench his hair, needing something to hold on to as he devours me.

"Harder," he says, breaking away from my core before diving back in.

I tug on his hair and another satisfied groan escapes him. He takes one hand off my hip and plunges his fingers into me, setting off a chain reaction. My hips fly up off the bed, my hands locked in his long strands while my climax catapults me into the stratosphere.

"Shit. Shit. Shit."

He chuckles and slowly licks me and twirls his tongue until I fall back to the mattress and expel the longest breath of my life.

Before I know it, he's off me and searching his bag.

I prop up on both elbows, my eyes not fully widening yet. "Did you come up here planning this?"

He shakes his head. "Nope. But a Boy Scout is always prepared."

"You forget that I know you were kicked out of Cub Scouts."

He laughs as he kneels in front of me, tearing open the condom wrapper and rolling the latex down his engorged shaft. I admire his long length and wide girth.

"Like what you see?" His arrogant smirk says how proud of his dick he is.

"Yes, because if I had to judge based on when we were six, I'm not sure we'd be here."

He falls on me, tickling, and I squirm to get out of his hold. "I think you should kiss it and tell him you didn't mean any offense."

"Um. No."

His fingers continue to tickle me until I'm squealing for

him to stop. But then the tip of his dick pierces my opening and things grow serious between us again.

Seth bites his lip and stares at me. "Still good with this?" He circles his hips and I moan, another jolt of arousal flowing through my body.

"You did promise me an orgasm that would shatter me inside and out."

"Such a smartass." His lips fall to mine and his tongue slides into my mouth as if we've done this a million times as he slowly fills me inch by inch.

With Seth, I feel a familiarity I've never experienced with anyone else. A comfortableness that's new to me.

He eases in and out of me in a leisurely yet torturous pace. I wrap my legs around him, and he groans from the reward of being deeper inside me. Tearing his mouth from mine, he nuzzles my neck. The soft sounds of his breath in my ear grow heavier and heavier as though it's a struggle to maintain control. My body tightens and throbs around him in preparation for my climax until I have no control and scream his name.

He growls as he thrusts, pushing off his knees and toes, grinding into me with a delicious force. I gasp as the sensation sets my nerve endings on fire.

"Fuck, Evan. You're so beautiful. This is just how I thought it'd be all those years I imagined it."

I'm sorry. What? Years?

But he doesn't look chagrined. Is this like the "I love you" people say during sex that they don't really mean? Lost in the moment and admitting things they don't really believe?

If he asked me point-blank, I'd never be able to fib and say I hadn't thought of him either. In high school, I'd watch him in the halls and wonder what he'd do if things were different. If we were two strangers and not mortal enemies.

"Jesus, you're so wet."

I grip his shoulder blades to hold on as his body drives into me over and over again.

"You feel amazing," I say, not nearly as good at the dirty talk as he is.

"I missed you. Your pussy is so tight I'm gonna come, so I really need you to go first."

I laugh, but he changes his position so that his pelvis grinds into my clit. As if he gave me some magic spell to make me come, every sensation stacks on top of the other and my entire body seizes, and I cry out.

He doesn't relent, hammering into me until one final push and a groan as he stills inside me. A drip of sweat falls between my breasts and the weight of Seth's body falls on me.

We lie there struggling to catch our breath for a moment. When he rolls off of me, I miss him immediately.

"I'll be right back." He disappears into the bathroom then returns and moves the bedding so we can slide in.

"I better go too," I say and climb off the bed.

I sit on the toilet and think about what just happened. There's no coming back from this moment. And the worst thing is Seth Andrews just gave me two of the best orgasms I've ever had in my life.

Once I finish my business then put on my pajamas that I left in here, I open the door to find Seth standing there in his boxers, his arms braced over the top of the door.

"You okay?" He brushes my hair off my shoulder.

I nod. "I'm good. It's just sex, Seth. I wasn't a virgin." I dodge his gaze and duck under his arm. "I'm super tired though. I can't wait to sleep in."

We get into bed and he lies on his back, kicking off his blankets. I lie on my side, facing away from him, because I'm certain he'll see my feelings on my face if he sets eyes on me.

The mattress shifts and I expect him to say he's going to

go out to the kitchen or something, but his arm wraps around my waist and he pulls me against him. "As my soon-to-be wife, you should know that I'm cuddler."

I giggle and his hand splays on my lower stomach, pulling my ass flush to his dick.

"And if you feel a pole poking you in the morning, it's just my morning wood. Feel free to do with it what you will."

"As in?"

"As in mouth, pussy, even ass if you're up for it."

I buck my ass into him. "Seriously, Seth."

He laughs and his arm tightens. Leave it to him to bring humor to an uncomfortable situation. He clears his throat. "Good night, Evan."

"'Night, Seth."

And soon my eyes grow too heavy and I succumb to sleep, determined not to worry about how what we did tonight might send our plan careening off course.

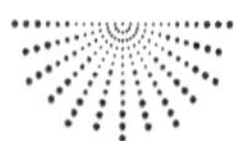

CHAPTER TWENTY-THREE

Seth

"Fuck! Where did you ever learn…" I grip Evan's ponytail, holding her mouth on my dick. "Tell me you read an article…" My eyes betray me and close from the sheer agonizing pleasure of having Evan's tongue twirling around my shaft as if she can't get enough. "And you practiced on a cucumber or something."

I grip her hair. Every ab muscle I have clenches and my hips jut forward as I groan until my cum shoots down her throat. She's a swallower, which I fucking love. She licks me clean and falls back to sit on her heels.

"So?"

Wiping her mouth, she rises to her feet. "What?"

"Where's your stash of vegetables you practice on?" I pretend to scour the area and she giggles, falling onto the bed.

I zip up my pants. If we didn't have to be at my parents' in twenty minutes for dinner and if her dad wasn't outside, I'd rock her world right now, even if I did just blow my load. But we're noisy fuckers and the last thing I need is her dad stomping up the stairs and throwing me out the window.

"I just have to finish this one inventory problem." She puts on a pair of glasses and sits at the laptop on her small desk.

I lie on her bed with my hands behind my head, completely relaxed. This friends-with-benefits thing is going well so far. "Bring those glasses to my house so we can play sexy librarian later."

She spins in her chair and waggles her eyebrows with them on.

"Or how about you just strip naked right now and I'll admire your body while you work?"

"You're incorrigible." She throws a pen my way. I watch her and she must see me in the reflection of her computer because she says, "Take a picture, it will last longer."

"I'd fucking love to photograph you. The question is would you let me?"

"I'm not sure I want pictures like that around. Plus, I don't own any lingerie."

"You don't need lingerie. The best photos I've taken only require sheets." I slide up to the edge of the bed and grab the back of her chair, pulling her toward me. "Come on. God, I'd love to see you through my lens."

"Seth, I'm not like that. I'm not comfortable."

She's crazy—half the time she's the one stripping her clothes off these days. She's even ridden my face and buried my face in her pussy. How is she self-conscious?

"You are with me. I promise it would just be for us."

"Us?"

I nod. "Well, photographer gets some rights." I grin.

"Uh-huh. I'll think about it, okay?"

I kiss her once before pushing her back to her desk. "Okay, but know it would just be me and you, and if you really don't want me to have any copies, I'd honor your wishes."

She nods and doesn't respond.

The last week has been pretty fucking fantastic. I think maybe I get the whole relationship thing now. Especially when it's Evan. I've dated women before, but it always came with a list of shit to do. Like going to chick flicks, eating at whatever restaurant they wanted to, picnics by the lake. Her telling me I wasn't romantic enough and me only wanting the sex and nothing else.

Which reminds me. "Frankie asked me to have you message her about that Thai restaurant we went to last night."

"Oh, okay. Did you tell her you hated it?" She laughs.

True, it was her choice... my mind pauses. Last night, we went to the new Thai place because Evan wanted it. Then we went to the movies—again, her choice—and she was just saying we should go on a bike ride along the lake. Motherfucker, I'm in a relationship. Except I haven't felt one ounce of unhappiness or dread while we've been doing all the stuff she likes.

I watch her work for another few minutes. "We should probably get going soon."

"Just one more minute. I swear I'm not sure how my parents would figure this out without me putting it all in Excel for them." Her fingers move across the keyboard and she clicks her mouse.

I contemplate how it is that I've found myself in a relationship. True, officially it's fake, but with the way I've been enjoying myself... no... I can't be falling for her. It's just our friendship being rekindled. And since we're adults, we can mix in a few sexual favors here and there. Yeah, that's definitely it.

"You good?" Evan's standing and looking at me. She folds her glasses and puts them in her purse as though she's up for playing sexy librarian later. "You're white as a ghost."

I look at her standing at the end of the bed, waiting. God, she's beautiful. "Yeah, I'm good. Let's get going so we can leave my parents' early and play a little. My books are overdue." I grab her coat and hold it out for her.

On the way down the stairs of her apartment, I spot both her parents' cars in the driveway. Eli is throwing his football in the air. I move over and steal it from him and tell him to run out for a catch.

Evan sits in the chair on the porch. Although it's grown colder, us northerners tend to make the most of the outdoors as long as we can until we're stuck inside all winter long.

Eli misses the ball and he smacks the ground. "I always miss it."

"It's okay, Eli," Evan says.

I glance back at her then at my watch. We have five or so minutes to spare. If we're late, it'll be okay.

I jog across the yard over to where Eli stands and have him hold his hands in front of him. "Now, touch your thumbs and your pointer fingers." I show him with my hands what I mean. "Spread the rest of your fingers wider. That's right. Now hold up your hands so that your thumbs and pointer fingers make a triangle."

He does it, but I correct his positioning a little to make sure it's right.

"Now I'm going to throw it. As soon as the tip of the football lands in that triangle, close your hands together."

Eli smiles and I place the football in his hands for him to close them over the leather and get a feel for what I mean.

"Yeah, just like that. You ready?"

Eli nods and I take about five steps away. I toss it lightly, but Eli misses it.

"Want to try again?" I ask.

"Yeah. I almost got it that time."

I throw from the same spot and it hits in his hands this time, but he doesn't close them fast enough. "Great. Now try to close your hands faster next time."

"Seth, honestly, we gotta get to your parents'," Evan says.

I hold up my finger to her. "Just a minute. Ready, Eli?"

He nods and I throw the ball again. This time it's right on the money and he catches it. Astonishment registers on his face and he smiles and yells, jumping up and down.

"Okay. Now I'm going to step back a little more, okay?" I walk backward a few feet. "Ready?"

He stays in place and holds up his hands. My aim is improving after a few throws now. It's been a while since I've thrown a ball—except for Thanksgiving morning, and even then Trevor always claims quarterback. We were both quarterbacks in high school, but age over beauty and all that.

"Seth?" Evan says, but I shake my head.

"Again, Eli?"

He nods and smiles, holding up his hands. I throw it and he misses it again.

"My bad, horrible throw." I pose with the ball in a throwing motion and Eli gets into position again.

This time, Eli catches it.

"Perfect. Perfect. Want to jog a little to the right and catch it on the run?"

"Um… are you sure?" Evan asks, fiddling with her phone.

"No belief in us," I say and shake my head at her.

She smiles and tucks her phone inside her purse and walks over to me, where she whispers in my ear, "You complete this pass to Eli, and I'll be the bad schoolgirl who needs to do some extra credit."

And now my dick is hard. "Deal."

"Now go slow, Eli. No need to run fast," Evan says.

He starts walking almost. Once I get his pace, I throw the ball and squint until it lands between his hands. He catches it and tucks it into his side. Obviously someone has taught him that. My money's on Mr. Erickson.

Eli screams and runs toward me, jumping into my arms. I'm not prepared, and I fall to the ground, laughing and cheering with him. He jumps to his feet, cheering and raising his arm in the air. I sit on the ground and wrap my arms around my bent knees. His happiness is contagious.

My gaze falls to Evan and her eyes aren't locked on Eli—they're on me. She mouths thank you, and I shake my head. There's no need to thank me. I loved helping him. Then she offers me a hand to get up, but I pull her down to me and place my hands on either side of her face and kiss her.

Eli jumps on us and we all laugh, rolling around on the hard ground. After I grunt from the weight of both Evan and Eli on me, we all stand. Evan's still looking at me as though I just bought her ten puppies, but it's the couple in the window who grabs my attention.

Mr. Erickson scowls while Mrs. Erickson beams.

At least I've won over one of them. Now I just need to work on the last one. With all the marketing for this Food Channel thing starting next week, Evan and I have our work cut out for ourselves because we never did take our businesses out of the show.

A car's squealing tires draws my vision to the driveway.

Evan slides her arm through mine. "Prepare yourself."

Elsie comes out of a small Volkswagen and slams the door. She stomps toward us, her eyes narrowed.

Eli cuts her off. "Seth taught me how to catch a football. Watch, Elsie." He jumps in front of her face, throwing me the football.

I fumble it and Evan steps away from me.

"You ready?" I ask Eli, and he catches again on the run.

"See, Elsie? I've been trying to get better and now I can catch. I can't wait to play with Henry at school."

"That's great, Eli." She turns to me. "So you're Seth, huh? My soon-to-be new brother-in-law?"

I hold out my hand and Evan steps up next to me. "Be nice, Elsie."

"I'm being nice. But just so you both know." She looks at the window where her parents are still watching. "You two are the ones being played."

"What?" Evan asks.

"Elsie!" Mr. Erickson calls to his daughter.

She moves to walk away but Evan pulls her back. We both lean forward.

"What are you talking about?" Evan asks.

"Meet me at the shop tomorrow around ten and I'll explain everything."

Evan and I exchange a look as Elise stalks into the house.

I high five Eli one more time before we leave. "Next lesson, you're throwing."

His eyes light up.

I link my hand with Evan's, and we walk down the driveway to my car. I can tell we're each preoccupied, trying to figure out what Elsie was talking about.

What the hell are our parents up to now?

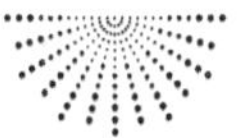

Evan

The Andrews' house is the same except their kitchen has been remodeled since the last time I was here. It no longer has beige appliances and red counter-tops. But pictures of Trevor and Seth still line every inch of wall space. She's got them at Halloween, Thanksgiving, Easter, and Christmas. I can't help but notice that Trevor has more pictures up than Seth.

"Mom? Dad?" Seth calls, leading me from the back of the house to the front. "We're here."

"Down here," his mom calls from the basement.

We walk down the basement stairs. I haven't seen Mr. Andrews since that day a few weeks ago when he and my dad tried to confront us, and we flipped the script on them. But when we reach the bottom of the stairs, we find Mrs. Andrews standing alone by the door of the laundry room. I hear Mr. Andrews grumbling through the doorway beside the stairs. Apparently, they've finished off their basement since I was here last as well.

"Hey, you two." Mrs. Andrews hugs Seth, then her arms wrap around me. "I was just talking with your mom about the engagement party and she said you two were on your way over."

"Sorry we're late," I say and give Seth the stink-eye.

"I was playing football with Eli," he says.

"That's okay. We're just trying to figure out something on the computer." She smiles, but there's a hitch in her voice that suggests it's not going well. She motions to Seth. "Maybe you could go over and help your dad?"

He walks into the next room and I struggle to come up with small talk.

"The space looks nice," I say.

"Yeah, the boys did it with Chris when they were teenagers. They spent every waking moment down here. Then Trevor moved down here permanently when Seth went to college. Which is why the computer is down here. Trevor used to handle all the books for us."

"Oh, well, it's a nice space for him. I'm above my parents' garage and we're getting to the time of year when I'll have to have ten blankets on top of me to sleep." I laugh uncomfortably. I'm apprehensive to talk about Trevor. What do I say?

She moves to a drawer, opens it, takes out everything, and throws it into a garbage bag.

"Dad, I have no idea," Seth's voice booms through the basement. "I could ask Evan. She does it for their place."

"Absolutely not!" Mr. Andrews yells. "She can't see our numbers."

Mrs. Andrews pats my arm and offers me a small smile before heading to another area of the room, opening more drawers and cabinets. "Trevor is coming home from rehab."

She has a stack of junk and I see the spine of a porn magazine. "I want all temptation out. You know?"

I nod like I understand, but I don't. Seth hasn't mentioned anything to me about Trevor returning. and although it's none of my business, I know Trevor works for Andrews Bagel Company. Maybe his parents fired him, but I doubt it.

"This is what they charge per item, this is what I sell at, and I sold this many," Seth says.

"And?" his dad snips.

"And what? Trevor told me he had this down and all I had to do was input the numbers, but that's not the case. It's a mess. Then again, why should I be surprised? He was probably snorting lines of coke while doing our books."

I wish they'd allow me to help, but I understand. My father would never let Seth see our books. In fact, if he knew I was in my apartment with Seth and the file was open, he'd probably strip the responsibility from me.

"Want to help me in the kitchen?" Mrs. Andrews asks. "I can finish this later."

"Sure."

I pull out my cell phone and find Mack Daddy. I really need to change his name in my phone. I text Seth the instructions to make a new formula for what I think his dad was talking about. He responds with a smiley face.

Upstairs, I help his mom with the salad. We talk about boring things like the weather and our trip to Maine last week. I leave out the part about her son rocking my world.

The men come upstairs and Mr. Andrews claps Seth on the back. "Seth figured it out. You should handle the books now," he says to him as though he's bestowed a great gift upon his son.

"I don't have time for that." Seth sits next to me and puts his arm around the back of my chair, his fingers playing with the ends of my hair. "Thank you," he whispers. The tension wracking his body could be felt in Russia right now. "I'm a photographer, Dad. I have a job."

"A photographer who takes pictures of naked women," Mr. Andrews says.

I place my hand on Seth's thigh to try to relax him.

"I don't expect you to understand," Seth grumbles.

"Can we just have dinner and talk about the engagement party? I have our list for you guys." Mrs. Andrews wipes her hands on her apron and digs into a drawer, pulling out a piece of paper that she hands to me.

"We really don't need a big party," I say, starting the same fight I have with my parents.

"Nonsense, you two are so happy, we should celebrate it." Mr. Andrews' fake enthusiasm screams that he knows this is a farce.

But how? We've been acting like a real couple for weeks. The more he and my dad call us out, the more I wish our relationship was real just to rub it in their faces.

"Very happy, ecstatic." Seth adds a couple more coals to the already raging fire. "But you and Mr. Erickson are fools for not doing the show."

Why is he bringing that up right now? Can't we at least do it *after* dinner?

"Not now, Seth," Mrs. Andrews says, turning away from mashing the potatoes.

"If you think for one second I'm going to team up with an egotistical…" Mr. Andrews glances at me and stops himself, for which I'm thankful. It's my dad he's talking about.

"It's national television. Your bagels on national television. Do you know what that could do for Andrews Bagel Company?" Seth sits up.

I tighten my hand on his thigh to calm him down.

"Andrews Bagel is fine. Trevor is coming back in two weeks and we'll pick up where we left off. And since you don't want anything to do with our business, you'll be free and clear. I already talked to the lawyer today about taking your name off the ownership papers once Trevor returns."

Seth sighs and sinks down in his chair. I don't think he knew his brother was returning. "You're being so stubborn about this. Trevor doesn't want to run the shop any more than I do."

Mr. Andrews only stays quiet for a minute before his irritation gets the best of him. "Not next to that man. Not so he can think that the recognition is only because of his cream cheese. When we owned The Bagel and Schmear Shop, he'd always say a bagel is plain and boring without cream cheese."

"Just use him for this opportunity," Seth says, exhaustion lacing his tone.

"And don't speak for Trevor. I talked to him last night and he said he's good to come back."

Seth inhales a deep breath and exhales slowly. "Fine. Then do the show for Trevor. To give him and your company the best shot it can have."

"Just stop. The answer is *no!*" Mr. Andrews' voice holds deep authority and it silences the room.

"This is ridiculous. Here I thought you were a rational man." Seth's chair scrapes across the linoleum and he holds out his hand for me. "We're leaving."

"No!" Mrs. Andrews whips around and shakes her head, her eyes pleading with me.

But I can't make this situation better. My being here is probably making it worse.

"Since this family seems to survive without me, we're going to head out. And you better get used to Mr. Erickson because you're going to be related soon." Seth drags me out the door and I say a fleeting goodbye to both of them.

Although I want to remind Seth that even though our engagement feels real, it's not, and Mr. Andrews won't have to deal with my dad soon, it's not the right time. Especially since we're in Seth's car and I have no idea where we're headed, but it's out of Cliffton Heights.

* * *

WE END up in historic Hudson Valley for the Jack-O'-Lantern Blaze. I haven't been here since high school. Seth parks, and although no one is here to play witness to our charade, he takes my hand. I don't object because I'm growing used to holding his hand. It comforts me in ways it shouldn't.

He's yet to say anything. I assumed that after fifteen minutes of silence he'd make a funny joke and we'd end up at his place, having sex. Never did I think we'd end up at a place full of carved out pumpkins artfully designed for us to walk through.

"I want you to know that I never did hate you. I wanted to… I just couldn't." His voice is low as we walk a path surrounded by thousands of jack-o'-lanterns.

I give his hand a squeeze. "I know. I was the same for a long while. But I think I changed you in my head over the years. Convinced myself you were a horrible person."

He chuckles. "Can I ask you a question?"

"Sure." I think it's rare for anyone to see Seth as he is right now. So low-key, emotional, and introspective. Something is bothering him and I'm sure it has to do with his family.

"Why did you switch lab partners sophomore year?"

I stop us for a moment and turn to face him. "What?"

"Science class. We were put together as lab partners and you asked to switch."

How does he remember that? I barely do. We start walking again.

"Because I couldn't work next to you."

He stops us—again—and tugs me away from the strangers so we're tucked in by a tree. "Why couldn't you work next to me?"

I'm not sure what answer he's expecting. We were supposed to hate one another. "How do you want me to answer that?"

He shakes his head. "Truthfully." His hands slide into my palms.

"I… I knew we might become friends again and I already…"

"Say it, Evan," he says.

"No." I shake my head. "I have no idea what you think I should say."

"Come on," he pleads. "Tell me I'm not alone."

"Does this have something to do with your parents and the fight just now?"

"Yes. Because I meant what I said to my dad. And I want to know if you changed lab partners because you couldn't handle being next to me because of hatred or something else."

"Something else?" My forehead wrinkles.

He blows out a breath, turning around and walking back toward the car. I follow him as he weaves through the throngs of families enjoying the show.

I grab his arm right before we reach his car. "What do you want me to say?"

He turns around so fast, I step back and almost fall to my ass. "I just want you to be honest with me."

I dip my head back and look at the sky, the stars sparkling. Fine. Let's do this.

I right my head and lock gazes with him. "I changed lab partners because I liked you. I was supposed to hate you, but I was still drawn to you like when we were kids, only it was different. We were older and I was drawn to you in a different way. And if I had to sit next to you, work alongside you, I would've crumbled, and my family was already in distress. Not to mention it's not like you felt the same—"

I'm cut off as Seth's lips land on mine in a claiming kiss. Our tongues slide together, and he spins us around so I'm pressed to his car.

"I had this whole plan back then. To ask you out. And bring you here. And then you switched partners and a younger, more immature version of me wrote you off. But I liked you so damn much."

I gasp, but he presses his body to mine, and I find that I can't get close enough to him.

"Come home with me," he whispers.

I nod, and he opens the door for me to slide into his car. On the way home, Seth is back to being handsy and flirty and we don't talk about the fact we had crushes on each other in high school. I knew feelings were developing and our relationship was shifting, but the last thing Seth is, is easy to read.

CHAPTER TWENTY-FIVE

Seth

"Don't wake up." Evan kisses me then rolls toward the edge of the bed. "I gotta go to work."

I pull her arm and yank her down, rolling so I'm over her. "I'm not letting you go." I kiss her long and slow as though she's got the time for me to really cherish her body.

"I wish I could stay, but The Bagel Place calls." She wiggles out of my hold.

I stretch out on the bed. She picks up her bag on the floor and I sit up, squinting at the clock to see that it's three in the morning. "I was thinking… you need to start figuring out what you wanna do after the show premieres and you gain your freedom."

Sadness dims the sparkle in her eyes. "I'm not even sure there will be a show. Our dads—"

"Hey." I rise out of bed and place my hand along her

cheek. "They'll get there. I promise. We'll talk to our moms. How about that?"

"Oh, that reminds me. We have to meet with my sister today."

I nod. "I'll be there."

Actually, after the fight with my dad and me turning into an emotional basket case last night where I demanded that Evan tell me she liked me in high school, I forgot about Elsie's demand we see her today. What is happening to me?

"From the sounds of last night, you're already free, what with your brother coming back." She pauses. "It's okay if you want to drop this whole thing, you know."

Her words hit me like a fist in the chest, but I don't want to examine why too closely. "You think just because Trevor is returning that I'd leave you high and dry? Not happening."

She smiles and leans forward, kissing me briefly. She doesn't answer what I said though. I'm going to have to prove to her that I'm not leaving her. At least until the show airs.

"I'll see you later," I say and open my bedroom door to walk her out.

Knox is just coming in wearing his street clothes, but his duffle bag says he worked last night and the bags under his eyes say it was a long shift. "Fuck, Andrews, I'm all for nudity but I do not need to see your dick this early in the morning. Especially after the shift I just had." He turns away. "Morning, Evan."

I look down, and sure as shit, I'm naked. But whatever, because I've seen Knox's ass more times than I care to. He loves public sex, or Leilani did maybe. I'm not sure, but those two were naked all the time.

"Go back to bed," Evan says to me.

"At least put some pants on," Knox says, dropping his

duffle by his door and heading to the kitchen, where he buries his head in the fridge.

I say goodbye to Evan and head back into my room to throw on a pair of pants. I could use some food to get my stamina back.

Knox clicks on the television and sits in the recliner, eating the leftover pizza from Pizza Pies Evan and I picked up last night. "So sleepovers, huh? That's all part of the arrangement?"

I knew Knox wouldn't let it go. Usually he barely sees Evan because he's working, and Evan leaves so early.

"We have an agreement." I shrug and take a seat on the couch.

He nods, but his expression says I've lost the battle already and should just surrender. Part of me feels like he's right, especially after my embarrassing episode last night. All I do is think of Evan all day long, and I know that's bad.

Very, very bad.

"Stop with the looks," I tell him.

"What looks? I mean, you were done for when you first saw her with Brock Floyd."

"What are you talking about?" My eyes narrow.

Knox chomps down on another piece of pizza. He lowers the volume on the television, swivels his recliner my way, and sets his gaze on me. "Listen. I'm not Jax. I understand love and I recognize when I see it. And I see it with both of you. But I also don't believe in all that unicorns, rainbows, and sparkles shit either since Leilani, so the last thing I'm gonna tell you to do is pursue her. Although I'm over Leilani, it fucking hurts thinking of her out there somewhere with God knows who after I felt like we shared something."

Maybe I should point out that he's not really free of Leilani yet. Not by a long shot.

"So love sucks and that's my advice, but stop being blind. Stop trying to deflect the seriousness of the situation you and Evan have put yourselves in. Because it might've started as a business proposition, a way to get both of you out of your families' bagel businesses, but it's transformed into something different and neither of you are just going to walk away after the show ends. Not without lasting effects. And if you're smart, you'd recognize that now because you're going to have a fight on your hands. You two against your fathers." He swivels back around and ups the volume on the television, grabbing another cold slice of pizza.

I sulk, leaning back into the couch and pondering everything he said. Fuck, he's right.

"I hate you," I murmur, heading back to bed and hoping this was a nightmare I'll forget when I rewake at a decent hour.

* * *

At ten o'clock, I walk into The Bagel Place, and Elsie and Evan are talking at the counter. Evan glances up and her smile at the sight of me is quick and wide. Tell me how I can ignore that? I can't, but Knox's words ring back at me. Love sucks and only brings heartbreak.

"What's up, double Es?" I ask and Evan hands me an empty cup.

"Ew, gross." Elsie walks into the back.

"Hey." I lean over the counter with puckered lips. Evan places her hand over my face and pushes me back. "What was that for?" I pick up the cup she gave me and head over to the machine to fill it with pop.

"I don't know. I just felt like giving you a hard time." She laughs.

I leave my pop by the machine. Since the place is empty, I

round the corner, wrap my arms around her waist, and lay her out on the counter, falling on her and kissing the hell out of her, leaving her breathless.

"Come on. I have a hangover and that's not helping." Elsie returns with a bagel and cream cheese.

Evan slides her now-limp body off the counter and smiles at me. Best look in the world.

"Come on, Els, spit it out. What did you have to tell us?" I ask.

"It's Elsie," she says.

"Not to me. Not anymore." I put a lid on my cup and a straw, then sip my pop.

She looks at Evan like "is this guy for real?" My girl shrugs because she knows me well. Elsie lets it go and glances out the window. Evan and I both follow her gaze. Holy shit, here comes my mom and Jenny Erickson, walking along the sidewalk together.

"I just had to get you guys here. Sorry, not sorry. If it makes you feel any better, I have to handle the customers while they talk to you." She points at both of us. "But if Mr. Tettlebaum comes in, I'm not helping him. He's a mean old fart." She stomps off into the back.

Talk about three siblings with different personalities.

Evan walks over to my side and my arm wraps around her waist, my fingers searching for the bare strip of skin above her pants to glide my fingers across. Evan leans in closer and I enjoy that we've grown comfortable with public affection.

"Any idea what the hell is going on?" I ask.

"None."

We wait for them to open the door.

"Mom?" we say at the same time.

"Jinx," I say, but Evan shakes her head. "That was your

chance to earn another sexual favor. You could've shut me up until I ate you out," I say in a low voice.

She whispers, "I think you'll go down on me anyway."

"Am I that transparent?"

Our moms wave us over to the first booth as though we're in a crowded restaurant and they don't want to disturb anyone. We sit across from them, and my hand lands on Evan's thigh. My fingers push into the space where her legs are crossed, and she sits comfortably while I imagine what I could do if she was wearing a dress.

"What's up, you two?" Evan asks.

"We wanted to let you know we're willing to help you get your fathers on board. We'll get them to agree to the collaborating Food Channel show," Mrs. Erickson says.

A wave of relief washes through me, but it's clear they have more to say.

"And?" I ask.

"Well, we want you to do something for us then," my mom says, making eye contact with us both.

Shit. This cannot be good.

"What do you want?" Evan asks, her voice laced with skepticism.

"We want you to promise us that you won't run away from this wedding."

Evan's body sinks back into the booth and I know it's because of guilt. I need to stop this conversation before she outs us. Everything is going perfectly right now. Our moms will get the show to go ahead. We'll each have our freedom. It's exactly what we wanted. I feel the guilt every time I look at my mom and see her hopeful expression, but we need to stay the course.

"Why would we run?" I ask.

My mom glances at Mrs. Erickson, and she nods. "Once your fathers find out the love between you is real, it's going to be horrible. For all of us. And you two." She says two but her eyes are on me. I'm the runner, after all. I just did it last night. "They still think you guys are faking, and when they realize that isn't the case, they won't want to deal with it. And your first inkling might be to run away because it will be hard. We'll help you if you promise not to run away when the big blowup comes."

"I don't understand," Evan says. "How come you two can be fine and they just continue to hate one another?"

My mom smiles and grabs Mrs. Erickson's hand. "Your mom and I never stopped being friends."

"What?" I ask, my voice low.

"We remained friends behind your fathers' backs," Mrs. Erickson says.

"But… you forbade me."

Evan's accusatory tone strips Mrs. Erickson's smile. "Because we didn't want to rock the boat. We're happy for you two, but you two falling in love has put a crimp in our friendship. Your dads are on high alert. We used to be able to sneak out and meet. That's becoming impossible."

"When?" I ask.

"Book club."

"Book club?" Evan says.

"It's not actually a book club. It's just the two of us meeting in Peekskill." Mrs. Erickson smiles.

"Except we did read that *Fifty Shades* book, what with all the hype around it," my mom says, though I wish she hadn't.

I shake my head. This is crazy. They've hidden their friendship for twenty years?

"Now is it a deal?" my mom asks and puts out her hand across the table.

Evan looks at me and opens her mouth to respond, but I beat her to the punch. "Deal."

I shake my mom's hand. Evan frowns and doesn't say

anything except that she has to go prepare the cream cheese for tomorrow.

Our moms squeal, oblivious to Evan's mood. Why isn't she happy about this? Our plan is coming together and now we have help. Isn't this what we wanted?

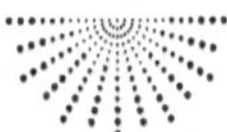

CHAPTER TWENTY-SIX

Evan

I'm thinking we made a complete mistake starting this train wreck of a plan. Every day a new revelation. Every day a new problem to fix. A new lie to tell. Now our moms tell us that they've kept their friendship a secret all these years? What the hell?

"Can you believe it?" Elsie asks when I reach the back. "Mom told me the other night, but only because I caught the two of them laughing over coffee at a diner in Peekskill."

Elsie doesn't care because it doesn't affect her life, but it does affect mine. I had to end my friendship with Seth because I respected my parents.

"Els, give us a minute," Seth says, joining us in the back.

"Um. No. This isn't your bagel shop." She shoos him away like a gnat. "Go to your own shop."

"Sure thing, and I'll take Evan with me." Seth smiles wide, taunting her.

She blows out a big breath. "You're going to be an infuriating brother-in-law, you know."

Seth puts his hands on either side of me on the butcher block counter in the kitchen, caging me in. "Don't worry, I'm really lovable," he says to Elsie's retreating back. "Hey, you." He dips his head to look into my eyes. "You good?"

I shrug. "I don't think I can do it. I feel spiteful now. I wanted to scream that they don't know anything because we're not real."

Dejection crosses his features for a moment. "That attitude's not going to get us to the end game."

That's right. It's a game. It's all a game. I nod. "But how could they keep their friendship going and—"

He steps closer and presses his finger to my lips. "I know. I know."

Does he? Is he just as mad that we didn't have to wait this long to explore our connection? That maybe we could've been one of those childhood-friends-to-lovers couples? Maybe he would've convinced me to go to college and not stay here. Maybe he would've stayed behind. Who knows what we could have been together?

His phone rings, but he doesn't answer it. "They're helping us, so let's play it cool for now. We'll figure everything else out later."

I have to wonder if "everything else" includes whatever is happening between us.

His large hand cradles my neck and his thumb runs across my collarbone. "I'm going to kiss you now."

"Thanks for the warning," I say.

Despite my mood, a laugh bubbles up—and he swallows it down with a kiss that I'm afraid one day I'll have to live without. Man, Seth Andrews gives the best kisses. Kisses that change your whole perspective on something.

"Now have a great day and meet me at the studio after

work. It's about time we do that shoot, don't you think? Plus, I had a cancelation and gave Madison the night off. So it'll be just me and you." He pecks me on the lips.

"And a bed and a camera," I deadpan.

He chuckles, stepping away from me. "And a bed and a camera. I promise I don't bite."

He winks and leaves out the back door before I can pull him back for another soul-crushing kiss.

* * *

I SET up the studio before Evan arrives. With everything going on, we both need a release, something fun. She's ready to spill our secret, and I'm worried that these feelings are setting me up for heartbreak.

Ever since she was here a few weeks ago, I've wondered what it would be like to shoot her. But I want her *au naturel*. Not with layers of makeup or outfits she doesn't usually wear. I want the real Evan Erickson lying in this bed, her naked body surrounded by silk.

"Seth?" she calls to me, inching the door open.

"I'm here." I step back from adjusting the lighting.

She's already biting her lip, and her hands are crossed in front of her stomach. She's worried and scared and I want to free her from self-consciousness.

"Come here." I hold out my hand and she eats up the distance between us.

"I stopped at the store and bought a few things. I know you said not to, but…" She's still in her jeans and T-shirt from the shop.

Once I get her in my arms, I kiss her neck and collarbone, unable to ever have enough of her. It's another troublesome sign, but I push it from my mind.

"Is this your way of telling me you want to wear lingerie for me outside of the studio?"

She giggles. "Maybe."

"I hope so. But first I want you in your panties and bra, if that's okay."

She groans. "I'm not sure about this."

"Just go behind the screen and undress. It's just me and you." I point at the room divider and walk out to the lobby.

I lock the front door and make sure the red light is on just in case. When I return and grab my first camera and lens, she tiptoes to the bed and crawls under the sheets.

"Oh, shy kitten," I say. "If I pet your pussy, maybe you'll open up for me."

She pulls the sheet down and her mouth hangs open. "Please tell me you do not say that to all your clients."

I wink. "Just my favorites."

She shakes her head. She's grown to understand when I'm joking and I fucking love that about her.

"Just be yourself," I say, and I snap a picture of her peeking out from the sheet.

"I can't." She throws out her arms and pounds her hands on the sheet. I snap a picture. "This is not comfortable for me."

"Think about last night when I stripped your T-shirt off and grabbed your tits."

A flush hits her cheeks and spreads down her body.

"Remember my fingers over your silk panties, coated with your wetness. The way I slid them to the side and teased you with my finger. Damn, you felt so fucking good."

My dick makes his presence known because he remembers and would love to repeat that act with him as the star, not my fingers.

I climb the ladder. One of her legs slides out of the sheet now, tan and toned and gorgeous against the white silk. I snap a picture. She's growing used to the sound of the camera because that time she didn't flinch.

"Evan, baby," I say in a soft voice, using a pet name for the first time. She looks my way and I snap the picture before she can cover her face or duck under the covers. "Pull the sheet just under your left breast."

She sighs but she does it, and I snap a picture of the black see-through bra with her hard nipple underneath.

"There you go. Can I get you to rise up on your knees?"

"Really?" she asks with a pained voice.

If I wasn't enjoying myself this much, I'd probably say we could stop. But I know she needs this. To get out of her head, out of everything happening around her and just enjoy this.

I nod, snapping one picture after another, climbing down the ladder and rounding the back of the bed to get her from behind. "So gorgeous. You're so gorgeous." Coming around the front, I continue to take pictures. "One strap, let it fall."

She pushes it off and my mouth waters at her delectable skin.

"Same with the other side." This time, the camera is rewarded with the best shy sexy kitten look I've ever seen. I swallow hard, ignoring the feel of my cock pressing against my zipper. "Unclasp your bra."

She sighs, a long breath leaving her pink lips, but reaches around to do as I instructed. I'm able to capture the moment just as the fabric falls off her breasts and her nipples are exposed.

"You're doing great. Can you grab the bar?"

There's a bar overhead and she wraps her hands around it.

"Arch your back."

She does.

"Jut your ass out."

She does, and damn, I'm never going to make it through this. I tear off my shirt and she giggles.

"Sorry, you're making me crazy right now," I say.

Another giggle. "How do you take pictures of women all day then?"

"They aren't you. I've never had this reaction while photographing anyone." It's like I'm thirteen and staring at my first pair of tits in a magazine. "Fair warning—this will end with both of us having a happy ending."

"Promises, promises," she says, but she lets go of the bar and slowly lowers herself back to the bed. "Come now."

I shake my head. "This might be the last time I get you in this position. Sit still. I'm going to change the backdrop."

She lies on the bed and fiddles with the sheet, her tits on display. Pride, or something like it, fills my chest that she feels comfortable like that in front of me.

"Nick Klein called today," she says.

"Oh really? What did he want? Something with the show?" I look through the backdrops to find the one I want.

She nods. "He said he's so happy that we're doing this, and he can't wait to work with us."

She says us, but I wonder how much of it is really about us and not just her. Nick Klein definitely wants her. I'd be lying if I said I wasn't jealous. At the moment, I'm only in a *fake* relationship with benefits. There are no strings between us, and whatever loose strings there are will be cut off after the show airs. I can't even think about that right now.

"That's good. Did he say what's next?"

"I guess they market it for the next month. Get the hype going, and he'll be in town the week before. He mentioned investors coming to the show. That I—we should be prepared to talk to companies that might want to buy our recipes and produce them on a larger scale."

"I didn't even think about anything like that." I change the backdrop to black. "I need you to ditch your panties."

She slides her black lacy panties down her legs and tosses them across the room but hides under the sheets right away. No argument. This is progress.

"Yeah, I didn't think of it either. I mean, what if someone wants to buy the recipe for your bagels or my family's cream cheese? That would amazing."

The shop talk helps as I shoot pictures of her in a black silk sheet and black backdrop with a low lighting I can enhance during editing. But eventually silence falls over us and my breathing labors from watching her shift and move along the silk. Her body parts sneak out and tease me. It's getting harder and harder to stay behind the camera.

Finally after I wipe the sweat from my forehead for the twentieth time, she gets up on her knees and crooks her finger at me. That's the last picture I snap before placing the camera down and jumping into bed with her.

She giggles as I kiss and fondle her while she makes quick work of my jeans. Before I can blink, my hard cock is poised at her entrance.

"Shit, we need a condom." I groan.

I shift, but she places her hands on my shoulders. "I have an IUD and I'm clean. I got tested two weeks ago."

"Me too. I go monthly with Knox and Jax."

She nods. "I trust you, and I want to feel all of you inside me."

The weight of her words hangs over us, but I refuse to let them pull me from the moment. "Your wish is my command."

I slip into her hot pussy and gasp from sheer pleasure. Holy shit. I've never been bare inside a woman before, and I wasn't prepared for the sensation that would hit every nerve ending.

"Are we going to move?" she asks with a smile.

I nod, but I close my eyes, trying to imagine my grandma's face. Shit. That's wrong.

"Seth?" she asks.

I nod again, more urgent, and concentrate on lenses and lighting and anything else in this room—anything except the fact that I'm bare inside Evan and can feel *everything*.

"Okay, I'm ready." I pull out slowly then thrust back in.

She moans. But this isn't going to be a marathon love-making session… I mean fucking. Because she feels too good. Everything about her is too much—her feel, her scent, the expression on her face.

At least I get her to come before I do, because no one wants to be even fake engaged to someone who can't. And the more we continue this farce, the more I realize that I really do care what Evan thinks of me.

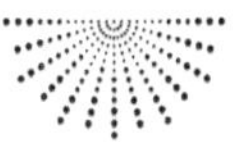

CHAPTER TWENTY-SEVEN

Seth

I stop by The Bagel Place since Evan didn't spend the night last night—okay, I'll admit it, I missed her. She's elbow deep in getting the morning orders out, so I grab a pair of plastic gloves and help. Her hair is braided down both sides of her head, but it's still tucked under a hairnet.

"You don't have to help," she says, shuffling racks of baked bagels into cardboard boxes.

"Yes, I do. We've been over this already."

"What did you do last night?" she asks a little absent-mindedly. I'm not even sure she's listening to me.

"Watched porn. I've got some new positions to try out."

She doesn't even flinch. Her mind is definitely some-where else.

"Earth to Evan!" I wave my hand in front of her face.

"What?" She tips her head back. "I'm sorry. I'm so distracted. Nick Klein called me again."

My jaw clenches. "Do I need to set the record straight with good ol' Nick that I'm the only man in your life?"

She smiles. "Only for another three weeks."

We're coming close to the end of our fake engagement and I'm scared shitless of what I'll feel like after it's all over. Will I be okay going back to my life the way it was? Because one night away from her and I'm waking my ass up at seven with the hope of finding her needing my help. It hurts that Evan seems a-okay with the fact that this thing between us will be over soon.

I'm beyond hopeless.

"What did he want?" My voice lacks any kindness. The man either wants in her pants or—I have no idea what else. But he's sniffing around like she's a freshly painted fire hydrant and he's gonna be the first dog to pee on her.

"He has a friend he wants me to meet."

"Oh," I say.

Her gaze meets mine. "I'm sure it's nothing."

"Why is he so invested in you? He hasn't called me."

She giggles like, "why would he?" and I want to say because I signed those papers too. I'm in the show as much as she is, and Andrews Bagel is a damn great product, just like Ericksons' cream cheese.

I stop my rambling mind for a moment. What the fuck? Where did that come from? Holy shit, it's like my father took over my brain for a second.

"He told me he felt pressured to be in his family business when he was younger too, so I think he pities me." She grabs the containers of cream cheese, pushing them into the indents in the packaging designed to hold them. "Nothing is going to come from it. I promise you that."

"So, there's a dinner tonight at my parents' for Trevor's return."

My brother is back, but I haven't seen him. My parents have kept him holed up in their basement like a prisoner. He'll eventually have to live in the world and learn how to function without using.

"Is there a question in there?" She smiles, taking handfuls of boxes to the counter.

"Come with me. Technically you're my fiancée, so you have to come. As long as Nick Klein hasn't already called dibs."

She scoffs and looks at me with disdain. "You can stop the jealousy act. We're not really engaged."

"So you keep reminding me."

It sure feels like we're in a relationship, but maybe that's just me. I touch her and kiss her every chance I get, whether we're alone or in front of people, but it's not like she's complaining. I mentally demand my hands and lips stay where they are when I tell her that I'll pick her up at five.

The fact that she doesn't try to kiss me goodbye annoys me, but she was busy.

When I'm back outside, my phone rings in my pocket and I slide it over without looking at the screen because I need any distraction I can get to get out of my head.

"Hello," I answer.

"Hi, is this Seth Andrews?" a woman asks.

"Yes."

"Great. My name is Ursula Dermak and I got your number from Blanca Mancini. You took the photos for their spread about New York City on their blog, correct?" she asks.

"I did."

"Well, I own a gallery in Manhattan, and I've been looking

for fresh artists. A friend follows the blog and showed me right away. I thought maybe you could come down and bring some of your work, check out the gallery. We're not the biggest or the best, but we do have a loyal client base. Maybe we can throw some ideas around about how we could benefit one another?"

Excitement lights a fire in my belly. "I'd love to."

We figure out what works for both of our schedules and arrange for me to bring some of my work to her gallery in two weeks. That will be the Monday after the engagement party—which is perfect, since I want to squeeze in a few more shoots and you never know what might happen with the weather. This might be the break that gets me out of the boudoir studio.

* * *

At five-thirty, I pull into my parents' driveway. Evan and I walk up the path and through the back door. Everyone uses our back door because everyone is family to us. Except Mr. Erickson, I suppose.

I grab Evan's hand. Ever since this morning when she reminded me twice that everything about us is fake, I've made sure I didn't show her any affection. And yes, I'm fully aware that I'm acting like a child who holds a finger a half an inch from his brother and says "I'm not touching him." Immature and annoying instead of just hashing it out with her. But the thought of pouring out everything that I'm feeling and her shitting all over it makes it easier to stay in our pretend bubble and leave it at that.

"Mom? Dad?" I call.

"We're already seated," my mom calls from the dining room.

When Evan and I walk in, they're halfway through dinner and there are no place settings for Evan and me.

"Didn't you get my text that dinner was earlier?" my mom says.

"No, I haven't checked my phone."

She stands and slides by us to the kitchen. "Hello, Evan." My mom runs her hand down her arm. "Let me fix you both a plate."

I step farther into the room. My brother stands to greet us, and I have to say, he does look healthier. His hair is cut, he's clean-shaven, and he's put on the weight he lost when he forgot there was anything else in this world but cocaine and whatever else.

"Hey, Seth." He rounds the table behind my dad and leans in for a hug. He's still got two inches on me, as if even God made sure I was the younger brother in every degree. "And Evan. Congratulations, I heard the news." Trevor moves from me to Evan.

"It's great to see you, Trev. You look great." She pats him on the back, and he returns to his spot at the table.

"We eat at four-thirty now because that helps Trevor," my mom says, buzzing past us with plates in hand.

"Yeah, the treatment place had us eat early and I kind of want to stay on that schedule until I get more comfortable being at home," my brother explains.

My mom sets down two plates and slides dishes around, making room for Evan and me.

"Thank you, Mrs. Andrews," Evan says.

My mom waves away her thanks. "You and the formalities."

Trevor cuts up his pork chop as we sit. "So tell me, how did all this transpire?" He points his fork from Evan to me and back to Evan. His smirk reminds me of Dad's.

"Oh, they've been hiding it," my dad says as though he still doesn't believe we're engaged.

"Really? For how long?" Trevor asks.

I shift in my seat, not wanting to lie. "A while. It's old news now." I shrug and cut my meat.

"Yes, we're having an engagement party. Trevor won't be attending, due to his sobriety and all," my mom says, glancing my brother's way.

"Understandable. Definitely." Evan nods a little too much. "We'd never dream of putting you in that position."

"For sure, no," I mumble over a green bean.

"I can't believe after all this time and all these years, you two are gonna get hitched. Seth, can you support her on your naked chick photos?" Trevor asks.

My dad chuckles. Evan chokes on her food but grabs her water and swallows it down.

"You okay?" I ask.

She nods, wiping her mouth with her napkin.

I don't even answer my brother's question.

"Stop teasing him, Trev." My mom covers his hand with hers and squeezes, not letting go for a while.

"I actually got a call today from a gallery," I say.

"Really?" Evan's head whips in my direction. "That's great. You didn't say anything on the way over."

I'd planned on telling her after dinner, but of course my brother makes me feel less than and I take the bait. But I nod at Evan because I'm not filling in my family on the specifics.

"I'm so proud of you." She kisses my cheek. It's the first affection she's initiated with me all day. I know I shouldn't be counting.

"Thanks."

"It is great, Seth," my mom says.

"So they'll hang the naked pictures on a wall for people to buy? Maybe you should snap a picture of me." Trevor grins.

Evan stiffens next to me.

"No one wants to buy a picture of a six-foot-four guy with a three-inch dick," I say and give him a serene smile.

"Seth!" my mom scolds.

My dad shoots me a dirty look.

"Oh, we both know I have the bigger dick in this house," Trevor goads.

"Boys. Evan is here," my mom chastises.

"Too bad you ended up with the wrong brother, Evan. You could be with the better brother right now."

I slide my chair back and my dad's chair flies out too, his hand on my chest. Evan grips my arm.

"We are not doing this!" my mom cries. "It's just one dinner."

"He started it," I say, pointing at Trevor's smug face.

"Your brother has been through enough these past months. Can you just sit and have a nice dinner?" my mom pleads.

"Whatever." I step back with my arms up, and my dad's hand lowers. "I'm going for a walk."

I stomp out the front door and down the stoop to the sidewalk. I'd rather leave, but my mom will call me until we make up. Maybe if I just cool off, I can go back in there and finish the dinner.

Evan opens the door, still sliding her arm into her coat, she jogs down to catch up to me. "Seth."

I shove my hands in my pockets and wait for her to catch up. All I want to do right now is leave Cliffton Heights.

"Come here." She rises on her tiptoes and wraps her arms around my neck, plastering her body to mine. "I'm so sorry, I had no idea you and Trevor didn't have a good relationship. Is he always like that?"

I wrap my arms around her and a calmness soaks in all my anger until I feel much better. "He's my brother. He'll always be my brother."

It's hard for an outsider to understand. I know why Trevor prods me on the naked women photography and wants to compare dick sizes in front of Evan. It's the same reason he used cocaine. His self-esteem, or lack of it. He's been like that since I went to college and decided to major in photography. He thought that if I was going to desert the family business, I should at least be a lawyer or a doctor. He resents me because he took over the family business.

"You wouldn't understand," I grumble.

"I understand he's an asshole."

I nod for us to walk, and she falls in line with me. "It's like you and Elsie. Can you tell me you don't resent her even a little? That she can go to college and get a degree and do what she wants with her life while you're stuck at The Bagel Place?"

She says nothing, so I know she gets it.

"Still, he shouldn't act like that," she says in a quiet voice.

I shrug. I would resent him too if the tables were turned. "He's been involved in the business for over a decade. As soon as he couldn't handle it and I had to step up a bit, I manipulated a scheme involving a fake engagement. What does that say about me?"

She slides her arm through mine and lays her head on my upper arm. "I'm sorry. And if it makes you feel any better, I know I got the right brother."

I look down and she's fluttering her eyelashes at me. "At least for three more weeks, right?"

She doesn't laugh. She stops fluttering her eyelashes and just looks at me. This is the perfect time to tell her I want more, that I want what we have to be real. Three weeks is going to fly by and I'm not ready to end what we started.

But instead I smile and turn us around so we're headed back to the house, ignoring the twisting in my gut that says I should tell her how I feel.

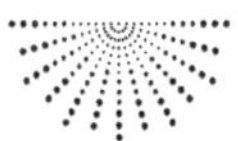

Evan

All I can think of is Seth's hands on me last night. The way his fingers glided over my skin sent shivers erupting along their path. The best thing about working here for so long is that most of my work is mindless and gives me a lot of time to think about being in Seth's bed. It took extra strength to slide away from the warmth of his body this morning.

I'm still annoyed with Trevor's behavior and the fact that Seth has to deal with his bullshit so as not to send Trevor over into using again. The entire family walks on pins and needles for Trevor. Then again, I've never known an addict either. Maybe when you love one, you'll do anything to try to keep them free of any triggers.

The door chime rings, and I wipe my hands, peeking out to the front. Nick Klein and another man in a suit walk up to the counter. I wash my hands and step out from the back.

"Evan," Nick says and rounds the counter, pulling me into a hug before he kisses my cheek.

Okay then.

"This is Cliff Daniels. He owns Daniels Foods."

I shake the hand of the man who's wearing a cowboy hat, slacks, and cowboy boots.

"So we need an everything bagel with plain cream cheese. Then if you could do a sampling of different cream cheese flavors with plain bagels, that'd be great." Nick smiles.

"Sure. Give me a minute."

I'm not in the back for more than a second before Nick joins me.

"Evan, this is huge. I'm sorry I didn't explain more, but Cliff likes to surprise people so that the items are authentic. He wanted to come by himself and be a secret shopper, but I convinced him to meet you and try your product in an official capacity."

"Why is he here?" I ask, obviously the last one on the train here.

He laughs. "To see if he wants to invest in your product. Maybe produce the cream cheese to sell to grocers. Could you imagine The Bagel Place cream cheese in grocery store fridges across America?" He puts his hands in the air and stretches them out as though it would be in lights on Broadway or something.

I have to admit the idea is exciting. "I didn't think that's what was happening today. I thought we had to wait for the show."

He shakes his head. "You'll still do the show, but if he likes what you have to offer, we need to get your parents in on this ASAP. This could free you of this place."

His smile says he's way more excited than me about the possibility.

"Okay, let me get the stuff together."

Nick puts his arm around my shoulders and tugs me into his chest. "I'm so damn excited. This is huge. I hope that is extra special." He points at the tub of cream cheese that I prepared this morning.

It was made while I was thinking about Seth, so it could be our worst batch ever since I was thinking more about his dick than the ratio of the ingredients.

"I'll be right out." I smile and hope Nick leaves because I'm a little freaked out right now.

I didn't know what to expect today because all Nick said was that he wanted me to meet someone. I wasn't sure if it was someone from the show, someone he was trying to set me up with, or what, but I never could have guessed that it would be this. I grab my freshest everything bagel, cut it in half, and slather on the cream cheese in an effort to make up for our bagels.

Once it's all done, I carry it on a tray to the front. "Here you go, Mr. Daniels."

"Please, call me Cliff." His cowboy hat sits on the bench next to him, showing off a head of salt-and-pepper hair.

"I'll be right out with the other items. Can I get you anything, Nick?"

"No, I'm good. Thank you, Evan."

I head back to prepare the tray of assorted cream cheeses. After being distracted by two more customers and a few pick-up orders—Nick stopped them to ask for glowing recommendations about us—I have everything ready.

"Here's the tray. I marked each flavor for you." I set it down in front of them.

Mr. Daniels, or Cowboy Cliff as I could refer to him, peers over the tray, picking up a piece of plain bagel and deciding where to dip. Not wanting to overstep, I return to the backroom to continue making the bagels for today.

Fifteen minutes later, Nick walks into the back. "We're

going to head out. He's super excited about this. He really wants to try Andrews Bagel Company as well, so we'll be in touch."

I smile and say my goodbyes even though I'm thinking that that's weird. Seth told me they hadn't reached out to him. Could he have been lying to me? He's good at lying. But then I remember his expression of betrayal when I told him about Nick calling me, so I shake my head of that thought.

Just like every other day, I make the bagels and dream of a life where I can stay in Seth's arms in the morning.

* * *

THAT SATURDAY, we're less than one week away from the engagement party and I haven't had to do much except buy a dress. Since Seth wanted to get more pictures of New York City and it's a beautiful day, I came with him to dress shop while my parents work at the store.

"Our parents are spending so much money on this party. Don't you feel bad?" I ask, gazing out the window of the train and seeing that we're almost in Manhattan.

"They wanted to do it, and since our dads already think we're faking our engagement, I say it's a lesson for them. Plus, they're using the Porterhouse and I know Linda is giving them a deal since we're having it on a Friday."

He has a point. And we're doing buffet and there's no dancing, but still...

"Do you want me to go shop and I'll call you when I'm done?" I ask.

"I thought I could join you in the fitting room," he says, his hand on my thigh.

Thankfully, things are back to normal with us. For a few days, Seth was acting really weird.

"Maybe you should be surprised when you see me."

"Or I could help you try on the dresses in case you need someone to zip you up," he says with a grin. "I should have the final say." He chuckles.

The train stops, and we leave the station hand in hand.

"How about one stop to get pictures, dress shopping, then some more pictures?"

"Sure." I've never seen Seth work at his actual passion, so I'm excited to see him in action.

We head to Teardrop Park, and as I sit on a rock, Seth's camera is faced up toward the buildings around us, never down. I watch him change lenses, fiddle with the shutter, and test areas, double-checking the picture then capturing another one. I can only imagine how wonderful they must be.

I can't believe our time is coming to an end and he's said nothing about continuing our relationship. I can't help but test the waters. "Do you think we should continue the relationship a little longer so that our parents don't question our motives?"

He sets his camera down and changes the lens. Glancing in my direction, he smirks. "Not ready to kick me to the curb yet, huh? I knew you'd have a hard time letting me go."

I lean back on my arms, letting the sun warm my face. The park is practically bare since the cold weather has arrived. A few kids bundled in big coats with hats and mittens on run around, but there aren't nearly as many people as there are during the warmer months.

"What can I say? I like to punish myself."

He takes a few pictures before he breaks the distance, leaning over me until his lips are almost touching mine. "Deal."

My heart feels buoyant. I'm happy that's out of the way since the thought of this ending was looming over me like a dark cloud before a thunderstorm. "Just like that, huh?

I'm thinking maybe *you* don't want to kick *me* to the curb yet."

"What can I say? You've got a great set of—" He motions to my breasts since there are kids around, and I pick up a small pebble and throw it at him. He laughs. "It's a compliment."

I've figured out when Seth is joking, even though more times than not, it's always a joke coming out of his mouth. But at first, I would've taken that comment to mean he only wants me around for sex. And even if he might think that's what he means, I know he doesn't. It's in his constant glances to gauge my reaction after he says something that's supposed to come off as casual. He checks my facial expressions because he wants to know what I'm thinking.

"I know." I turn my head back toward the sky. "Did you make up with Trevor?"

"Not really. Mom made him apologize and I apologized back. It's the same as always. Nothing new."

"That sucks. I'm sorry."

"Stop apologizing for my relationship with my brother. It's not your fault." He sits on the rock with me, cracking his neck. He knocks his knee to mine. "Thanks for coming with me."

"You're welcome." I knock my knee to his. "I enjoy seeing you so focused. It's kind of hot."

"Hot like at the studio a few weeks ago?" His hand slides up my thigh.

I place my hand over his. "Hot like we're in public though I wish we weren't. Speaking of, I haven't seen any of those photos yet." I raise my eyebrows.

He chuckles. "They're in good hands. Promise. I just haven't had a ton of time to edit all of them."

"Edit? As in correcting?"

He lays his forehead to mine. "As in touch-ups. Lighting

and shit. Don't worry, you look delicious in them. I've beaten off to one already. It's taking me a little longer because they get me all hot and bothered."

I giggle and push him back with my hand on his chest. He grabs my hand and pulls me to my feet. I jump off the rock and allow him to lead me wherever he wants. As we walk through the city, Seth stops us every once in a while and takes a picture.

We find me a dress that costs way too much for a fake engagement party. Seth does sneak into the dressing room once before the saleswoman knocks on the door.

We end up in Central Park for the rest of Seth's pictures. Although I've sat most of the day, I've never enjoyed myself so much. Watching him do something he clearly loves is addicting. It makes me want to do some soul-searching and find my own desire.

My phone dings with a text and I pull it out since Seth has ventured farther away to get a new angle for a shot.

Nick Klein: *Great news. Round up your parents because you've got a deal in the works.*

Me: *This is going to be a hard sell.*

Nick Klein: *Just wait until you hear the news. Cliff had to head back to his office but he's coming back next weekend with his wife. He wants to meet at two pm Friday at Porterhouse.*

Me: *Can you tell me anything else?*

Nick Klein: *I don't have final numbers or anything. He's talking to his business associates this week, but he'll be presenting a contract on Friday. So you need to work on your parents.*

Me: *I think I'm going to be sick.*

Nick Klein: *Relax Evan, this is all good news. I promised we'd get you out of there.*

I've heard that same thing from Seth, but our route was much more complicated than Nick's.

"Evan!" Seth yells.

I look up to see him waving at me from the bridge. He's got two pretzels in his hands. I tuck my phone inside my jacket pocket, grab my bag, and head in his direction. This is our day and I'm not going to mess it up by talking about business.

He kisses me when I accept the pretzel from him. "Thanks."

"Anything for my girl."

My stomach flips with his declaration. I'm not sure when I'll ever be able to end this fake relationship. It all feels so real.

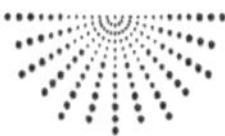

Seth

The day of the engagement party, I'm sitting at Ink Envy while Dylan and Jax are working. There's no Frankie since she had to drive Jolie to her grandma's so that she could come tomorrow night.

"So… fake engagement party, huh?" Jax says. "I mean, you clearly like the girl. Are we still pretending you don't?"

Dylan chuckles.

"Why do you think I like her?" I ask, although he's right. I really, really like her. Last weekend when she asked about keeping this charade going, I wasn't about to say no. I just don't know if she asked because she doesn't want it to end either, or because she's concerned about what our parents think.

"The chick is at our place all the time. She should be paying rent."

"You never even see her." I fight the accusation because

usually Evan comes when Jax is still "out" and she leaves while he's sleeping.

"I hear her. You two must be the loudest fuckers ever. And I had to listen to Dylan and Rian." Jax bends forward, telling his client that he speaks the truth.

His client turns and smiles my way.

"What can I say? Our sex life isn't boring."

"Is that a dig at me?" Dylan asks. "Because I had no idea the shit I was missing out on with relationship sex. I mean, the shit we've done…" He shakes his head.

Jax eyes me. "Are you doing weird shit like Dylan and Rian?" His voice sounds so polite, I'm thrown at first.

"More shit than I've ever done with a woman from a bar. Or any other relationship I've had." I sit back and chew on my inner lip.

"Because you trust her. I'm telling you, it's the trust thing. She trusts you, so she opens up sexually. It's the best thing ever," Dylan raves as if he's acting in a commercial for monogamy.

"Maybe because you got a good one. Could you imagine if you fall in love with someone who sucks in bed? Imagine fifty years ago when you got married before you even slept together. It's like fucking Russian roulette." Jax shakes his head as if the concept is foreign to him.

"Newsflash, there's still a large population of people who remain virgins until they marry," I inform him.

"Shame. Dumb fucks," he says.

"Now we've gotten off track…" Dylan cuts in. "I get that you guys agreed to add sex to your fake relationship, but you tagged her in your Instagram feed last weekend. You seem to be at her bagel place more than your parents'. Give it up, man, you're in love with the girl."

All my muscles seize, and pain stabs me in the chest. "No way, man. You're crazy."

Dylan raises his eyebrows. I wish I knew the reason I can't face my feelings for Evan. The thought of not having her in my life makes me feel as if I'm suffocating, so what's keeping me from just laying out my hand to her? I guess it's because I don't know how receptive she'll be and I'm being a complete pussy about it.

"Just tell the girl," Jax says. "You're acting like a drooling dog following his master with a steak hanging out of his pocket. I guarantee she knows how you feel. If I do, she does."

But if she does and hasn't even broached the subject of making this fake relationship real, doesn't that say something?

The door chimes and in walks Brock Floyd. *You've got to be kidding me.*

Jax stands. Dylan stands next.

"Relax, I'm not gonna do anything to your boy. I just wanted a word." Brock raises his hands in the air.

"I'm not fucking talking to you."

"It's important."

The seriousness on his face makes my gut churn and I wonder if it has something to do with my brother. So I walk outside, and Brock leans against the brick wall in the alley next door to Ink Envy.

"What do you want, Brock?"

"I heard you and Evan are moving pretty fast? Engagement party already?"

I nod. "None of your business though."

"I could tell from the way she looked at you at that gala that she wanted you. Congratulations, you win." He puts out his hand as though he came all the way down from his hill to say *good job, you win*. But that's not Brock's style.

"Why are you here?"

"Well, I just thought you should be warned."

I arch an eyebrow.

"Nick Klein scored a deal for The Bagel Place." He chuckles when he sees what must be confusion on my face. "So I was right, and she didn't tell you."

Sourness coats my throat. "Tell me what?"

"That Daniels Foods is buying their cream cheese recipe. They're meeting today at two o'clock at Porterhouse to sign the contract." He leans in close. "See, she's not all that, right? She just used you to get what she wants. Same as she did with me to get closer to Nick. The apple doesn't fall far from the tree."

My hands fist at my sides and it feels as if the ground drops out from under me.

He steps back and looks hard at my face, then laughs into his palm. "Oh fuck, you actually care about her. At least to me, she was just a good lay. Can she give a blow job or what? You should thank me—when she started with me, she was pitiful. I taught her how to do it just how I like it."

I don't even think before my fist flies at his face. I can't stop myself. All I see is a veil of red. He tries to fight back, landing a couple good blows to my ribs and my face, but I'm in control. The next thing I know, Dylan is pulling me off of Brock.

"Fuck you! I was just being nice and warning you." Brock spits a glob of blood on the sidewalk. "If you don't believe me, go see for yourself."

"What the hell is he talking about?" Dylan asks.

I straighten my shirt and walk down the street to my car.

"Seth, do not listen to him," Dylan calls behind me.

I wave and slide into my car to find out what I should've found out years ago.

* * *

My DAD IS about to put the closed sign on Andrews Bagel Company as I approach the front door. The shop is closing early since we'll all be at the engagement party.

"Seth? Shit, what happened to your face?"

He disappears, so I take a seat in a booth until he returns with a bag of ice.

I place it on my now-black eye. "Dad, I gotta know."

"Know what?" He slides into the booth across from me.

"Why did you and Mr. Erickson have the falling out? What was it about?"

All my life, all I heard was that they argued a lot and they each had "the product." Sooner than later, it turned vicious.

"I don't think today's the day. It's your engagement party," he says and runs a hand through his matching brown hair.

"Please just tell me."

He lets out a breath. "Are things okay with you and Evan?"

The high pitch of his voice says he still believes the entire thing is a farce. But I'm not telling him shit until I find out if Brock was telling me the truth.

"They're fine. Just tell me."

I wait as he collects his thoughts. "Well, it's hard to explain the entire thing. It was twenty years ago. Even my memory is sketchy. But we went in as partners. This guy came in one day, couldn't stop raving about our product. Of course, we did the whole 'I make the bagels and he makes the schmear' thing. It was an ad line we kind of did that people enjoyed. The guy turned out to be from the city and he wanted to invest and franchise us. I was on the fence because I wanted us to do it ourselves. I felt like if that guy could do it, so could we. But Vic was set on the deal."

"So that's what it was about?"

"Yeah, I mean, I said no, Vic got mad, said I was taking money away from his family. The investment guy ended up walking because he wanted both, not just one of us. A huge rift happened. Which is why the whole show thing is a sensitive topic. I know you guys worked on your moms and it's happening anyway, and I suppose it will be good, but I hope you understand after that show airs, it's over. We're back to being Andrews Bagel Company and The Bagel Place."

I nod.

"Good, because I cannot do business with that man."

"The way you hated one another, I thought it wasn't just business and maybe you swapped partners or some *Jerry Springer* shit."

My dad shakes his head. "You and your jokes."

It wasn't really a joke, but I'll keep that to myself.

"All right." I move to slide out, but he puts his hand on mine.

"Mind telling me about the shiner? It wasn't Evan, was it?"

I shake my head. "Nah, just some prick." He raises his eyebrows in question, but I'm not ready to tell him anything yet, especially since I don't need a scene at our engagement party tonight. "I'll tell you later. I gotta go."

He allows me to leave, and I head to Porterhouse since it's almost two, crossing my fingers I won't find her there. She'd tell me something like this, wouldn't she? I thought we were a team. Then again, people like to hide things from me. Trevor hid his drug problem. Mom hid the fact she was still in contact with Mrs. Erickson. Why would I be surprised if Evan is hiding something from me?

Because you trust her.

I push the thought from my mind as I push open the door of Porterhouse. It's a fancy steakhouse, so I'm not surprised that she might be meeting a bigwig business guy here. Heading over to the bar, I can see through the opening to the restaurant, but they'll never see me. And sure as shit, there's

Evan, her dad, Nick Klein smiling next to Evan, and an older man with one of those cowboy ties. Nick appears to run the conversation and keeps touching Evan's arm.

My jaw clenches and my hands fist at my side.

The bartender blocks my view. "What can I get you?"

"Beer. Whatever you have on tap."

"Oh, honey, let me get you some ice. Someone got a hold of your face."

I touch my eye and flinch. With everything going on, I completely forgot about my black eye. She disappears, so I'm happy.

The guy with the cowboy tie pulls something out of his bag and passes it to Evan. She and Vic lower their gazes to read what I'm guessing is a contract. Nick hovers over them, pointing and explaining. He leans even closer and puts his arm on the back of Evan's chair, pointing with his other finger now. She looks at him and smiles. Mr. Erickson never looks up and continues reading the contract.

They talk, and it's clear Evan is asking questions because Nick is answering them. He laughs at almost everything she says. Anger fills my veins, singeing me from the inside out. Meanwhile, Mr. Erickson sits there, going page by page, reading the contract as if he's a lawyer.

After a long pause, Mr. Erickson puts down the contract. They all toast with their glasses, Nick hugging Evan to his side.

I stand and tuck in my chair, having seen enough. She trusted the wrong guy. Or maybe I trusted the wrong girl.

Good luck with Nick Klein, Evan, because Seth Andrews just signed off.

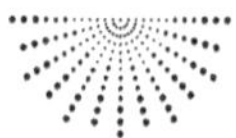

Evan

My dad and I leave Porterhouse, and Nick Klein and Cliff Daniels, behind.

"Let's take a walk." Dad motions with his head toward the lakefront.

"It's a little cold, no?" I say, zipping up my coat and pulling out my mittens.

"Humor me. It's good for my heart to walk."

"Okay, but you know Mom will be upset if we're late. She's got hair and makeup coming for tonight."

I should be filled with anxiety about having to pretend to be Seth's fiancée tonight, but I've been counting down the minutes until I see him. After he agreed to continue this arrangement a little longer, the dread over the engagement party and the show filming finally lifted.

"Is this business with Daniels something we should do?"

"You're asking my advice?" I look at my dad and his eyes soften.

"Yes. You're an integral part of The Bagel Place and its future."

I love that he trusts my opinion, but at the same time, I hate that he assumes I'm a part of the shop's future.

"I don't know." I shrug. "I hate the idea of just handing over our recipe and not having anything to do with it. It's nice to hear the praise from something we've made and see our customers' faces light up on their first bite. As cocky as it sounds, it's the one thing that's kept me…" I stop because I would've finished that thought with Seth, but not with my dad. I'm not going to make him feel guilty.

"From going? Because The Bagel Place isn't your dream." He knocks his shoulder to mine.

I look at him, a lump forming in my throat. "Am I that transparent?"

He chuckles and puts his arm around me, pulling me closer to place a kiss on the top of my head. "I know your mom and I have put too much on you. And I apologize for that. I think we just started living day by day and you handled it all so well. Took the reins without much guidance or grief. But we should've noticed and done something about it. As sad as it is, it was Seth's appearance in your life that made us look harder at everything."

"Seth? But you hate him."

He chuckles and motions toward a bench. "I don't hate Seth. Hell, I don't even hate Chris. Not anymore, at least."

"But I thought you think the engagement—"

"Is fake. You guys concocted the whole thing. I'm not stupid, Evan."

I don't know what to say. I feel more put on the spot in this moment than I have the entire time we've been lying.

"Right?" He dips his head to meet my eyes.

I nod, looking at the lake. "I'm sorry. I can't even tell you how it all happened. It sort of snowballed. But we really wanted the show and the show wouldn't do it until we were partners and we thought—"

He places his hand on my shaking leg. "It should have never come to that. Your mother and I should've made it easier for you to come to us. To explain what a great business opportunity it was. We should've been able to see past the fact that we were doing it with the Andrews. I'm sorry we weren't what you needed. But I will say I'm not mad that you're with Seth rather than that Brock Floyd."

I laugh and throw up my hands.

"The guy is a loser and he didn't appreciate you. Now Seth…"

"It's fake, Dad. It was all an act." The guilt lifts as the words fall from my lips, but a deep sadness settles in at calling Seth's and my relationship what it is.

"Fake." He shrugs. "An act?" He shakes his head. "That boy loves you and I'm willing to bet our recipe that you love him too."

I say nothing. I'm well aware of my feelings for Seth—I just don't want to admit to them. Because if I put it out there, then I need to do something about them. And I have no idea how he really feels about me.

"Yeah, I liked calling your bluff, but I think by doing that, you two just clung closer and now I'm really in jeopardy of having the Andrews as in-laws. Damn Chris, it was his idea. He thought Seth would fold." He chuckles.

"Do you think… I mean, if we did make this thing real, could you accept it?"

He nods. "I don't think we'll ever be best friends again, but your mother's been keeping her friendship with Deb for twenty years. They always were smarter than Chris and me." He leans forward on the bench and fishes out the contract that's sticking out of my bag. "But you need to know, this will change things." He holds it out. "I'm betting money Seth knows nothing about this?"

I shake my head and he sighs.

"Not good, Evan. You guys were partners in this. I'm not the best example, I know, but you owed it to him to tell him."

"I just wanted to hear what they said first. I have no idea if they're offering Andrews Bagel something too."

He raises his eyebrows. "I'm fairly sure that Nick Klein guy was only interested in you."

"And our cream cheese," I add.

He shrugs. "Both, but he seemed to put extra attention on you. Listen, you're twenty-nine now. I think it's time you do something for you. So…" He hands me the contract. "If you want us to do this, then I'm in. But I want you to think hard and make this decision, because this could change your relationship with Seth. Especially if he gets wind of this before you tell him."

He pats my knee and stands. "I have a lot of regrets in my life. I'm not proud of some of my actions. It was a quick revelation when I had the heart attack that you don't have all the time you think you do to make things right. You're supposed to teach your children to learn from your mistakes. I don't think I've done a good job of that. Until now. Make this decision for yourself. And hell, this isn't the nineteen-fifties—if you love the boy, tell him. Don't wait for him to tell you." He touches my shoulder and walks down the path toward the car.

I stare at the contract in my hands. The buyout alone would put my entire family in a much better financial position. We wouldn't have to worry about Eli's medical bills and therapy sessions. Elsie could leave community college and go to a four-year school with room and board. And I'd be out of the bagel business. No more early mornings and hairnets or cramps in my hands.

But all that flashes in my mind is Seth. I know he'd understand if I did this.

Fishing my phone out of my purse, I pull up his contact, smiling at the fact that I never changed his name.

Me: *Can we meet before the party?*

The three dots appear but disappear immediately. I wait for a text to come through, but it doesn't. I thought he said he wasn't working today. This entire week, he's ventured out to take pictures of Cliffton Heights for his portfolio for the gallery on Monday. Maybe he's just busy.

Me: *Call me when you can.*

I stuff my phone into my purse, walking around the lake and trying to remember what it is I love to do. When the possibility of starting on a path toward your dream career is placed in your lap, it's hard to figure out what would bring true happiness. Especially when my mind is preoccupied with Seth and how much I love him. My dad saw right through me and I'm thinking everyone else did too. Everyone but Seth.

* * *

LATER THAT EVENING, I still haven't heard from Seth except a message to say he's running late and he'll meet me at Porterhouse.

I drive over with my parents and Eli, wishing it was Seth I was pulling up to the restaurant with. The sensation in my gut says something isn't right. But maybe it's just because after this party, I plan on telling Seth exactly how I feel about him. I have no idea what my future looks like, but I want him in it.

Once we're in the banquet room, I take in the purple and silver decorations our moms put up. With my purple dress, it feels like it's my sweet sixteen and we color-coded the entire thing. I only picked purple because Seth said I looked stunning in it. If this was his sick twisted joke, I'm going to punch him.

"Evan!" Rian and Dylan walk toward me. "You look gorgeous."

I hug them both. "Thank you. Have you seen Seth?"

Dylan looks around and shakes his head. "Not yet. I'm gonna go get some drinks."

Rian nods and waves to him, linking her arm with mine. "I need more cream cheese and more flavors. That cinnamon one was perfect. Have you ever thought about making frostings?" She smiles at me, but my eyes are following Dylan.

He was acting weird. He tucks himself into a corner of the room and pulls out his phone. That sour feeling in my gut comes alive again. Something is up. I should've known when Seth never called me back. I dismissed it as the artist version of him being distracted, but I think I was really wrong.

"So come by next week so we can talk, okay?" Rian says.

I nod, but we get swallowed up by the rest of Seth's friends, who hug me and offer their congratulations, knowing full well that this is all a lie. Looking over Sierra's shoulder, I see all the guys huddled together with their hands stuffed in their pockets and shaking their heads.

"Have you guys seen Seth?" I ask.

Blanca looks at Sierra, and they both shake their heads.

"I'm sure he'll be here soon," Bianca rushes to add.

I nod because that's all I seem to be able to do.

Mrs. Andrews spots me and waves, breaking the distance between us. "Oh, sweetie, you look so beautiful." She wraps her arms around me. "You all do."

We all gush over her dress—which isn't purple.

"Have you seen Seth?" I ask Mrs. Andrews.

She shakes her head and my shoulders fall.

We go through the entire cocktail hour and everyone's trying to paste on their best smiles, but I see the concerned whispers. Where's Seth? Why isn't he here yet? What could have kept him?

When the banquet guy asks everyone to be seated, Seth finally walks in the room. But he's not dressed in the suit he said he would be wearing. His hair isn't gelled back, and he hasn't shaved. He looks as if he rolled out of bed and hit his face on the corner of his nightstand, because he has a black eye to boot.

Dylan grabs Seth's arm and drags him out before he can reach me, but I excuse myself from our family table and meet them in the small waiting area outside the banquet room. Dylan has his fists in Seth's shirt, his voice low and stern, though I can't make out what he's saying. Seth pushes Dylan away, then he spots me.

"What's going on?" I ask, walking over to them.

"Don't do it, Seth," Dylan says.

Seth pushes Dylan and meets me halfway. "I thought we were a team?" He's slurring and I realize now that he can't really stand up straight.

"What are you talking about?"

He laughs and almost topples over. "I saw you with your buddy Klein. Secret deals under the table, huh?"

And now that sour feeling in my gut makes sense.

"It's not what you think," I say, reaching for him. "Let's go outside and talk about it." Some crisp air might help sober him up.

He pulls his hand from mine and my arm flies in the air. "It's fine. I mean, this entire thing was fake anyway." He looks over my shoulder, where I'm sure a line of guests are taking in the show. "Yep, folks, that's right. Our entire engagement was fake and didn't mean anything because we all know the Ericksons just like to think about themselves."

"Let's talk about this," I say. "What exactly did you see?"

"I saw it. I saw it all. His arms on you, touching you. You laughing with him."

"What? Nick? He was happy that we got the offer, but I didn't take it. I don't want it."

A hollow laugh rings out in the small space, and our parents step up to our sides as Seth says, "I find it funny that I'm always the last one to know everything. I upended my life to help you get out of the business. Pretending you were my fiancée. I foolishly thought we were in this together. Do you think I would've been mad if you got some deal?"

I look at my feet because I'm ashamed. In the weeks I've grown closer to Seth, I've discovered that he harbors feelings about being second best.

"First, I'm the last one to know my brother is so high on coke he's stealing to support his habit."

His dad puts his arm on Seth's forearm. "Let's go, son."

But Seth shakes his head and dislodges his arm from his dad's grip, turning his ire on him. "Come on. This entire town knows. Even after he stole from you and broke into the store, you still put him above me. Fuck, I just wanted a better life for myself, so I went to college. Why is that so fucking bad? But then you treat me like some outsider. The jokes between you and Trevor, always ganging up on me. You'd think you'd be proud of me for getting a fucking degree. And yeah, I know I take boudoir photos, but it's a legit business. I'm not stealing to support a drug habit. So tell me, Dad, how do I end up the asshole?"

"Seth," Mrs. Andrews says. "It's time to go."

He laughs and looks at his mother. "And you. You have a friendship going with Mrs. Erickson for twenty years behind your husband's back."

Her eyes fly to her husband's. I'm guessing from the look on Mr. Andrew's face that she wasn't as upfront as my mom was with my dad.

"You told me we hated them. That I wasn't to talk to the Ericksons," Seth continues.

"I never said that," Mrs. Andrews says.

"You implied it. Suddenly I couldn't go over to Evan's and she couldn't come to our place. No one told me why, just that things changed, and our dads weren't friends anymore. What was I supposed to think? I was nine."

His mom blows out a breath.

"And then I come to find out you were secretly meeting with her behind everyone's back? Fuck, Mom, did you ever stop to think that maybe I wanted to see Evan too?"

"Seth, let's just go talk somewhere." I place my hand in his. He's self-destructing right in front of me, and I can't bear to let him do it in front of all these witnesses.

"And now you." He narrows his gaze on me.

Knox steps in and puts his hand on his friend's chest. "Enough, Andrews, let's go."

But Seth weaves around him. "Now you. Why couldn't you trust what we have? Why would you not be upfront with me?" His voice is pleading, and it stabs me in my heart.

Knox grabs Seth's arm and tugs him. Seth's shoulders sink like he's done.

Just as they reach the door, Seth wiggles free and holds out his arms, facing everyone. "Happy, Dad? You were right. It was all fake and I got played by an Erickson too." He sets his eyes on me. "While she was making chess moves behind my back, I fucking fell in love with her. Now she broke my damn heart."

Knox gets a hold of him and pulls him back.

"I fucking loved her," Seth tells his friend.

Knox just nods and pushes him out of here. Dylan and Jax jog after them. The rest of Seth's friends follow, the girls giving me fleeting looks before walking through the doors.

Somehow I make it to the bathroom before my legs give out and I crumple to the floor. He declared his love for me. But what runs through my head over and over was that it was in the past tense. I burst into tears and wish we'd never devised this plan in the first place. It was inevitable that we'd end up here.

CHAPTER THIRTY-ONE

Seth

"Man, you make me happy I'm sober." Trevor kicks the side of my bed.

I blink to see that I'm in my apartment. Sliding up my bed, I look down at myself with blurry vision to find that I'm dressed in jeans and a T-shirt that smells like vomit.

"What the hell happened?" My voice is gravelly. I sit up and put my pounding head in my hands.

"I wasn't a witness, but some are calling it a mental breakdown and others are referring to it as a drunken rant. You can pick your preference." Trevor sits at the end of my bed.

"Shit. I didn't?"

"Oh, you did. You told off Dad, Mom, threw some truth bombs out about me, and worst of all embarrassed Evan in front of all your guests."

My stomach rolls over on itself. "Fuck."

"Listen, I talked to Mom and Dad last night about what

you said when they got home and told me what happened. I owe you an apology."

I roll off the bed to get out of my T-shirt because I'm going to throw up again if I have to keep smelling it. "For what?"

"For being a prick. For making fun of your job." He sighs and remains quiet for a minute while I pull on a new T-shirt. "You know it's only because I'm jealous, right? I mean, you got to go to college, and I got to learn the family business. No one asked what I wanted to do. Truth is, I was a lazy mother-fucker when I graduated high school. Already on my way into a heavy addiction. But don't throw your life away because of me."

I shake my head.

"I'm serious. Mom and Dad treat me with kid gloves. Like the minute something bad happens, I'm gonna run for drugs. I can't promise I'm gonna stay clean, but I'm the only one who has control over that. I think they just want us to be perfect and I tried to fit into that role because I'm jealous of you. You've got a great life. You live on your own. You have a job and now the art gallery opportunity. But it was finding out you were engaged to Evan that made my self-destructive asshole tendencies come out at dinner."

My eyes widen. "Evan? Please don't tell me—"

"Hell no. She was always yours. But your life kept moving forward and I feel like I'm stalled." I open my mouth, but he continues. "Which is my problem. I have to be the one to get myself out there. And as far as you being the last to know about my drug problem, hell, man, you were the last person I wanted to know. You still thought of me as your strong, older brother. You were one of the last people who still saw me, how the drugs made me feel —invincible."

Sadness for how my brother sees himself weighs heavily

on my shoulders. I sit down next to him. "I still see you as my bigger, older, stronger brother."

He shakes his head like he doesn't believe me and pushes me with his shoulder. "You stink. Go take a shower." Standing, he hesitates by the door. "And go get your girl back."

He walks out and shuts the door.

I sit there thinking about everything he said, deciding that no matter how hard it might be, I'm going to start fresh with my brother. I don't want to be like my dad and harbor animosities for years.

I check my phone to see my mom and dad's missed calls. But there's nothing from Evan. I head out of my bedroom to take a shower and find Knox getting ready to leave for work.

"You fucked up," he says.

"I know."

"Fix it."

I nod, and he opens the door and leaves.

* * *

AFTER I SHOWER and feel slightly more human, I head over to Evan's place. Bits and pieces of what I did have come back to me and the sinking sensation in my stomach has been getting worse. I'll be lucky as fuck if she accepts my apology. I'm surprised when she opens the door the first time I knock. She's wearing flannel pants and a long-sleeve T-shirt, looking like she hasn't slept all night.

"Can I come in?"

She nods and opens the door wider.

Once I'm inside and she's closed the door, I meet her gaze. "I'm sorry. I shouldn't have confronted you like that in front of everyone."

"You shouldn't have, no. But I should have been open and honest with you too. We were both wrong."

She sits in her desk chair, and I sit on the edge of her bed.

"I'm not sure of everything I said, but I know one thing I said is true. Somewhere through all of this, I fell in love with you. And I know after last night, you probably want to throw me out the window. I'm sorry. I should've told you about my feelings earlier and I think that's why I thought you lied to me…"

She stands and turns away from me, but I see her back shaking with sobs. "I didn't lie. I dragged my heels, but I was going to tell you. I think the real reason you can't trust me is because my last name is Erickson. With our families' past, maybe we'll never be able to fully trust one another."

"That's not true." I walk over to her and put my hands on her shoulders. "I trust you."

She shakes her head. "You don't, and maybe you have a reason not to. Maybe the whole business thing with our parents has everything to do with it. Maybe we're just destined to be enemies forever."

I urge her to face me with my hands on her shoulders. "You can't possibly believe that."

She stares at me, bearing no expression. A shrug is all the response I get.

"I think it's the opposite. I think we're destined to be together. To find our way back to the friendship we once had, and that friendship grew into love. We can't just turn our backs on that because of one misunderstanding."

Tears slip from her eyes. "It wasn't just a misunderstanding. You're right—I was terrified to tell you about the offer because I thought you'd think I was selling out or using you as a backup plan to make my exit from the business. And I didn't know if Nick was after Andrews Bagel too. I thought maybe you were keeping that from me. As long as our families are working in competition with one another, how can we be together? Think about it, Seth."

"So you're okay to just walk away from this?"

She looks over my shoulder so we're no longer making eye contact. "I don't see another choice."

I close my eyes as the pain of her words settles in my chest. "You're not going to fight for us?"

"It's a losing battle. We didn't even trust each other enough to tell the other one we were in love."

"I was scared you didn't feel the same way. That has nothing to do with trust." I step closer and dip my head until our eyes catch. "Meet me halfway here."

"I'm sorry, Seth. I think it's better if you go now."

"What? No." I shake my head.

She wiggles out of my hold and opens the door for me to leave. A cold rush of air whooshes in and chills my shattered heart.

"I thought you were a fighter like me. That you'd go toe to toe. I guess I was wrong." I walk out of her apartment, down the stairs on the side of the garage, and to my car.

Eli spots me from the yard and runs over with his football. "Hey, Seth? Want to play?"

"Not right now…" But I stop and hold my hands out for him to throw the ball.

He gets it right on target and he must register my surprise. "My dad's been working with me."

"Great throw." I signal with the ball for him to go out for the pass. "Right there."

I toss it and he catches it, jumping up and down like the first time.

"Way to go, Eli." My eyes instinctively move to Evan's window and find her watching. "I gotta go. See you later."

My voice breaks on the words because I know that might very well be another lie.

CHAPTER THIRTY-TWO

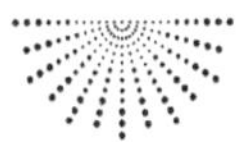

Evan

There's not much to be said about breaking your own heart other than it sucks. A lot.

Seth left my apartment and never returned. Our moms ended up doing the Food Channel show and were a hit. We didn't sell to Daniels Foods, so I'm back to running The Bagel Place, which is busier than ever. Giving ownership of our product to someone else, even if it was a good opportunity, just didn't feel right. So after all of that, nothing has changed in my life except that now my heart is broken. Great job, Evan.

Early one morning, after the rush, my mom comes into the shop with Mrs. Andrews.

"Hey, sweetie," Mom says. "Come sit with us."

I desperately want to ask Mrs. Andrews how Seth is doing, but that's none of my business anymore, so I politely slide in across from them.

"Oh, cheer up. Things are about to get better." Mrs. Andrews pats my hands and I sit up straighter.

"So we're closing The Bagel Place," my mom says.

"And we're closing Andrews Bagel Company," Mrs. Andrews adds.

My jaw is practically on the table. "What?"

They share a look and laugh.

"You don't want to do this for the rest of your life. We're setting you free." My mom smiles as though this is the best news ever.

It was only months ago, I concocted a plan with Seth that's now ended in disaster. So now not only is my heart is gone, my financial security is too.

"What do you mean you're closing the shops?"

"You go and do what you love. Everyone is in agreement —we're joining forces again, but this time it's the two of us." Mrs. Andrews motions between her and my mom. "The way it should have been from the get-go."

"Definitely," my mom says.

"Really?" I'm shocked that these two families with so much baggage between them can overcome everything and start another business together.

"But we would like you to continue to help with the books for a while. Maybe you could teach us," my mom says.

"What about Trevor?" I ask.

"He's decided to head south to Florida." Mrs. Andrews shrugs. "Wants to do something, anything other than run a bagel shop."

"He's moving?" I ask.

She nods.

"Don't look so upset. If you want to work with us, you're more than welcome to," my mom says.

"Yes, we're not kicking you to the curb." Mrs. Andrews laughs.

I sit in the booth as they go over possible names for the bagel shop and all the things they've wanted to incorporate throughout the years.

"How did you guys keep your friendship going after the fight?" I ask, pulling them out of their bubble of happiness.

Mrs. Andrews laughs. "I should probably go." She winks just like Seth does, and longing and sadness fill my veins.

"No. Stay," my mom tells her. "You're an integral part of our story, and I think she's asking for more than just her curiosity."

I say nothing.

Mrs. Andrews nods and looks at me. "We just kept it going. It was our husbands' problem, not ours." She shrugs.

"But the trust between you..." I'm starting to hate that five-letter word.

"Trust? I've always trusted Deb. I knew she had to do things for the business and we never talked about it unless we were complaining about work or discussing you and Trevor taking over our businesses. But we concentrated on what we loved, which was each other." My mom grabs my hands. "I know you're struggling right now, and I've tried to give you your space, but can the daughter I know and love show up? The one who meets a challenge and conquers it?"

My nose tickles and my throat closes up, tears threatening to fall.

"You love Seth, and that's not going to change. I promise you. I've been trying to give you time to get comfortable with the feeling because I know it's new and scary for you. It's hard to make yourself vulnerable and put your heart in someone else's hands." She looks at Mrs. Andrews. "We both know that. And I'm probably biased because my best friend raised the boy you love, so I can't help but believe he'll hold that heart with tender hands."

The tears fall and I wipe them away with the heel of my palm.

"He's a good boy. I promise. This was just a misunderstanding. You two are young and foolish. You're supposed to be. This is your first time experiencing something so magical and life-changing." Mrs. Andrews covers my mom's and my joined hands. "And your mom is right. It's scary, and when things are scary, you're not always rational. But the two of you not pursuing your love is foolish."

I sit back and think about Seth and how I ache for him every second of every day.

"If you two hadn't joined forces, none of this might have happened," Mrs. Andrews says. "Our friendship wouldn't have come out of the darkness. We wouldn't be combining the businesses again. You wouldn't be free to pursue your own happiness. That's the power of love. It trumps all."

I sink into my seat, pressing my heels into my eye sockets. I ended it. How could I have been so stupid? He'll never take me back now.

Mrs. Andrews sighs. "My son hasn't been the happiest of people lately, even though his own dream is coming true."

"What does that mean?" I whisper, removing my hands from my eyes.

"He got the gallery spot and his show will open this Thursday evening."

"So soon?"

She laughs. "The owner had a cancelation—some artist who lost their muse or something—and decided that since Seth had so much to show, she'd showcase him."

I smile. The first real one since everything fell apart between us. I'm happy for him.

"But the problem is, he's not truly appreciating it because his heart is somewhere else." She pats our hands. "It's with you, sweetie. He misses you."

"Come on, Evan. It's time for you to live. Go," my mom urges.

Mrs. Andrews digs into her purse and slides an invitation toward me. It's clearly not for me, something she probably carries around to show off. "Go see what happens. He could use all the support he can get."

I read the invitation and nod. "I'll be there."

No matter what Seth thinks of me, I'll make him see that we're too good to give up. I know the real thing when I feel it.

CHAPTER THIRTY-THREE

Seth

I'm at the studio with the coordinator, Ursula, in the private viewing room.

"This is truly one of the best displays I've seen in my career. Thank you for allowing me to view it. I understand why it's intimate to you, and if you choose not to allow the public in, I understand. Your other work on landscapes is magnificent as well. I'm sure we'll find some buyers tonight. You're like a little treasure I've uncovered." She pats my arm and walks out of the blocked off room.

I'm embarrassed to admit I've spent more time on the photos here than I did on what the public will see. It was therapeutic, to say the least.

After walking into the main gallery, I position the closed sign in front of the velvet drapes and straighten my suit jacket. A few people are sprinkling in, but no one I recognize yet.

I always hate when I go to a gallery and the photographer is there schmoozing, so I stand back from the crowd and observe for a while, looking over my work. It only reminds me of Evan.

"Hey, man." Knox squeezes my shoulder. "Did you call her?"

I shake my head. "If my mom did her job right, she'll be here. I have to trust that."

Giving my mom the invitation on the sly when she stopped by the studio a few days ago should guarantee Evan will receive it. My mom can't keep her nose out of my business.

I had thought about sending one to Evan myself, but it felt forced. I want her to come because she wants to. Because she misses me and misses us. Because she's over the family bullshit and wants to start something real between us.

"I'm proud of you for fighting for her. It takes guts." Knox accepts a glass of champagne and leaves me to wait impatiently on my own.

All of my friends come in support, each one "oohing" and "ahhing" over each photograph because they're my friends and they have to be sweet like that. Adrian purchases the one of the Brooklyn Bridge at night for a hefty amount. I told him he didn't have to purchase it, that'd I make him a copy, but he wasn't having it.

"Nonsense, I'm supporting my friend," he says.

Sometimes I feel bad for Adrian because I wonder if he feels like the outsider since most of us have been friends for so long.

"Thanks, man," I say.

"The Brooklyn Bridge at night holds a lot of great memories for me. You captured it perfectly." He puts his arm around Sierra, and she looks at him with so much love, I grow nauseated at the thought that I threw away that possibility.

They walk away and I keep glancing at the door, hoping to spot Evan.

My parents and Trevor come, and I'm surprised when Mr. and Mrs. Erickson walk in right behind them. I watch from afar as my mom and Mrs. Erickson walk with linked arms and champagne glasses, stopping to comment on each photo. My dad and Mr. Erickson linger behind, holding a civil conversation. Trevor goes off on his own and ends up finding a woman to talk to.

I'm still shocked he decided to leave Cliffton Heights. Said there's too much bad here for him and he needs a fresh start. I'll miss him, but hey, a place to stay in Florida is nice too.

Another hour ticks by and most of my photos have sold, which is crazy for my first showing. But there are still two hours to go.

The doors open, and as if my body just knows, I turn to find Evan walking in. She's wearing a black cocktail dress that dips to reveal her cleavage, and her heels show off her amazing legs. She smiles and gives her name to the person at the door. I can tell she's surprised to find she's already on the list. She shrugs out of her shawl and hands it to the coat check girl.

I wait for her to look up, and when she does, her gaze finds me immediately. I should play this cool. A million jokes fly into my brain as a way to lighten the mood, but I stop myself.

Allow her to see me.

All of me.

We walk toward one another, and I place my half-finished champagne on a tray. My heart beats like a drumline when she's right in front of me.

"You came," I say.

"Is it okay? Your mom—"

"Yes. I'm glad you came."

She looks around and smiles and waves to our friends and family. They can't stop their stares from lingering on us.

"I guess I'll just walk around. Congratulations."

"Can I walk you through?" I ask.

She smiles a little shyly. "I'd love that."

I place my hand on the small of her back and lead her to the front. She compliments my work, and we talk about the day I took some of these pictures.

"It's all so beautiful," she says. "I can't believe I was sitting on a rock and you were seeing all this when all I saw was a building."

I laugh. "It's the angle and the lighting."

"No, you're truly talented."

I don't respond to her compliment because I want her to reserve her opinion until I show her the part I'm really proud of. "I have one last part to show you."

"Okay." She places her now-empty champagne glass on a tray and I slide my hand into hers.

"Is this okay?" I ask.

She gulps but nods. "It says closed." She points at the sign in front of the room that's sectioned off.

I weave us around the sign and slide through the curtained area. "Not for you, it's not."

She steps in, and I release her hand once we're in the middle of the room.

Her hand flies to her chest. "Oh, Seth."

CHAPTER THIRTY-FOUR

Evan

The room is filled with pictures of me. From the first time he snapped that picture of me at the studio, to me lying on a rock in the middle of Central Park. The candid pictures are mixed with the boudoir ones he took in the studio. The walls are covered in a light pink fabric, and the photos are a mixture of black and white and muted colors. Rose petals in shades of pink line the floor with twinkle lights weaved between them.

"It's beautiful," I say.

"Before you get worried, I've only allowed the gallery owner in here. This is for you first and foremost, and if you want to keep this between me and you, that's okay."

I turn around, lost in a world of me. "Why did you do this?"

I step closer to a boudoir picture, my arm stretched toward it. My hair is spread out above my head and all my private parts are hidden behind the silk sheet. All that shows is a scrap of my stomach and one leg.

"Because I want you to see yourself like I do. I know things with us are rocky, but I heard about our moms' plan. And I know you're lost right now. That you don't know what you want to do. But this is the woman who has kept a bagel shop open for the last decade. The woman who took the brunt of the storm for her family. This woman is a boss. And I'm not sure you see her when you look in the mirror."

I shake my head, and tears flow down my cheeks as they have been for the last two weeks.

"Out there, you asked how I was able to see that building for the photograph it could become. Don't you see? The camera never lies. The woman staring back at us right now is the same woman I see every day when I look at you. I want you to believe in yourself and see what I do." He steps back as though he's scared to get too close.

"Thank you." Those two words don't come close to what I'm feeling.

This is exactly what I needed. To be reminded of the trust I have in him. Of the girl who fell in love with him a little bit every day. Our moms were right—I can't throw that girl away because of a misunderstanding. For the first time, I think I finally understand what Seth sees when he looks at me.

"I'll leave you alone," Seth says after I stand there admiring the room for a moment.

I spin around. "No. Why?"

"I figured you'd want some time without me." He shoves his hands in his pockets.

"You couldn't be more wrong," I say.

His eyes widen, and a startled expression falls over his face. "I am?"

"I'm not lost." I walk toward him. "I was." I stop when I

come face to face with him. My hand glides down his tie. "You found me. You found her." I point at the photograph while my tears cascade down my face.

"I never wanted to make you cry." His hand cradles my face and his thumb swipes at a tear.

"Say the words," I practically beg.

"I love you, Evan Erickson."

I nod. "I know you do. And I love you, Seth Andrews."

"Are you saying what I think you're saying?"

I nod, and he pulls me flush against his body, his hug so tight I can barely breathe but I'm not about to complain. He draws back and his lips capture mine in a kiss that's sweeter than any other we've shared.

"Look, all that planning on your behalf paid off. You finally caught me." He winks.

My stomach flip-flops like a giant fish is struggling to breathe in there. "Hey, Mack Daddy, let's not start by rewriting the past. You caught me."

"That's not the story we're telling our grandchildren. Just imagine their faces when I tell them their grandma wanted me so badly, she baited me into a fake engagement and used her magical powers to make me fall in love with her."

I roll my eyes and shake my head, not annoyed at all because this is Seth, the man I love. He takes me in his arms once more and I sigh at the feeling of finally being here again.

"Don't worry, I'll tell them Grandpa was trying to get caught by Grandma because he's loved her for as long as he can remember," Seth says.

"Uh-oh, you're growing sentimental on me."

"I guess love has that effect on people." He presses a kiss to my forehead.

We exit the private room hand in hand, and Seth hollers

to Blanca, "Redo on the *Newlywed Game* because things just got real."

I gasp when he dips me and kisses me as everyone claps.

Who would've guessed an Andrews and an Erickson could fall so madly in love? Maybe our stars really were aligned this entire time.

EPILOGUE

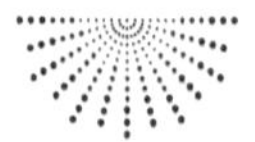

Two Months Later…

Seth

"I have to go to work," Evan whines, stretching her body like a cat beside me.

"I'll go make us some coffee, then I'll walk you to work." I flip off the covers and put on a pair of boxers.

"Really? Walk me to work?" She laughs, climbing out of the bed. She stands naked in the room, grabs her robe, and walks toward the bedroom door.

She works at Sweet Infusion with Rian. Well, she rents a space from Rian to make her cream cheese concoctions. Evan's started her own little company called Spreads, and so far, she loves it. I think she enjoys the business aspect of it more than actually making the product. More than anything, I think she enjoys the fact that she has a choice and the freedom to do what she wants now. If she decides to pack it in a year from now and try something else, I'll support her.

I block her with my body. "Where are you going?"

"Shower," she mumbles. She's not much of a morning person since she doesn't have to wake up before dawn anymore.

"Come back to bed. I'll do that thing you like." I waggle my eyebrows.

"Tempting but no." She rolls her eyes and slides me out of the way. She walks out of our shared bedroom in our one-bedroom apartment and heads to the bathroom.

"You know seeing you naked gets me all hard, and now my big dick will be dangerously close to the oven while I cook your breakfast. Maybe you should solve this problem before you lose your favorite lollipop."

She peeks out of the bathroom. "Is this you asking me for a blow job?"

For some reason, her words trigger a memory of what Brock said that day.

"Hey," I call. "Where did you learn to give such a great blow job?"

She raises her eyebrows. "Why are you asking?"

"Just curious."

She tilts her head because I can't get anything by her. She might know me better than I do myself.

"That fight with Brock, he said something." I shrug.

She walks out of the bathroom without her robe, sauntering over to me. Her finger runs down my chest until she cups my groin. "What do you think?"

"I like to think you learned by watching porn or something. You're a smart girl. I'm hoping you watched a tutorial."

She laughs and bites her lip. "I can assure you I never went down on Brock Floyd. Does that make it better?"

"Really?"

She raises her eyebrows and I know it's because I'm questioning her.

"Never mind." I grab her hips and hoist her onto the counter, wiggling between her thighs.

"This is very unsanitary," she says.

"I'll clean it after." I bend down, bringing her legs over my shoulders so I can show her my own oral skills. "Breakfast of champions."

"Good thing we make our own hours," she says.

And I am thankful to no longer be doing boudoir shoots, concentrating on architecture photography and showing them at exhibits Ursula keeps allowing me to have. Plus, I've had a few other people reach out. I was suspicious when someone asked me about a photo of Evan. It wasn't for sale, just on my Instagram feed. I'm pretty sure it was Nick Klein.

A pounding so loud you'd think it was the Incredible Hulk's hand banging on our door sounds.

"What the fuck?" I say, ready to ignore and feast on my girl.

"Answer it," she says.

I groan, dislodging her legs from my shoulders. "If this is some ding-dong ditch, they're going to see my fist."

She slides off the counter and runs to the bathroom for her robe. Another bang.

"Open up, Andrews!" It's Jax.

Once Evan's amazing body is hidden, I open the door. Jax is in his boxers, his tattoos on full display.

I glance over my shoulder at Evan. "Close your eyes."

She shoos me away and comes to my side.

"Fuck, you're never gonna believe this. Get over to Dylan's now!" He runs back down the hall.

We were fortunate to get the apartment across from Ethan and Blanca, next to Dylan and Rian. I was skeptical at first because of times like this when I could be eating Evan out but instead we're all rushing to Dylan and Rian's apartment for God knows what. But Evan seems to enjoy it. The girls have wine nights where they watch new Netflix shows. She fits in perfectly with all of them, and I think it's something she needed in her life—honest and true friendships.

Blanca stumbles out of her apartment, her eyes blinking while Ethan looks as though he's been up for hours.

"Seriously, is there a fire?" Blanca asks Evan and hooks her arm through hers.

"I have no idea," Evan says. "I was getting ready for work."

I glance back and Evan smiles at me. I won't make a joke. I'll let that stay between us.

Dylan and Jax are out on the balcony overlooking Ink Envy and Sweet Infusion on the other side of the street. My stomach drops, hoping something didn't happen to the building overnight. I see the reflection of blue and red lights on the windows of the condo building above the small businesses.

Ethan's phone rings. He answers and hands the phone to Blanca.

"What happened?" Blanca sounds as if she's had five bottles of wine. "It's so early, what?"

Jesus. I walk out to the balcony and look at what Jax and Dylan are so interested in. Rian is on the curb, watching from outside Sweet Infusion since she does start work before the sun comes up.

"Shut up!" Blanca suddenly sounds perfectly awake and alert. "No way."

"What am I missing?" Evan says, coming alongside me. "Knox is arresting someone? Isn't that kind of his job?" Evan cops an attitude with Jax.

I put my arm around her and smile although the situation isn't funny. I'm kind of proud of my girl's sarcasm.

"He's arresting Leilani," Jax clarifies.

"Who's that?" Evan asks.

"The girl who fucked him up in the head," I say.

"What could've happened?" Blanca leans forward to get a better view.

Dylan turns her way. "Rian said she saw Knox pull his car over to the curb and was just going to go say hi when…"

He doesn't fill in the rest because Knox must feel all our eyes on him. He looks up with a handcuffed Leilani, holding her arm and escorting her to the back of his police car.

"Do you think he had to frisk her? That had to be uncomfortable," I remark.

Jax laughs next to me.

"Fuck, just as he was getting back to his normal self," Dylan says.

We watch Knox put his hand on her head and lower her into the back of his squad car. He doesn't look up again as he rounds the back of the car and climbs into the driver's seat. We all watch him drive away.

Nothing good can come from Leilani coming back into Knox's life.

"So should we plan a welcome back party for Leilani?"

The End

Seth and Evan's story was our first attempt at the star-crossed lovers trope. As most of you long time Piper Rayne readers know, we try to think of new tropes we've yet to write in order to challenge ourselves and keep things fresh. Of course, we have our ole' faithful's like enemies-to-lovers (we really can't get enough of this one). So it was awesome when we wrote this story because we could have that hatred and pent-up sexual energy brewing between them in the beginning, but then allow their friendship to rekindle, shifting us into friends-to-lovers, and ultimately settling on star-crossed lovers as the story progressed. It was such a nice story flow and once we figured out the logistics it was so enjoyable to write.

That said, this storyline didn't come easy for us and we went through so many iterations of Seth and Evan's story. Some hit the page and some didn't. Rayne thought she had a gold mine of an idea (that Evan would be pregnant with Brock's baby and Seth would raise the baby as his own. Nice in theory but that wasn't the story for Seth and Evan). Sometimes you only realize that once you start writing and so the first five thousand words had to be scrapped. Which meant an emergency meeting was in store. Although we like to tell you guys we have it all plotted and figured out, the cliffhanger at the end of The Rival Roomies put us a little bit in the corner that we had to find our way out of.

In the end, it all worked out. And once we realigned the conflict and goals, words came fast and furious and Seth and Evan bounced off the pages. Now all we can hope is that we can pull off Knox's little cliffhanger at the end of this book!

Fun facts: Piper & Rayne both eat everything bagels. If you ever see us in the morning when we're together whether at a conference or a signing, we'll more than likely both have an everything bagel. Piper's with butter and Rayne with cream cheese. Maybe that's where the idea for competing bagel shops came from. LOL

None of this would be possible without our amazing team!

Danielle Sanchez and the entire Wildfire Marketing Solutions team.
    Cassie from Joy Editing for line edits.
    Ellie from My Brother's Editor for line edits.
    Shawna from Behind the Writer for proofreading.
    Hang Le for the cover and branding for the entire series.
    Wander Aguiar for the amazing photo of Seth and Evan.
    Bloggers who consistently carve out time to read, review and/or promote us.
    Piper Rayne Unicorns who shout from the rooftops about our new releases and love our characters like we do.
    Readers who took a chance on our book with so many choices out there.

We think we're really going to throw you on the next book. That was quite a cliffhanger we left you guys with at the end. As for what's in store for Knox? We can't really say much more without giving anything away. But we're rubbing our hands together excited to flip the script!

XO,
   Piper & Rayne

ABOUT THE AUTHOR

Piper Rayne, or Piper and Rayne, whichever you prefer because we're not one author, we're two. Yep, you get two USA Today Bestselling authors for the price of one. Our goal is to bring you romance stories that have "Heartwarming Humor With a Side of Sizzle" (okay...you caught us, that's our tagline). A little about us... We both have kindle's full of one-clickable books. We're both married to husbands who drive us to drink. We're both chauffeurs to our kids. Most of all, we love hot heroes and quirky heroines that make us laugh, and we hope you do, too.

www.piperrayne.com
Amazon
Goodreads
Facebook
Instagram
Pinterest
Bookbub

ALSO BY PIPER RAYNE

The Rooftop Crew

My Bestie's Ex

A Royal Mistake

The Rival Roomies

Our Star-Crossed Kiss

The Do-Over

A Co-Workers Crush

The Baileys

Lessons from a One-Night Stand

Advice from a Jilted Bride

Birth of a Baby Daddy

Operation Bailey Wedding (Novella)

Falling for My Brother's Best Friend

Demise of a Self-Centered Playboy

Confessions of a Naughty Nanny

Operation Bailey Babies (Novella)

Secrets of the World's Worst Matchmaker

Winning My Best Friend's Girl

Rules for Dating your Ex

The Modern Love World

Charmed by the Bartender

Hooked by the Boxer

Mad about the Banker

The Single Dad's Club

Real Deal

Dirty Talker

Sexy Beast

Hollywood Hearts

Mister Mom

Animal Attraction

Domestic Bliss

Bedroom Games

Cold as Ice

On Thin Ice

Break the Ice

Box Set

Charity Case

Manic Monday

Afternoon Delight

Happy Hour

Blue Collar Brothers

Flirting with Fire

Crushing on the Cop

Engaged to the EMT

White Collar Brothers

Sexy Filthy Boss

Dirty Flirty Enemy

Wild Steamy Hook-up